DIANE CAPRI

GET BACK JACK

DEDICATION

For Lee Child, with unrelenting gratitude

GET BACK
JACK

CAST OF PRIMARY CHARACTERS

Kim L. Otto
Carlos M. Gaspar

Charles Cooper

Frances L. Neagley
Karla Dixon
Jorge Sanchez
Marion Morrison
Margaret Berenson
Edward Dean

Jacqueline Roscoe

and
Jack Reacher

Bad Luck and Trouble
by Lee Child

2007

Reacher had served thirteen years in the army, all of them in the military police. He had known Frances Neagley for ten of those years and had worked with her from time to time for seven of them.

There was a lot he didn't know about her, despite their ten-year association.

If she felt something was right or necessary, then she was uncompromising. Nothing stood in her way, not politics or practicality or politeness or even what a civilian might call "the law."

She impressed him, deeply. Sometimes even came close to scaring him.

Chapter 1

Friday, November 5
11:10 p.m.
Washington, DC

What would Jack Reacher do?

Sanchez considered the question again for a moment before he ignored orders and executed the scumbag with a single shot to the head.

At close range, any gun might have done the job. Sanchez had chosen a Glock 19, Gen 4. Utilitarian, tough, reliable. Comfortable grip, controllable recoil, easily concealed. Used by law enforcement because of its stopping power.

A perfect choice for a man anticipating precisely this situation.

Six and a half long seconds later, Sanchez punched the off button on the military grade speakerphone.

Connection terminated.

* * *

Twenty-two floors below, the gunshot exploded through the eavesdropper's equally high-tech headset, traumatizing her eardrums almost as if *she'd* been standing in front of the bullet.

The crisp audio feed she'd appreciated for the past eighty-seven minutes and seventeen seconds was gone, as though she'd been dropped head first into a vat of clammy marshmallow cream.

Could Sanchez have gone off the rails at the very first obstacle?

She increased the audio to maximum volume and strained to hear his explanation, but heard only the severed connection's silence.

She jumped up, ripped off her headset with one latex-gloved hand and flung it to the floor of the four-by-four janitor's closet.

Christ!

She might have screamed.

Thoughts slammed like racquetballs inside her skull as she stormed back and forth in the hot, tiny closet. Even if she could've heard them, her sweat-soaked coveralls and paper boots no longer rustled crisply with each step as they had earlier in the evening. Behind her surgical mask, she sucked deep breaths and shouted silenced, frustrated curses.

She forced herself down into her guerilla training. Allowed fifteen more seconds to assess, analyze, plan, and perform.

Assess and analyze.

O'Donnell should have seen it coming. She felt slightly less stupid because O'Donnell had missed the obvious, too. Sanchez was far wilier (and certainly far crazier) than she'd believed. But O'Donnell had known Sanchez better than she did and O'Donnell was now dead. It was entirely possible that O'Donnell had committed suicide by allowing Sanchez to kill him now instead of torturing him later.

The two remaining targets could disclose what O'Donnell had refused to reveal.

Which meant her goal was still in play.

O'Donnell had made either a stupid blunder or a stupid choice, but his death didn't compromise her ultimate mission. She could still acquire what she'd come to collect. Her plan was altered, but not irrevocably thwarted.

Still, Sanchez's unsanctioned killing of O'Donnell was nothing short of disaster. For him. He had to know that, too. Which brought her back to the fact that Sanchez was far from okay. She must have missed something important about him. Something that might present a bigger problem. But what?

She hurried through her recall of the meeting she'd overheard. The erratic shuffling of Sanchez's shoes as he paced O'Donnell's office, pouring out his woes. At the time, she'd been impatient, stewing in her own sweat in the airless closet, willing Sanchez to get the hell on with it. She hadn't paid close attention to his ramblings. Mere impressions stuck in her memory. She ticked them off rapidly.

Sanchez increasingly distraught as he explained his plight, his anger growing while he recounted his five-year ordeal.

O'Donnell expressing shock. (Maybe he wasn't lying.)

Sanchez blaming O'Donnell, who claimed surprise. (Maybe he'd been a bit contrite.)

She cringed, recalling Sanchez's sudden switch from rage to whining pleas, begging O'Donnell to save him this time, as O'Donnell and the rest of their crew had failed to make the smallest effort to do five years before.

O'Donnell claimed he couldn't supply what Sanchez needed. (Almost certainly lying, of course, as thieves everywhere do.)

Sanchez's ordnance replied.

Then what?

Seven seconds before she'd recovered her wits enough to check the timer.

What happened next?

She'd been partially deafened by the blast. Her experience told her bullets blasted predictably into bony skulls, through gelatinous brain and out again, carrying moist soft facial tissue along with them. She could almost smell the gunshot, the metallic scent of blood.

Now, the office was no doubt a gooey mess, Sanchez was gone, and their perfect plan compromised. She'd failed. She'd need a plausible solution before she reported the damage, but that would come later, when she'd removed herself far enough away from the scene.

Now she was pacing again like an outraged tiger. She rubbed her face, and memory-pain sliced afresh; she jerked both palms away from the long-healed scars as if they'd been inflicted again by Sanchez's betrayal.

She sat on the janitor's stepstool, becalmed, ignoring the timer, backhanded the sweat from her brow and then stroked the narrow scar that stretched from the corner of her left upper lip to the outside corner of her left eye. Her index finger rested on the bump of keloid above her cheekbone, massaging absently, seeking comfort and clarity.

Rehearsals proved she could disappear in ninety-five seconds leaving no trace evidence. She should be outside the building in less than three minutes. But then what? Her escape plan was compromised because Sanchez couldn't be trusted.

Plan and perform.

Eliminate the hostages in Mexico. At least one. Immediately. Sanchez needed to know she was a woman of her word, to believe she'd kill the others if he stepped out of line again.

She'd intended to kill all of the hostages anyway. Right after Sanchez collected what he'd been sent to retrieve. His wife and brats would be of no use then. Sanchez's failure meant she was forced to revise—terminate one hostage a little early—and delay progress toward the goal, but only slightly.

Damn Sanchez. He was too smart to have failed so spectacularly. He'd no doubt planned everything. What about her hostages? Had Sanchez planned a rescue? Changes were now required there as well.

Sanchez should never have betrayed her. She knew precisely how to deal with him. She challenged herself to remain still, kneading the pea-sized keloid like a prayer bead, while her mind raced methodically as if the devil himself snapped her ass.

Go now. Go now, her intuition prodded with each beat of her pounding heart inside the steamy, sweat-soaked cocoon that enveloped her.

Forty-two seconds after the gunshot, she was ready. She pulled off the wet protective gear, ripped the paper wall coverings down, stuffed it all along with the listening equipment into her oversized litigation bag.

A soaking wet woman fleeing a murder scene would be noticed and remembered in this neighborhood. She'd need fresh clothes immediately. She had none. She shrugged into her overcoat and turned up the collar. For now, she'd alter her planned route as she could and her overcoat must suffice.

She took one last look around the room, satisfied she'd sanitized as well as possible. She flipped off the lights, pressed the knob's center button to lock the door from the inside, and closed the janitor's closet solidly behind her. Sliding her gloved hand into her pocket, she slipped down the hall into the lobby and out into the Friday evening pedestrian traffic less than three minutes after Sanchez killed O'Donnell.

Six blocks away, cloaked by the late night crowd waiting for traffic to clear before entering a crosswalk, she heard her own voice murmur, "What the hell was that soldier thinking?"

Her chance to ask him came sooner than she'd expected.

CHAPTER 2

Thursday, November 11
5:07 a.m.
Washington, DC

The untraceable cell phone vibrated itself almost to the hotel's bedside table edge before FBI Special Agent Kim Otto awakened. She watched the wretched thing snag against the table's lip and let it dance an unrelenting jig for a few more moments before she chose to answer.

Only one person could be calling and he wouldn't give up.

Her assignment was off the books—not stated to her as a mere preference, but hammered home. He wouldn't have allowed anyone else to use his secret phone inside or outside the Agency.

Kim slid her arm outside the cozy warmth of the down comforter, and brought the viper to her ear. "Don't you ever sleep?" she asked, not caring about the edge in her tone.

The Boss ignored her question and her foul mood. "How many times have you seen him in DC this week?"

"Why?" Not even bothering to ask whom he meant or how he knew she'd seen Reacher at all. She'd found staying under the radar a monstrous challenge in the era of constant surveillance, and had experienced the consequences of failure too many times already. She kept her conversations to a minimum; her face turned away from cameras, and used only the most secure connections possible. Even so, she was only too aware that more than one pair of eyes was watching her every move.

"Get in and get out today," the Boss said. "And watch yourself. He knows who you are and what you're doing now. He won't like you messing with his team."

Kim had already seen the results of things and people Reacher disliked. Not pretty. "Can't see that we have a choice, given what you've supplied us to work with."

Ten days ago, they'd been tasked with completing a background check on a subject being considered for a special assignment. Routine. Except the assignment was classified above her clearance and the subject was Jack Reacher and someone had worked very hard to ensure every paper trail ended with his discharge from the Army fifteen years ago.

For the first five days, she and her partner believed Reacher dead. For the next five, they'd learned so little about him that he might as well have been. Today, they planned to change their luck.

"You could tell me what you know," she said. "Or give us access to his existing files. Or do anything remotely helpful."

She listened to silent breathing for a moment, then tossed off the duvet and shivered with the cold shock. High-tech microfiber pajamas might be great for travel packs, but they certainly weren't warm. If she didn't get back to her Detroit apartment soon, shopping would be unavoidable.

"Check your mail," the Boss said at last, as if he'd only made up his mind to send her something during the call. "And be guided accordingly."

After that, she heard nothing at all. She threw the cell phone across the room, where it hit the wall and bounced onto the carpet. With luck, maybe the damn thing would never ring again.

Sleep was now impossible.

Three hours later, showered and dressed and fully briefed on the short report the Boss had sent, Kim opened her door after the first knock. Room service. She signed for her meal, ushered the server out, and poured more strong black coffee. She snagged a piece of toast and spread a bit of jam over it. She wasn't really hungry, but bread would soak up the two mini-pots of coffee already in her stomach and reduce her antacid consumption. Maybe.

The next knock on her door marked the arrival of her new partner, Carlos Gaspar.

"Let's ignore the dead ones for the moment," she said as he walked in. "Any brilliant ideas about the others?"

Both had dressed for the same work day—hours of interviews in the business districts of DC and New York—but Gaspar's relaxed khaki was all casual Miami, and Kim's tailored black suit was pure, stodgy Detroit. They looked exactly like what they were, Kim thought. She found that refreshingly unusual.

"Look on the bright side," he joked. "Fewer interview subjects means less work. We'll make it home for Thanksgiving."

Kim's relationship with Gaspar mirrored the paradox of their assignment. Straightforward, but complicated. Easily stated, but impossible to predict. Reliable, but dangerous. In some ways, Kim felt she knew Gaspar well because of everything they'd already survived. In other ways, Gaspar remained nearly as much a mystery to her as Reacher himself.

Gaspar stood facing the window, watching the cold, grey November sky, preoccupied. His wife was very pregnant and alone in Miami with Gaspar's four daughters. Kim knew he wasn't happy about being away from Maria and the girls. And something very negative had happened yesterday in Gaspar's Cuban-American community while they were in Virginia following up a lead on Reacher. Something that worried him. Gaspar didn't tell her about the problem and made it clear he didn't want to discuss his personal business with her. She was glad. She had enough on her plate already.

"I'm waiting for that brilliance," she said.

Gaspar shrugged. "Brilliance? Such as?"

Kim watched him a moment. She was lead on this assignment and it was up to the leader to make sure all the players were fit for duty. Events had already proved the job was a challenge for Gaspar, given his injuries. Today's plan was routine pavement pounding and interviews.

Before the Boss's call, she'd thought she could afford to give him twenty-four hours to figure things out at home. After that, if the assignment continued, he needed his head (and as much of his body as he could muster) in the game. For now, she'd let that plan stand. But she'd do whatever she had to do, including replacing him, if it came to that. She wouldn't work with Gaspar if he couldn't do the job.

Like her mother insisted, when there's only one choice, it's the right choice.

With exaggerated patience, Kim recapped what Gaspar seemed to be ignoring. "Reacher's old unit had nine members, counting Reacher. We've spent two days trying to track them down. We were only able to locate three. We're set to meet the first two of those this afternoon. You were supposed to come up with a can't-miss approach for today's two. What are we going to say?"

Gaspar's tone was clipped, as if he were reciting the phone book. "We're doing a routine background check on Jack Reacher for the FBI Special Personnel Task Force, updating his personnel file since he left the Army. We want to know, soup to nuts, what they can contribute to our almost non-existent data."

"Just like that?"

"Why not? The guy's a licensed P.I. and the woman's a forensic accountant. Both ex-Army police. They'll get it."

Kim drained the coffee cup and refilled. She felt taut as a drawn bowstring.

"He didn't call you?" she asked.

"Sure, he called," Gaspar told the view out the window. "He warned me about Reacher coming our way. He sent the report. I've read it. Nothing worth getting our panties in a wad over. Let's not get off course again just because he's yanking our chains, okay? We tried that last week and it nearly got us killed."

Now that they had at least an understandable plan, Kim wanted to stay on track, too. Despite running into dead ends everywhere they turned, they'd managed to uncover bits of Reacher's Army file that the Boss had refused to supply. They'd already tracked down two of Reacher's prior commanding officers. Both generals now, and both tight-lipped. Deliberately unhelpful, beyond suggesting they interview members of the elite special investigative unit Reacher had recruited and trained. For two years, the team had been inseparable, a force to be reckoned with, never messed with. If Reacher had kept in touch with anyone, the two generals said, it would be the eight other members of that unit.

Given what she knew about Reacher so far, Kim had her doubts. But a group of people once that tight could be a gold mine of information. Maybe. Besides, neither she nor Gaspar had identified any viable alternatives.

So, after unencrypting the Boss's early morning e-mail, they had even fewer.

She asked, "I wouldn't feel too optimistic about my life span if I were in Reacher's old unit, would you?"

Gaspar shrugged again, distracted, still gazing out the window—or at his reflection. "Special investigative units are manned by soldiers with a death wish, Sunshine," he said. "Volunteers for extremely hazardous duty. Natural risk-takers. Adrenaline junkies. They continue risking life and limb after discharge, too. Predictably, they don't live long."

She nodded. "True. But, Reacher's team never lost a member while they were handling the Army's extremely hazardous duty. They leave the service, and now four of the eight are dead, another is presumed dead, not one has died of natural causes, and their leader can't be found."

Gaspar shrugged. "The first one died in a car wreck. Car crashes kill plenty of Americans every year."

As if he'd said one member of Reacher's unit had died on a trip to Mars, she asked, "You believe that was an accident?"

At long last, he turned to her. "You don't, I suppose," he sighed.

"Let's say you're right. One car wreck. What about the others? Five years ago, one member of the unit disappeared and three more members died. All within days of each other. All three of the known dead tortured, their legs broken to immobilize them. And then each one dropped, still alive, from a helicopter miles above the desert floor. That is not normal risk-taking, adrenaline-junkie death-defiance, Chico. No way."

The data they'd uncovered on Reacher's army days had, as usual, revealed too little. He had never been popular with his peers. As a military policeman, Reacher was in trouble often and he'd made enemies.

But he'd been discharged fifteen long years ago and a lot of those enemies were dead or not interested in Reacher anymore. Unlikely Reacher would hide from anyone out to hurt him, anyway, based on the little Kim knew of the man. He was more of a confront-me-if-you-dare type.

So why was he living so far off the grid not even a sniffing bloodhound could find him? There had to be a reason, and the one she'd reluctantly reached was as good a working hypothesis as any.

Gaspar shrugged, wagged his head back and forth. "It bothers me that I'm starting to understand you. You're actually thinking Reacher killed four members of his own unit? Oh, and maybe five while we're at it, counting Jorge Sanchez, who hasn't been found yet." His tone conveyed precisely how preposterous he thought her suspicion was. "The Boss sure as hell didn't tell me that. Can you prove it?"

She said nothing.

"That's what I figured, Susie Wong." He grinned. "And

what about the remaining three? It's inconvenient for your theory that psycho-killer Reacher didn't off them, too, isn't it?"

She replied, "We haven't actually laid eyes on them yet, have we?"

Kim wasn't joking. She'd believe they still walked the earth when she actually saw and spoke to them. All she could say for sure at this point was that she hadn't located death certificates for them. Where Reacher was concerned, the absence of records proved nothing.

Dave O'Donnell was first on today's interview list because he was located right in Washington DC. The other two, Karla Dixon and Frances Neagley, resided in New York and Chicago, respectively. Kim and Gaspar would be visiting Dixon as soon as they finished with O'Donnell, then back here tonight and head to Chicago for Neagley in the morning.

Gaspar turned from his window-gazing. "Don't worry so much. Mucking around with 15-year-old contacts will probably be another waste of time. But I get it. Interrogating the last three unit members is the only plan we've got. Let's just waste our time with O'Donnell and then we can move on wasting it with the last two. Have I mentioned lately how much I love this job?"

Kim didn't expect to get much help out of O'Donnell or the others in tracking Reacher down, either, but she didn't have any other ideas. They'd finish the interviews in forty-eight hours or less. At that point, she'd demand that the Boss give her the resources they needed to accomplish the job or relieve her of the Reacher assignment. She had better things to do with her time and Gaspar was practically desperate to get back to Miami. This was bullshit.

She glanced at her Seiko. 9:43 a.m. They'd booked a 3:30 flight out of National to New York City to interview Dixon. That gave them plenty of time to interview O'Donnell and get to the airport. She grabbed her overcoat and headed toward the door. "Come on, Cheech. Let's get this show on the road."

"Yes, Ma'am, Boss Dragon Lady," Gaspar said. His tone was light, but Kim noticed his limp was more pronounced this morning, which too often meant he hadn't slept enough.

She was worried, even if Gaspar wasn't. She didn't for a moment believe the Boss had called this morning to warn her about provoking Reacher because he was concerned for their safety. Whatever the Boss was up to, her experience proved she'd need to keep her wits about her to deal with it. And she'd need a full-bodied partner, too.

She reached into her pocket for another antacid and held it in her mouth as the elevator dropped forty floors in twenty seconds.

CHAPTER 3

Thursday, November 11
10:30 a.m.
Washington, DC

A small, square sign on the wall to the left of the door-knob proclaimed, "David O'Donnell, Discreet Inquiries by appointment only."

Everything seemed quiet enough.

Gaspar turned the knob, pushed O'Donnell's office door open and entered the interior lobby with Kim three steps behind.

A middle-aged woman, maybe about seventy, give or take a decade, was seated behind the reception desk. She glanced up from her computer screen and peered over the bright, orange-framed readers perched on her nose. The readers magnified her flawless complexion. Her eyes rounded and she hesitated a moment too long, shooting a quick whiff of discomfort through Kim.

The woman cleared her throat. In a voice that seemed to croak from disuse or maybe nerves, she said, "May I help you?"

Kim nodded. "We'd like to see Mr. O'Donnell, please."

"Do you, uh, have an appointment?" Her left hand trembled as she reached to the side of her desk, maybe feeling for a calendar that wasn't there.

"No," Gaspar said.

"I'm afraid Mr. O'Donnell isn't available." The more she talked, the more Southern her accent became.

"No problem. We'll wait," Gaspar said, settling himself into the closest chair and adopting his usual waiting posture. Legs outstretched, crossed at the ankles, hands clasped over his flat stomach, eyelids sinking, if not yet closed. He wasn't sleeping, but if he sat there more than five minutes, he would be.

The secretary cleared her throat again. "He, uh . . . ."

"I'm sorry," Gaspar said, glancing lazily around her desk, as if he were looking for a nameplate or a business card. "I didn't catch your name. Mrs. . . . ?"

Curiously, she didn't fill in the blank. Maybe she'd noticed they hadn't offered their names, either. Instead, she replied, "If you could just leave your contact information, that would probably be best."

Gaspar said, "Glad to wait. Go ahead with your work, Mrs. Droptini." His eyes settled closed.

Startled that Gaspar had somehow discovered her name, she said automatically, "Mrs. Droptini is my mother-in-law."

Gaspar grinned. "You prefer Myra Dale, then?"

Myra Dale shifted uncomfortably in her chair and turned her attention to Kim, who smiled blandly as if she, too, was content to wait for O'Donnell's appearance.

Kim glanced around the small lobby, ignoring Myra Dale Droptini even as she could feel the woman watching her.

Something was not right with the woman. Or the situation. Kim's discomfort level rose as the Boss's early morning warning about Reacher resurfaced. But at the moment, she saw very little out of the ordinary.

What did she need to learn here? She didn't know. Her

entire assignment had been contained in a single thin file. Too thin. O'Donnell could fix that. He'd known Reacher reasonably well back in the day. O'Donnell could add some color, if nothing else, to her black-and-white knowledge. But would he? After the first few questions she'd prepared for him, she'd follow wherever the interview led. She expected to have plenty of time and to exhaust everything O'Donnell knew, even if he didn't realize he knew it.

Was it possible that Myra Dale Droptini knew anything useful about Reacher? She seemed like a woman who would know what was going on in her boss's business. Kim made a mental note to ask Myra Dale after she questioned O'Donnell.

O'Donnell's private office down the interior hall was likely more spacious than the lobby, which was little more than an anteroom outfitted with two sets of armless chrome and black leather chairs separated by 12-inch glass-topped pedestal tables. There might be a small conference room, maybe another smallish space somewhere for a coffee pot. She sniffed. No coffee aroma floating around. Too bad.

Kim had no access to banking records so she didn't know how successful O'Donnell's business actually was, but he seemed to be doing all right.

The office suite was large enough for a solo private investigator in the nation's capital. Class A space was notoriously pricey in DC; she didn't hold it against him that his lobby was compact by her Detroit standards. One high-end piece of artwork hung on each narrow white wall, furniture was minimalist but expensive, and the carpet had been upgraded.

In her prior life, had she been auditing O'Donnell's financial records, she'd have approved of his choices in quality and quantity. Good enough to inspire confidence; not so showy as to invite distrust. Precisely the correct mix for his probable clientele.

Current issues of political magazines rested on the tabletops along with small dishes of individually wrapped hard candy. Kim snagged a couple, unwrapped one, and popped it in her mouth, puckering up when the sour apple flavor hit her salivary glands.

O'Donnell wasn't hiding from anyone. His current private investigator's license was discreetly displayed near the door. According to official databases, O'Donnell had first obtained the license immediately after his Army discharge and had maintained it consistently since. His number was listed.

He also had a concealed weapons permit and several registered firearms, according to public records.

If he had a wife and kids, or even an ex-wife or step-kids, that information was missing from the files she'd located. Nothing about the immediate décor suggested O'Donnell was tethered to anyone in particular, but Kim noticed more framed objects on the walls of the corridor leading deeper into the suite. Family snaps?

When she wandered toward them, Myra Dale stiffened in her chair and made a small, choked sound. What was wrong with that woman? Kim kept walking and Myra Dale did nothing to stop her.

The most interesting photo was at least fifteen years old. A group of nine soldiers, two women and seven men, taken while they were on active duty. All nine looked different from their Army personnel file headshots, but they were recognizable. The giant in the middle was unmistakably Reacher. The rest were the eight members of his special investigative unit, including the ones who were now dead or missing, as well as O'Donnell, Dixon, and Neagley.

The other frames held flashy photo ops of O'Donnell with various politicians and prominent celebrities, suggesting he was well connected, too. Yes, O'Donnell was doing okay after leaving the big green machine.

Reacher might be doing okay, too, she realized. It was a new idea where Reacher was concerned. Maybe Reacher had enough money to buy his privacy. Could that be true? It was as likely an explanation for his success at disappearing as any other she'd considered.

In some ways, a wealthy Reacher made more sense.

She'd traversed the interior hallway almost to the last door on the right, which was cracked open. O'Donnell might be there, might've just instructed his secretary to say he was out. She and Gaspar could get this interview over with and head to Dixon in New York. Otherwise, they could flip the interviews: go to Dixon now, come back for O'Donnell tomorrow morning.

She'd taken another step toward the doorway when she heard Myra Dale's voice behind her.

"Please," she said, a bit more loudly. "Please don't go in there. The officer said she'd be right back."

The officer?

Kim didn't look back, and didn't stop. She counted on Gaspar to deal with Myra Dale Droptini. He said something and Myra Dale answered, but Kim paid no attention.

Just as she pressed against the door, she noticed the yellow crime scene tape that had fallen onto the carpet and been kicked aside. *What the hell?*

When the door swung open, she confirmed enough space to enter O'Donnell's personal office and stared at the cold, dried, bloody mess blanketing the room.

The next few minutes passed with glacial speed.

Kim's experience said the scene was at least five days old. Maybe more. It fell into the familiar gap between before and long after murder. Which explained why the office felt not quite abandoned and not yet restored to whatever it would become. Probably helped explain Myra Dale's odd behavior, too. Trapped out front in a workspace that seemed normal while incessantly aware that horror reposed down the hall.

Had Myra Dale been the one who discovered the body? Or had she been here when he'd been killed? Either way, Kim understood Myra Dale's nervousness now and felt sorry for her. Some people recovered from such experiences, but many did not. Myra Dale seemed less resilient than she needed to be.

Kim's experience supplied the warm, acrid scent of blood and bone and grey matter and guns attacking her nostrils as it had at fresher crime scenes. She imagined slimy specks clinging to her face and clothes. Even as her skin crawled, she felt separated from the atmosphere inside the room by the time gap between murder and what cold evidence remained.

Out of habit, her mind reconstructed the killing. The victim was most likely Dave O'Donnell. The blast had propelled pieces from the front of his head around the room, and blood had continued to flow from his head wound afterward as his heart kept pumping. Judging from the amount of dried blood covering his desk, around the outline of his fallen upper body and beyond, O'Donnell's heart had been strong. Crime techs must have worked here for hours collecting evidence amid the gory mess.

Gaspar approached, glanced around the room, and then his gaze met Kim's. "Droptini says she's been closing out the confidential files this morning. An officer has been watching her to be sure she didn't destroy evidence. Officer stepped out to get coffee. Expected back any second."

"I'll hurry," Kim replied, grabbed her smartphone, glanced at her watch, and videotaped the scene, dictating just-the-facts into her official report.

"Thursday, November 11, 10:58 a.m. FBI Special Agents Kim Otto and Carlos Gaspar on the scene of what appears to have been a murder committed several days ago."

Kim allowed the video to record the room's contents. She left no time gaps that might provoke questions later. She panned the desk where the blood evidence suggested the body was found and thought hard about the audio report, what to leave in, what to leave out, before she spoke again.

"The victim appears to have been seated at the desk at the time of death and based on the estimated amount of blood loss and outline of the body's position was probably male. Evidence of a single bullet removed from the wall directly in front of the desk chair suggests one shot in the head, back to front, at close range. Death was likely near instantaneous, although the gunshot was followed by a continuing heartbeat for several seconds."

Muffled footsteps approached along the hallway carpet. Gaspar turned to block the visitor's view, but Kim knew she was out of time.

"Report concluded 11:02 a.m." She switched off the video and slipped her smartphone into her pocket just as a uniformed officer arrived at the doorway.

Gaspar engaged her to allow Kim a few more moments. Standing amid the bloody chaos for a final look, Kim noticed the high-tech speakerphone on O'Donnell's desk.

Fingerprint residue blackened the buttons.

Had crime scene techs found evidence to identify the killer there? Could the victim have been conducting a telephone call at the time he was killed? If so, who was the caller and when, exactly, had he disconnected? More unanswered questions she filed away for later.

"Agent Otto, this is Officer Pat Schofield," Gaspar said when she joined Gaspar at the threshold.

"Sorry, but I need to see some ID." Schofield said it pleasantly, though. If she'd been wary upon arrival, Gaspar had somehow put her at ease already.

They showed their badges. Local law enforcement worked well with the FBI in DC and paths crossed often, although neither Gaspar nor Otto had met Schofield before. Satisfied by whatever Gaspar had said, Schofield didn't seem overly concerned to find two agents in O'Donnell's office.

"Why are you interested in the victim?" Schofield asked.

"We came to interview David O'Donnell about another case," Gaspar explained. "Was he the victim?"

Schofield nodded. "So I'm told. This is my patrol area, but I wasn't on duty Friday night."

"You didn't know O'Donnell, then?"

Schofield wagged her head. "No. You?"

"No," Gaspar said. "What happened here?"

Schofield said, "Wish I could tell you. They just asked me

to come up this morning while the secretary collected files."

"Any reason we can't talk to her about it?"

"She left when I came in. She wasn't here when it happened, anyway. You'll need to ask the detective in charge."

"Do you know who that is?" Gaspar asked.

Schofield wagged her head again. "Just call the station. They'll want to talk with you anyway."

"Right," Gaspar said. "Why hasn't this place been cleaned up?"

"Sometimes it takes a while to get a crew out here," Schofield said. "Or maybe the techs aren't done. Like I said, I wasn't on duty Friday night."

Kim followed Gaspar out of the office and back through the door they'd entered forty-eight minutes earlier, heading downstream, away from the crime scene.

Could she have saved O'Donnell? Maybe. Not that it mattered now. O'Donnell could no longer be saved except, perhaps, by God. Which, under the circumstances, seemed unlikely.

Gaspar kept up a strong pace as they crossed the building's main lobby, controlling his ever-present limp fairly well. He said, "Want me to call?"

Kim stopped at the glass exit doors. She knew what Schofield meant. The detective on the case would call them in after he heard from Officer Schofield. Expect them to explain themselves. That could not be allowed to happen. They needed high-level preemptive action to make sure they were never officially connected to O'Donnell or his murder.

"We've got a narrow window here, Sunshine," Gaspar said.

She sighed. Nodded. He opened the untraceable cell. She heard him say, "Requesting interference."

Kim tuned out the rest, pushed through the doors.

The more distance they put between O'Donnell and themselves, the better.

Once again, they were mired in death. Hardly surprising, though. They had come to expect violence in Reacher's wake.

Had Reacher been here? Made sense.

Had he killed O'Donnell? No evidence to suggest otherwise.

"Still think Reacher's old unit is just a bunch of unlucky ex-grunts, Cheech?" Kim asked when he'd finished his call, head bent against the icy rain pelting her face and slickening the sidewalk.

Gaspar ignored her question, hunched deeper into his overcoat against the biting November wind and speed-limped as swiftly as possible to catch up. Slightly breathless, he asked, "Where's the fire?"

She kept her stride. She wanted to get away from O'Donnell's office, and she felt an illogical urgency to reach Dixon. Whoever had killed O'Donnell had a six-day head start. If he'd left O'Donnell intending to kill Dixon, they were already too late.

After three more blocks at a near jogging pace, Gaspar grabbed her arm.

"Look," he said, chest heaving, staring directly into her eyes. "Yes, it pisses me off that everyone we want to interview is dead before we get there and the Boss hides facts we need to know. Yes, it's dangerous to ignore the implications."

His breathing had slowed a bit. He lowered his head closer and softened his tone, too. "That said, you've got to know there's probably no point in getting to Dixon at all, and there's certainly no rush to get there."

"You could be right. But what if you're not?"

They might have argued further, but the icy cold made sparring on the sidewalk bone chilling.

He flagged a taxi. "Come on. There's an earlier flight to Kennedy. We can catch it if we hurry. We don't have time to go back to the hotel for our bags. We'll do without them until we get back tonight."

Kim said nothing, but she entered the cab and tried to focus on Dixon instead of the many ways a commercial pilot could screw up when flying an airliner through an ice storm.

CHAPTER 4

Thursday, November 11
11:22 a.m.
Washington, DC

Gaspar said, "Reagan National, please."

They settled into the back seat for the short drive along ice-slicked streets. Kim glanced at Gaspar and allowed her anger to surface. "He knew about O'Donnell when he called this morning. Otherwise, he wouldn't have lit such a fire under us to get there. But no warning at all. Not a word. Why not?"

Gaspar nodded toward the taxi driver, reminding her of the dashboard camera before he replied, "Because he wanted us to stay on course."

"Why? We didn't learn a damn thing. Nothing but a waste of time."

"Ours is not to reason why . . . ." She glared at him. He shrugged. "You're losing your perspective, Sunshine. This is just business as usual."

Kim said nothing. She was no mind reader, and Gaspar

wasn't either. The Boss had his own agenda. Whatever that agenda was, it didn't include sharing information vital to their assignment. She'd already learned that lesson the hard way. Still, she wasn't used to working for a man she didn't trust with a partner she didn't know on a mystifyingly dangerous assignment where people attempted to thwart her at every opportunity. The assignment was more than a challenge. So far it had been a constant ten-day nightmare.

When the taxi dropped them off at the terminal, Gaspar paid the driver before joining her on the sidewalk, where they stood a moment in silence before he asked, "Now what, Suzy Wong?"

Their assignment was to be completed in as close to total secrecy as possible, revealing their identities when required but never the true nature of their mission. Which was okay because neither Kim nor Gaspar knew the truth anyway. Their cover story was difficult enough and they disclosed it only when unavoidable. Staying off the grid was a constant struggle, but it was the only piece of the job that made Kim feel safer.

Surveillance at Reagan National was perhaps the most comprehensive in the country. There was no way to stay off camera but they could slow the hunters down by refusing to provide audio instructions to go with the video. A weak grin lifted the right corner of her mouth. Whoever wanted to know where she was going next would have to do a bit of digging to figure things out. *Keep 'em guessing as much as possible* was not much of a plan, but it was the only one she'd come up with so far that occasionally worked.

Gaspar could figure things out. They entered the terminal building. He approached the ticket counter and returned saying, "We're departing in twenty-minutes."

They hustled through security, passing their guns and badges to the TSA officer, and were the last two passengers aboard the plane. As usual, Gaspar relaxed into seat 1A while Kim chose a seat a bit further back in the first class cabin where she couldn't see and hear too much of what was going on with the flight crew. She popped two antacids, gripped the seat's arms, and closed her eyes as if she might save herself from disaster only if she didn't see it coming.

After they reached the appropriate altitude, the flight attendant announced electronic devices could be used. Kim loosened her death grip on the armrests and reached for her laptop. A bolt of panic stole her breath before she remembered she'd left everything she owned back at the DC hotel. She didn't even have a charger for her phone, meaning she couldn't afford to drain its remaining energy by working on the inadequate keyboard.

Which left her no choice but to do the one thing she avoided whenever possible while flying: think without the benefit of distraction.

An hour and fifteen minutes later, Gaspar was still sleeping when she tapped him on the shoulder to disembark. He yawned, stretching long arms and long legs across the entire bulkhead before he stood, slouched into his overcoat, and limped out behind her onto the jetway ramp.

New York's JFK airport was no better place for a private conversation than Reagan National, so Kim saved the benefit of her flight wisdom for a safer location. The Boss, his enemies, and Reacher himself could all be listening or watching or both. They'd done it before.

The ice storm they'd left in DC was worse here. After another, much longer ride into the city in silence, the taxi driver deposited them a block away from Karla Dixon's apartment. Again, Gaspar paid the fare in cash and was not offered a receipt. By tomorrow, there was an excellent chance the driver would have forgotten them completely.

Hours of pelting sleet coated New York in clear ice that glistened like cellophane gift wrap. They slipped and slid along the sidewalk toward Dixon's apartment building, as alert as possible to their surroundings. Half a block away, Kim spied as good a briefing location as they were likely to find.

"Let's stop in here for a couple of minutes," Kim said, tilting her head toward the door of the café. She was chilled and wet and she wanted a chance to talk.

They entered a surprisingly busy eatery of indeterminate ethnicity. People packed the front, waiting out diners reluctant to leave the fragrant warmth inside for the inhospitable November storm.

Kim wiggled to the side of the crowded holding pen and leaned against the wall, allowing her to see toward Dixon's apartment outside the plate glass window. Gaspar followed, leaned next to her with a view of the café's entrance while he bent his head closer to hear her.

Quietly, beneath the chatter buzz, Kim offered the results of her mental heavy lifting while he'd napped on the plane.

"Given O'Donnell's execution, I think we proceed under the assumption that both Dixon and Neagley are either dead or about to be, too. We could barge in and confirm that's the case with Dixon, but that would only light us up on the radar."

"Agreed," Gaspar said.

She didn't know who was watching Dixon and Neagley other than the Boss. But she knew it was safer to assume others were engaged in the same surveillance. Reacher could be watching, too. She'd seen him three times in the DC area recently, including the night O'Donnell was murdered. The last time, Reacher was headed north. It wasn't foolish to consider that he'd come to New York for Dixon. It would be foolish to assume otherwise.

"Maybe Reacher killed them all," she said. "Maybe not."

"Agreed," Gaspar said again.

"If he didn't kill Dixon, he'll want to see the crime scene for himself before he makes any decisions."

Gaspar's right eyebrow popped up. "You think so?"

"He was a homicide investigator. That's what you and I would do."

A group of four finally departed. They opened the door wide just as Kim inhaled, filling her lungs with cold New York fuel exhaust. She controlled her cough while she exhaled long and slow.

Gaspar shrugged. "And if Reacher shows up, knowing she's dead or not, he could get pissed off."

"Reacher gets pissed off?" she cracked. "What makes you say that?"

"Besides the dead bodies, not to mention the maimed and mangled? Ignoring fires, explosions, and various other forms of destruction we've found in his jet-stream over the past ten days alone?" Gaspar grinned, wagged his head. "Nah. No anger issues with this guy."

Kim chuckled. "Maybe he is a little angry. Now and then. When provoked."

Gaspar guffawed, which made Kim feel better. But his laughter also drew stares from the immediate crowd, which didn't. They didn't need to be remembered at a place so close to Dixon's apartment. Maybe they weren't that hungry. She stood quietly for a moment, allowing patrons to return to their private conversations, before she said, "Let's go, okay?"

Outside, they faced the blustery ice showers once again as they slid along carefully toward their destination.

Karla Dixon's business address was also her apartment, located in a tony area of midtown Manhattan. Normal Midtown traffic around the entrance; no official vehicles or other obvious indicia of criminal activity within the building. They stood shivering outside the entrance, simply processing this lack of abnormal activity. Which might be okay. Or not.

Gaspar stamped his feet in what she recognized as an effort to generate body heat. "We're not going to learn anything standing out here, Sunshine. What's your pleasure?"

Kim took a last look around the immediate area to confirm the surveillance camera locations she'd spotted and the absence of discernible human surveillance. If Reacher or anyone else was watching from between buildings or behind vehicles, she didn't see any sign of it. She led the way through the heavy glass door into Dixon's building.

A private security guard talked on the phone behind a

desk twenty feet inside the entrance. He was about 5'9", early 60s maybe. Gray hair, brown eyes, rimless glasses, and a growing paunch still comfortably covered by his uniform shirt without gaping spaces between buttons. He was unarmed, which might have rendered another man useless against threats more serious than tenants irate over delayed deliveries from Bloomies. But Kim's quick appraisal revealed this guard wasn't just another rent-a-cop.

She'd seen men like him all over New York, DC, Chicago, even Detroit and smaller cities, since the events of 9/11 and the wars that followed. A plastic nameplate pinned above his blue shirt's left breast pocket said simply "H. Silver," but his bearing and general appearance all but flashed the neon warning: "Col. US Army, Ret."

Dixon would feel comfortable with an Army veteran manning the security desk for her building. Not that some regular Army retiree would represent a challenge for Reacher, should he decide to get past.

Retired Army or no, Mr. Silver didn't seem at all concerned when a uniformed bike messenger slipped by Kim and Gaspar, waved and continued past his station toward the residence elevators without stopping. Dixon's killer could easily have done the same.

Silver finished his call and asked Gaspar, "How can I help you today?"

Silver's assumption that Gaspar was in charge because he was the male half of the duo might have rankled at another place and time. As it was, Kim recognized the value of the man-to-man approach and stood aside, giving Gaspar room to talk them past Dixon's gatekeeper. It was a short, fruitful conversation. Silver waved them by as breezily as he had the messenger, which made Kim feel uneasy.

The elevator ride was express to the top floor, a distance they covered in forty-five seconds. Kim worried about airplanes, but never about elevators. Elevators were tethered by cables. They went straight up and straight down, and they were inspected regularly and maintained properly. If they fell, which rarely happened, well, they only dropped as far as the basement. She wasn't claustrophobic or even particularly fearful. But she was aware of life's risks. Riding elevators in city skyscrapers wasn't risky enough to worry about. No elevator had ever crashed into an office tower and killed 3,000 civilians.

"What did Colonel Silver have to say?" Kim asked.

"Dixon isn't home, but she left him a standing order to allow visitors up to her floor once he'd screened them."

"That's curious, isn't it?"

"He said she's running a business and her clients expect constant access. Sometimes, they meet here when she's away." Gaspar shrugged. "Maybe she's expecting someone in particular. Anyway, she hasn't been here for the past three weeks. He doesn't know where she is. She travels on business." Gaspar hesitated, glanced at her and finished his report. "We're not the first ones to ask the question."

"Who else was asking?"

Before Gaspar could respond, the elevator doors opened silently on the penthouse floor and the messenger Kim had seen pass through the lobby downstairs was waiting to enter for his return trip. He was lanky, Caucasian, brown eyes, brown hair. Maybe a little old to be riding a bike around the city in an ice storm, but fit enough. He wore a navy and white polo shirt with a *Reliable* logo across the front and back. He carried a bright yellow helmet, wore black bike pants, fitted bike gloves, and shoes with rubber soles. Kim wondered why he wasn't dressed in heavier clothes, given the winter wonderland he was pedaling through. He nodded at them as they disembarked, but said nothing. They waited for the doors to close behind him and the elevator to begin its descent.

Kim counted six apartments on this floor; the messenger could have delivered to any of them.

Dixon's apartment was to the right of the elevator. Like O'Donnell's lobby, this hallway presented nothing to indicate a crime scene, fresh or otherwise, waited on the other side of the door.

Given how chummy Gaspar had become with Colonel Silver, she figured he'd probably have mentioned a murder in Dixon's apartment.

Gaspar punched a code into the keypad on the wall above the doorbell. The front door clicked, he opened it, and they entered.

"How did you know the code?" Kim asked when the door was safely closed behind them.

"Think about it a minute," Gaspar said.

"Silver told you?"

Gaspar frowned. "He was in Special Ops for forty-six years. Those guys don't reveal much."

Kim let the question go because at that moment she stepped into Dixon's apartment and was knocked back by the breathtaking view of the New York skyline through the windows opposite the entrance.

"Wow," she whispered.

Kim waited, admiring the vista's glistening structures while Gaspar made a quick sweep through the pricey apartment decorated with expensive furnishings. He returned to stand in the middle of the room to stare at the magnificent view while Kim had a look around.

Karla Dixon lived literally and materially so far above anything Kim had expected that she couldn't quite comprehend even as she walked from room to room, taking everything in like a child's first experience with astonishing high-wire circus performers.

Kim pulled out her phone and captured a quick video, mindful of her rapidly dwindling battery power, as she made a second, slower trip around.

Although the decor was a bit too modern and minimalist for Kim's taste, everything in the apartment was also relatively new and barely used.

Dixon's bedroom was larger than Kim's entire apartment in Detroit and Dixon's shower was large enough to accommodate Reacher's giant body engaged in all sorts of contortions. Surprising, unless she regularly entertained such giants, since Dixon was almost as petite as Kim.

Dixon's clothes were of the bought-this-season designer variety. Kim didn't wear designer anything, but she recognized the costly stuff. What did a forensic accountant need those clothes for? And more importantly, how could Dixon afford them? Kim had been a double major, herself. Accounting and law. She knew the salary ranges accountants were paid. Dixon's income level must have been well above normal because she didn't come from a wealthy family, according to her Army personnel file.

Kim found a number of framed photographs on the walls in Dixon's home office. She recognized a duplicate of the special investigative unit group photo she'd seen this morning on O'Donnell's office ego wall.

Kim took still shots of the photo before she continued.

Dixon's home office was as neat as the rest of her apartment. No computer or printer or phone. Only an open desk with no drawers. No visible papers of any kind. Kim realized she was actually standing amid the very first paperless office she'd ever seen. Until now, Kim had suspected a "paperless office" was akin to a golden unicorn. Everybody talked about such a beast, but nobody had ever laid eyes on one.

So Dixon was a neat freak of the highest order, too.

In the kitchen once more, Kim opened the big side-by-side refrigerator. The middle shelf held two cartons of Greek yogurt, two weeks out of date, a six-pack of still water and two large bottles of nice champagne. Otherwise, the refrigerator was as perfectly empty as the day it had been installed.

Quickly, Kim opened cabinet doors and closed them again. She moved through the remaining rooms opening every storage spot she found. She finished, returned the smartphone to her pocket, and joined Gaspar. Her entire apartment search lasted maybe ten minutes, max.

"No blood, no body, no sign of foul play, as they say in the old detective movies," Kim said as she approached him.

"Looks like O'Donnell's killer failed to add Dixon to his resume."

Gaspar continued staring out the window as if he could see answers on the enormous glass windows like words projected on a teleprompter. "Or he did the deed elsewhere."

Kim's stomach growled, reminding her that she'd had nothing to eat since the miniscule hotel breakfast hours ago. Gaspar must have heard, too, because he turned and said, "How about a cup of clam chowder? We're not too far from the Oyster Bar at Grand Central. We can talk there, too."

They let themselves out and rode the elevator to the lobby, where they found Colonel H. Silver, US Army, ret., occupied with another visitor. He barely waved when they walked past him out to the street.

"Next time, I'll input the code to open Dixon's front door," Kim said.

Gaspar grinned, turned up the collar on his overcoat, and moved off the curb to hail a taxi.

Traffic was busier now and the weather was worse. Every cab that passed was occupied. Kim ducked further into her upturned collar, stuffed her hands deep into her overcoat's pockets, moved from foot to foot to keep as warm as possible, and glanced at the surrounding buildings while she waited.

Street vendors had closed up for the day, if they'd ever opened. Parked cars lined the curbs. Pedestrians hurried along, shuffling across the slippery sidewalk, heads bent against razor-sharp sleet that slashed facial skin left unprotected for more than a brief moment.

As alert as she could be with cold wind gusting sleet into her watering eyes, Kim thought she recognized one pedestrian moving toward her.

She blinked away the ice forming on her lashes. She wasn't sure. Could it be the same messenger who had passed them twice inside Dixon's building?

He seemed to recognize her, too, because he turned away from Kim, hugging closely to the building, and headed back the way he'd come.

Gaspar continued attempting to flag a taxi. Kim called to him, but he'd stepped further into the street and didn't seem to hear over the noise of afternoon traffic. The messenger was farther down the block. Soon, he'd be too far ahead. She gave up on capturing Gaspar's attention and slid her feet along the sidewalk toward the messenger. He glanced back, saw her following, and shuffled faster. His foot slipped on the pavement. He grabbed for the building to steady himself, and kept moving. Kim slid along toward him with her hand also riding the building's exterior for balance.

Glancing back, Kim was glad to see that Gaspar had either heard her call or simply checked and followed. Not that he was making much progress, slide-stepping along the sidewalk with his injured leg.

Returning her attention to the messenger just in time to see him duck into a crevice between two buildings, Kim reached inside her coat, located her gun, and moved into the grim slice of alley after him.

CHAPTER 5

Thursday, November 11
3:35 p.m.
New York City

The sleet-slickened pavement along the dim alley was cracked and marred by potholes, giving the messenger's feet purchase where he'd had none on the sidewalk. He'd entered the alley and put on speed. By the time Kim reached the alley, his lead had grown enough to place him almost half a block ahead. Knowledge of the gloomy terrain provided him a second advantage.

Twice she yelled, "Stop! FBI!" He didn't hear or he ignored her and she didn't know which and it didn't matter. She chased him, but his longer stride and head start proved decisive. As he reached a lightless stretch in the alley ahead, he slipped out of sight and never reappeared.

Kim reached the spot a few moments later and stood searching fruitlessly for the messenger's escape route until Gaspar caught up with her.

"What the hell were you chasing him for?" Gaspar said,

both annoyed and breathless. He'd fallen on the ice at least once because the entire right side of his trousers and overcoat were covered in alley slime. He bent over and slapped at his clothes, attempting to knock some of the ruin off, but the effort was not productive.

"Why the hell was he running from me?" Kim replied, anger bubbling over. "Come on." She turned sharply, stuffed her gun back into its holster, and stomped carefully back the way she'd come.

"Where are you going now?" Gaspar called to her back.

"To ask your buddy Silver the right questions this time," she snapped. After a moment, she heard his careful footsteps following behind.

She retraced her path in the alley quickly enough, but when she reached the corner and stepped onto the icy sidewalk her leather-soled shoe slipped and she fell, hard, against the wall. She leaned her shoulder against the building and pressed it there as she covered the remaining distance lest her clothes end up in worse shape than Gaspar's.

By the time they reached Dixon's building entrance, unrelenting grey skies had turned the late afternoon to early evening. Sleet continued to pelt the few visible travelers. Pedestrians were scarce. Perhaps the usual mob of city dwellers had taken the subway or managed to hail cabs. The result was eerie, as if the city were abandoned.

Dixon's building lobby featured dim interior lighting that cast shadows into corners, which was okay because Gaspar's filthy overcoat would be less noticeable in the gloom. Kim pulled the heavy door's handle and Colonel H. Silver looked up from whatever he'd been doing, probably because an electronic noise or light or some alert happened at his desk when the door opened. No one else was in the lobby and this time Silver wasn't talking on the phone. He focused full attention on them.

Kim approached the desk, pulled out her badge wallet and showed its glinting gold. "FBI Special Agent Otto," she said. "You've met my partner, Special Agent Gaspar." She inclined her head in Gaspar's direction.

If Silver was surprised to hear her official identification, he didn't show it. "How can I help you, Agent Otto?"

"When we were here earlier, a messenger from *Reliable* went up to the penthouse floor. What was he doing here?"

Not many gatekeepers in Manhattan jousted with anything the FBI requested these days and Silver was no rogue. "*Reliable* comes in several times a day."

"Do you have that particular messenger's name and his contact number?"

Silver clicked a few keys on his keyboard. "Regular visitors register the first time they come in. I'm sure we've got him in the system. I need to find his first visit."

"Who on the penthouse floor uses *Reliable*?"

Silver continued to check his computer, "Ms. Dixon, usually. Could be others. *Reliable* is one of the more common services in this area."

"Ms. Dixon has been traveling for three weeks, you said," Gaspar reminded him.

"Right." Silver didn't look up. "But she gets deliveries when she's gone, too."

Gaspar's gaze met Kim's, his right eyebrow raised. She nodded, asked, "So the messenger service enters her apartment when she's not there?"

Silver raised his head this time, stared straight at Kim. Frowned. "That would be up to her, but yes, she could arrange to receive deliveries when she's away."

"You said she accepts visitors when she's not here, too, right?"

"Those are her orders. But you're only the second visitors she's had this time."

Gaspar's eyes met hers. She nodded.

"Was the first visitor an exceptionally big man?" Gaspar asked. Kim held her breath. Reacher could have been here, she knew. But she'd been hoping he hadn't.

Silver wagged his head back and forth. "Not that I saw. I'm only here on the day shift, but I remember a man and a woman. Maybe a week ago? I can search for their names if you want."

When neither Gaspar nor Kim replied, he turned his attention to the keyboard once again. "Don't ask me why visitor names aren't recorded in a searchable database. I've gone back two weeks and haven't found the *Reliable* guy yet. But the other two were here on November sixth. Mr. & Mrs. Edwards."

"Any chance you've got surveillance photos of all three of these visitors?" Kim asked. "And any others looking for Ms. Dixon during her absence?"

"I can get that for you, but it'll take me a couple of hours to pull it together."

Kim tried not to groan. She'd planned to be out of New York before nightfall. Best laid plans.

"Tenants don't provide you with specific dates when they're planning a long-term absence?" Gaspar asked.

"Optional. Ms. Dixon usually doesn't. We don't do any security monitoring on the residence floors." A moment later, he glanced up, clearly pleased with his efforts. "Okay. Here we go. The messenger's name is Downing and I've got a cell number for him as well as for the Reliable office he works from, but no street address."

Gaspar took both numbers and the name and placed the calls while Silver continued looking for the names of the other couple.

"No answer," Gaspar said.

"Why am I not surprised," Kim deadpanned. She pulled out her business card and handed it to Silver. "Give me a call when you have those photos. Or if the messenger comes back." She turned her gaze out into the darkness. Streetlights glistened off the steadily falling sleet. "And can you call us a cab?"

"I'll start on the photos as soon as my replacement gets here at six so I can leave the desk. Shouldn't take too long. I'll probably have them by seven or so. I can e-mail or text them to you at this number?"

Kim nodded.

Silver said, "But you'll never get a cab out there tonight in this weather. We've got a car service. Can we drop you somewhere?"

"Grand Central Station," Kim said. "We should be able to get out of the city from there after we have a bite to eat."

Silver wagged his head again. "You'd be better off staying the night. Flights have been delayed all day and the storm has been getting worse. Temperatures are falling, too. They'll probably close the airports in an hour if they haven't already."

Great, Kim thought. That's just perfect.

CHAPTER 6

Thursday, November 11
5:45 p.m.
New York City

Kim's toes had finally begun to thaw. Settled at a back table inside The Oyster Bar at Grand Central Station, she and Gaspar were on their third cups of hot coffee and working their way through bowls of steaming clam chowder.

She was tempted to book rooms upstairs at the Grand Hyatt, buy new clothes, and figure out the rest tomorrow, but they'd optimistically booked a flight back to DC at 9:45 p.m. instead. Storm gods willing, they'd actually be asleep in a somewhat familiar DC hotel before midnight and have clean clothes tomorrow. She'd collect her laptop and have access to secure files as well. For now, she wanted to eat and figure out what the hell to do next while they waited for Colonel Silver to send the photos he'd promised and for the storm to release them.

Gaspar looked more exhausted than she felt. The alley grime on his clothes had dried and begun to smell.

"Where are we?" Kim asked.

"Same place we were this morning. Nowhere."

Kim might have argued if Gaspar wasn't so obviously correct. She applied her attention to the chowder and considered what she knew, what she'd guessed, and what she still needed to find out.

Reacher's behavior had become her fixation since she'd received her assignment. Kim had spent years studying human behavior. She knew what was reasonable and what wasn't. Sometimes, she could tell what criminals would do before they did it. And she could analyze their activities exceptionally well afterwards, which was not as good, but still helpful. She wasn't a profiler by training, but what she had was an odd, savant-like talent based on instinct and experience. She'd honed the talent over the years to something akin to a fine art form. She couldn't explain it or defend it, but she relied on the ability as she relied on ever-present oxygen.

She wished she could see Reacher's face up close, though. And hear him speak. She'd never heard his voice. She'd seen him move on videotape once and she replayed the video in her mind.

At this point, she knew she would recognize Reacher in a dark alley when he was completely shadowed. But if she could meet him, study him, she would memorize his smell, his gestures, his voice timbre and cadence and syntax.

Did he have an accent? What kind? Was his voice gravelly and rough? Or smooth? What did the texture of his skin say about his physical activities? His hands were the size of shovels, but were they roughened by heavy work? Or softened by disuse? Did he have good teeth? She'd never seen him smile broadly. Army dental records suggested he'd had the usual cavities for a kid before Fluoride became ubiquitous. Had he worn braces? Have an overbite? A lisp?

She heard herself sigh and felt her shoulders sag with fatigue and disappointment. The problem was the same as it always was with this assignment. She just did not know enough, and she was battling on two fronts that she simply could not control. One, acquire more data. Two, face Reacher.

Preferably in that order.

The server approached with more coffee, which both Kim and Gaspar accepted. "Would you like dessert? We have terrific pie."

Kim looked down. She'd finished the last of her chowder without realizing she'd eaten it all. "No. Thank you."

Gaspar said, "Sure. Apple? With ice cream?"

The server collected the empty chowder bowls and before she hurried away said, "Coming right up."

Gaspar rested his forearms on the table and leaned toward her. "Figure everything out yet?"

"It would help tremendously if we knew why the Boss wants Reacher's file completed."

"No kidding."

She knew the Boss well. He had a reason for this assignment and the reason wouldn't necessarily be kosher. Which was okay. It was the not knowing that was not okay. Not knowing could get her killed. It almost had already.

"I was running the video we saw of Reacher head-butting that dude through my mind again," she said. They'd been given only one opportunity to watch the video, without sound, before it was taken from them. But Kim could remember every frame as if the short video were running on a continuous loop in her head.

In her mind's eye, she saw Reacher hitchhiking along the deserted country road. She watched as he caught a ride in a small sedan driven by an attractive young woman with a young boy in the car. The woman was distracted by the child and rear-ended a truck. The truck driver jumped out, pulled the woman from the car and attacked her. Reacher bolted from the vehicle and stopped the attacker with a quick, vicious head-butt. The attacker fell to the ground and cracked his skull on the pavement. Reacher left the scene, headed toward New York City.

Just two days ago.

"And?"

"Compared it to the first video we acquired." Last week, they'd seen and studied a better quality video in Margrave, Georgia. A man they'd thought was Reacher impersonated a U.S. Marshall to break an inmate out of the local jail.

"And?" Gaspar asked again.

She shook her head slowly. "Definitely not Reacher on the Margrave video."

"Because?"

She shared each comparison point slowly, even though she felt confident in her conclusions. The knowledge might save both their lives. "Reacher's taller, broader, looser limbed. His posture's better and his hands are bigger. Gestures more contained and defined. No wasted motions."

The server brought Gaspar's pie, a piece big enough to feed Kim for a week. Then she refilled their coffee mugs and left them alone.

Gaspar dug into the pie like a man who hadn't eaten in decades. His appetite amused and amazed Kim every time she witnessed it. If she ate in one month the amount of calories he consumed in one meal, she'd be as big as one of her mother's Buddha statues.

As it always did, her mind returned to Reacher. He was starting to feel very familiar to her, even though she had uncovered only a limited number of data points. She wasn't sure if that was a good thing or not.

In a moment of unanticipated confrontation, such familiarity might save her life, or cost it. Impossible to tell in advance.

But when there's only one choice, it's the right choice.

The only thing she could do was keep working on the puzzle, one interlocking piece after another, until she could see the entire picture. When would that happen?

"Any flashes of brilliance over there, Sunshine?" Gaspar asked, talking around his mouthful of pie and ice cream, as if she'd solved their knotty problems when he knew damn well they'd acquired precisely nothing of use this entire, miserable day.

She smirked. "Absolutely. I figure Reacher will be joining us for dinner three days from now at 7:32 p.m. at the Capital Grille in Chicago."

Gaspar's right eyebrow shot up in a perfect demonstration of his quizzical nature. As if she'd been dead serious, he swallowed and replied, "I've got fifty bucks that says you're right."

She laughed out loud, which, strangely enough, made her feel a bit more normal. Finally.

"Is Dixon with Reacher?" Kim asked.

"Too many variables to hypothesize at this point, don't you think?"

"I don't like it."

"Like what?"

"Probably two and maybe three of Reacher's special unit left, and we can't find even one of them. It's not normal."

"There is nothing normal about this entire assignment. We established that a long while back, Sunshine."

"This is beyond abnormal."

"How so?"

"Nine soldiers survive long stints and tough jobs in the Army. They get out and survive a long while. Later, in no special order, one disappears off the planet and five are dead, none by natural causes."

"As far as we know," Gaspar reminded.

"Right."

"Like I said, it's beyond abnormal. Weird, in fact. Outside of Mafia crime families and gang wars, I can't think of any reason why that many members of a single group of any kind would find themselves in this situation. Can you?"

He seemed to consider her question and finally said, "No."

"Right," she said again. "If we have any prayer of learning anything useful about Reacher from his Army buddies, our last clear chance is Frances Neagley in Chicago."

"And we need to get to her before she ends up dead or missing, too."

"So you agree that Reacher's on his way and has a three-day head start, then?"

Gaspar shrugged. "Who knows if he's with Dixon or Neagley, neither or both?"

Too many mysteries, unanswered questions, unbelievable situations. All of them revolved around Reacher. That was the only part lacking surprise.

The server came back with the coffee pot, the check, and unwelcome if not surprising news. "You folks aren't flying anywhere tonight, are you? Just heard they've closed the airports until tomorrow morning. A big jet slid off the runway and they've got a mess with cleaning that up in addition to the sleet storm."

Kim didn't even bother complaining. Sometimes, it just wasn't worth the effort.

She pulled out her phone and pressed the redial on the number for the Grand Hyatt Hotel to confirm the tentative reservations she'd already made. Before she could make the connection, her screen reflected a new message from H. Silver, with attachments.

CHAPTER 7

Thursday, November 11
8:55 p.m.
New York City

While Gaspar completed the paperwork for check-in at the hotel, Kim found a small shop at Grand Central geared to travelers, where she bought two phone chargers, deodorant, and a T-shirt to sleep in. They'd rely upon the hotel to supply the remaining necessities. While Gaspar rebooked their flight back to DC for the morning and sent his clothes to the laundry service, Kim had also stopped at the business center to print the three photos Silver had forwarded before joining Gaspar in his room.

Kim handed one phone charger and the three printed photos to Gaspar. He studied them while she rooted around the room until she found an empty outlet behind the television.

Gaspar studied the messenger's photo. "Friendly-looking fellow," he said.

After a few pretzel-like contortions, she connected the

second charger to her smartphone, which had depleted its final gasp of reserve battery power downstairs when she downloaded Silver's photos.

The room's Asian decor suited her size better than his. Courtesy of her German-American father, Kim was all lithe, lanky, and stubborn blonde, but only on the inside. Outside, she was shy of five feet tall and just as shy of 100 pounds, courtesy of her Vietnamese mother. The combination was seldom ideal. This hotel room furniture was a rare exception. She couldn't be blamed for savoring it, could she?

She plopped down in the room's only chair. Gaspar had stretched out on the grey leather divan, which barely accommodated his length. Wearing the hotel's skimpy robe, he looked uncomfortably cramped. She noticed him wince every time his weight shifted to his right side.

"Great cover, isn't it?" he said, holding the photo of the messenger up to her. She'd examined it on the way upstairs. It was a surprisingly clear full-face headshot, almost as if the messenger had posed for it. She'd already committed his face to memory. Brown hair. Dark eyes. Freckles. Big smile. Friendly-looking, indeed.

Gaspar spent more time with the second and third photos. These, too, were clear for surveillance cameras, though the two subjects were obscured. They'd either been lucky, which was unlikely. Or they'd expertly avoided clean headshots, which meant this couple was worth investigating.

"One of these shots was taken in the lobby and the other in the elevator," Gaspar said. "Not even an ear is exposed."

Kim mentally reviewed both photos. The man and woman stood close together. She was looking down, wearing a scarf covering her head, and sunglasses. He wore a wide-brimmed hat and an overcoat with its collar up. His face was turned away from the cameras, which had captured only the back and side of his head under the hat.

"Notice the time stamps," she said.

"The messenger's first visit was quite a while back. It's stamped October 3, 9:16 a.m. For the couple, less than forty-eight hours after O'Donnell was killed. Monday, November 8, 14:32 p.m. and 14:36 p.m. Guess these two didn't spend much time with Silver in the lobby, did they?"

Kim had noticed that, too. "Why do you think that is?"

Gaspar glanced up. "They must have done what we did. Given him ID he felt comfortable with. Wonder what that was?"

"And if the messenger is somehow involved with this couple or with Dixon's disappearance, he's been running his game for weeks. That suggests a certain level of sinister we hadn't expected," she said, thinking out loud.

"But he could be just a messenger," Gaspar suggested. "Dixon's stop could be on his route. Maybe he ran from you today because of something unrelated to Dixon."

She'd rejected this possibility hours ago, on the sidewalk when she'd seen the alarm in his eyes at the moment he noticed she'd recognized him. "Because I'm so big and scary, you mean?"

He grinned. "Well, you've got a scary gun and you were chasing the guy, after all."

She'd have punched him if he wasn't all the way across the room. Instead, she slouched as if he couldn't rile her with foolishness.

Gaspar asked, "Is this all Silver sent? No photos of the pair going in and out of Dixon's apartment? No elevator or lobby departure shots? No timeline or anything?"

"Dunno. My battery ran out of juice before I could check. But Silver included the names and contact information they gave him. Video, too. We'll be able to download it shortly when my phone is working again. I don't want to rearrange the furniture to look at it while it's charging, do you?"

He said, "Maybe the video will at least show us something about their body sizes. No rush. Let's rethink this a bit while we wait. The glue holding everything together is Reacher's old army unit. What do we know about them?"

Kim agreed they'd had very little opportunity to compare notes and analyze what they'd learned so far. "Not as much as we need to know."

"Right."

She gave up her pout and straightened up in the chair as she recounted the early facts. "Stanley Lowery was the first one to die. Alleged car accident victim, quite a while ago. His obituary said he was one of those back-to-the-earth types. Moved to Big Sky Country to raise sheep. There was a valid Montana death certificate."

"He got hit by a truck," Gaspar reminded her. "And nothing to suggest Reacher was around at the time or had any motive, let alone caused Lowery's death. Let that one go."

She wasn't willing to accept the easy answer, but for now she simply nodded. "Okay, chronologically, who died next?"

Gaspar said, "Couple of years later, Tony Swan, Manuel Orozco, and Calvin Franz all confirmed dead under fairly suspicious circumstances within a few days of each other. Maybe in that order, but it's hard to know based on the information we've got."

He waited a moment, as if they had not digested and disagreed over this data before. Kim waited until Gaspar filled the silence. "I suppose it's prudent to list those three as potential Reacher victims, but the idea doesn't sit right with me."

Kim felt the same way, but she wanted to hear Gaspar's take on it. Gaspar was the closest thing to Reacher's mindset she could get for now. On paper, Gaspar and Reacher's resumes were similar until they both left the Army. And they shared that Y chromosome thing. She had three brothers and had worked around men all her life, but male-think often confounded her. She'd be a fool not to exploit Gaspar's thinking. "Because?"

He wagged his head back and forth slowly as if it might help him to work out the kinks in his thinking. "Reacher was an Army officer. West Point graduate, no less. Not only that, a military cop. Hunting down U.S. Army-trained killers and bringing them back for court martial is a tough, tough gig. I know. I've done it. And Reacher chose his own team. Each of these soldiers must have saved Reacher's ass dozens of times. And vice-versa."

Gaspar leaned forward and studied her face as if he could persuade her to his point of view if she would only pay attention. "After all that, I'm sorry, Sunshine, but unless we can prove he's certifiably nuts, I just don't see the guy betraying members of his handpicked special investigations unit at all. Ever. No matter what."

"It's not the Marines. No *Semper Fi* and 'once a Marine, always a Marine' and all of that," Kim reminded him quietly.

He seemed to consider her comment seriously, but soon rejected it. "These nine had formed a special unit. They not only worked together, they relied upon each other for everything. That sort of bond—I don't know if it *can be* severed."

Gaspar had offered no new facts, nothing Kim didn't already know, nothing she hadn't already rejected. "All things are possible, Chico. Maybe the question we should be looking at is how that bond *could have been* severed. Because something out of the ordinary definitely happened."

He shook his head hard, even more firmly entrenched now. "Reacher might be hunting and taking out their killers. That makes a certain kind of sense. But you want to assume that Reacher killed members of his own unit?" He stood to pace the room in his slow, limping way that suggested pain Kim couldn't fathom.

Gaspar continued pacing and as always, the stretching seemed to lessen his pain and give him more control over his right leg. Kim had determined to let him tell her about his disability in his own way and his own time. But they'd been together ten days now and he hadn't once acknowledged the weak leg at all. How much longer should she wait? She didn't know, but she felt now was not the time. Something else was bothering him, too. So she waited. For now.

He grabbed a bottle of water and settled again onto the inadequate divan. Finally, he said, "About the only wild ass guess I can come up with is maybe—maybe, mind you— unavoidable self-defense *might* make Reacher kill his team.

I'm not persuaded, though. I don't see how that could happen even once, let alone repeatedly and separated by years of time and miles of distance."

"I agree," she said.

"Why the hell let me struggle with that, then?" His face suffused red and his nostrils flared and real anger bubbled over, which confirmed her gut. Gaspar was struggling with something. This was the first time she'd seen him so volatile. But she felt certain it wasn't her theories on Reacher that caused his reaction. What had pushed his buttons?

She waited until he managed to control himself once more, then said, as if he'd never lost his Latin temper, "Because I love watching your mind work. Or not work."

Ignoring his glare, she went on. "The theory's an obvious non-starter because it skips right over the most relevant issue in your setup. Basic criminal law. You know it as well as I do. Killing isn't self-defense unless the opponent presents an immediate threat of deadly harm. Meaning Reacher couldn't kill his team in self-defense unless they attacked him first."

She paused to give her point a fighting chance to breach the steam fairly billowing out of his ears and land in his brain. "Despite your unflagging belief in my creative abilities," she said, grinning at him, "I can't figure anything their former leader might have done to incite a cold, lethal mutiny in Reacher's team. Can you?"

Gaspar leaned his head forward and rubbed the back of his neck with his right hand. He squeezed his eyes shut as if forcing them closed might somehow reinvigorate him.

Kim had been studying Gaspar in the way she wanted to study Reacher. All of Gaspar's data points were melding together like molten chocolate she could smell and almost taste. He was slowly becoming predictable, which she found comforting. Predictable meant reliable in Kim Otto's world.

She wondered what he really thought about Reacher's old unit. Were they as loyal to Reacher as Gaspar seemed to expect? Maybe they were. Maybe that's why they were dead.

Maybe Reacher didn't kill them literally, but maybe something they learned from him or about him had proved fatal.

Gaspar said, "Let's move on. There were eight plus Reacher originally. We've accounted for half of them. What about the remaining four?"

"Well, Jorge Sanchez disappeared around the same time Swan, Franz and Orozco died," Kim replied.

Gaspar raised his eyebrow again. "Could be your answer right there."

Kim wagged her head. "Not likely. It's possible Sanchez *could* have killed the first four. Once Reacher found out about it, he *could* have made it his business to avenge his team. *If* we assume that happened, then Sanchez would have been a walking dead man for a very short while until Reacher caught up with him and made it a permanent condition."

"What's wrong with that? I like that idea. Makes sense."

"No, it doesn't." Kim stood up. Stretched. Gaspar was tired. She was tired. They weren't going anywhere tonight because of the storm and the analysis wasn't going anywhere, either, as far as she could tell. Maybe it was time to give it up. But then again, what else did they have to do? "If Reacher killed Sanchez five years ago, who killed O'Donnell last week?"

Gaspar opened his eyes. "Reacher again, most likely. Maybe he finally figured out that Sanchez and O'Donnell worked together to kill the others."

"Wow, Chico. Tangled web you're weaving just so you can give Reacher the benefit of the doubt."

He shrugged. "Killing any one of those three dropped from the helicopter was definitely more than a one-person job."

She nodded to concede that point. "Which means Reacher would only have needed the right accomplice to help him. Sanchez, say, who Reacher then takes out after he's through with him. And then maybe O'Donnell looks into it and gets too close, so Reacher takes him out, too. We could look into O'Donnell's notes, look for signs of him sniffing around the other killings."

"Who's got the tangled web now?" Gaspar said. After a second or two of brow-knitting, he shrugged. "Mostly, I just don't like to think about criminal behavior by military personnel at all, and certainly not distinguished officers like Reacher. Or military cops like his team."

She felt the same. Kim was a cop, too. And a damn good one. She worked side-by-side with some of the bravest veterans anywhere in the world. She didn't like chasing these angles, either. But it would fit the facts and she knew she'd be a fool to ignore them. She'd learned the hard way to take the facts as they came.

Kim moved on. "Whatever happened to Franz, Snow, and Orozco, only three and at most four members of the unit remain alive. Reacher, Sanchez, who is almost certainly dead, Karla Dixon, who is probably dead." Kim took a quick breath before concluding: "And Francis Neagley."

Gaspar noticed. "What scares you about Neagley?"

"What do you mean?"

He flashed her his knitted-brows-over-the-nose thing, which she knew was annoyance, but said nothing.

She laughed at him. "Does that stink-eye work to keep your kids in line? That's the best don't-mess-with-me look you can manage?"

A small grin parted his lips and wrinkled his nose. But he didn't back off. "What's your problem with Neagley?"

"Oh, come on. You can't tell me you think she's anything but an enormous toxic problem. Even you aren't that clueless, Cheech."

Gaspar shrugged. "Of course not. I'm not sure what's wrong with her, but I agree she's far from whatever passes for normal in a woman with her resume. But what's your problem with her?"

Good question. At some point, she might answer.

Before she'd been ordered not to do so, Kim had pulled Army personnel files for all the members of Reacher's Special Operations Unit. All would have been immediately expelled from the Gandhi School of Change by Passive Resistance, but Neagley's file was particularly disturbing. Perhaps more disturbing than Reacher's, depending on why you were comparing the two.

Sergeant Frances L. Neagley was a small but frightening woman. She'd refused Officer Candidate School four times during her years in the Army. That was odd, right there. Ten of those years were spent in close proximity to Reacher. From the files, it was impossible to determine which one had influenced the other. Reacher chose her for his Special Operations Unit, where she excelled during two crucial years. He'd praised her performance as smart, resourceful, thorough, and one particularly worrisome phrase that even now sent a taser-like charge up Kim's spine: "strangely uninhibited."

Neagley had been fearless herself and frightening to others. Early on, a few complaints of excessive force were lodged and dismissed when the facts showed a much larger man grabbed Neagley first. Several reported that Neagley didn't seem to move a muscle, but suddenly, they found themselves falling. Later in her Army tenure, word had gotten around and men had stopped touching her, for their own safety. Kim found the list of busted heads had overshadowed almost everything else in Neagley's file, and the woman's behavior was too often lethal for Kim's taste.

Maybe the most interesting point about Neagley was that she seemed to be the closest to Reacher. The crucial years she spent in his unit paired them together on every tough case the unit handled. When Kim asked one of the generals, he said there had been an odd connection between Reacher and Neagley that wasn't sexual. Which, Kim felt, was odd in itself. From what she'd seen so far, Reacher seemed to relate to women as sexual partners or rescue victims, and sometimes both. Neagley was neither. Not even close.

All of which meant Neagley was an enigma greater than Reacher himself. In a contest between Reacher and Neagley, Kim would have bet on her.

Bottom line? Neagley was unpredictable, and unpredictable meant terrifying in Kim Otto's world. Confronting Neagley would be foolhardy at best. Kim had deliberately planned to approach Neagley last, hoping the interview would not be necessary. But now Neagley was the only member of Reacher's unit left and Kim had no choice.

One choice, right choice.

Maybe.

What was her problem with Neagley? What wasn't? For now, though, she chose to change the subject. "I suppose you think Dixon and Reacher were lovers."

His eyebrow popped up again. "You think otherwise?"

"Just confirming how your mind works, Chico."

He laughed. "Don't think I failed to notice how you dodged my question."

Kim shrugged. Said nothing.

He said, "Check your phone, will you? Let's get a look at the rest of Silver's stuff so I can get some sleep. Long day tomorrow."

Kim bent and twisted and practically stood on her head reaching behind the television to check the battery level on her phone. She saw the little icon just as Gaspar's personal cell phone chimed a salsa tune across the room. She pulled the plug on her charger and stood, feeling a bit lightheaded.

He said, "I need to take this call and it'll be a while. Do you mind?" The salsa tune chimed again. "I'll call you when I'm finished, if it's not too late."

"No problem. I'll download Silver's stuff and forward to you. Digest it. We can't do anything more tonight anyway. We can talk in the morning."

Another salsa chime interrupted and this time he nodded and brought the phone to his ear.

"I'm here," he said quietly.

Kim let herself out and checked to be sure the door locked behind her.

Gaspar's physical handicaps made him about half the partner Kim needed even when he wasn't distracted by personal matters. Whatever his wife was calling about, Kim knew the problem was serious. Definitely something to worry about. Phone calls on the job can get people killed. No cop's wife ever calls his work with good news. Good news from home can always wait.

She wrestled with her decision as she slid the key card to unlock her room. Loyalty went a long way with Kim. Gaspar hadn't failed yet and he'd managed to be there whenever she'd needed him so far. He deserved the benefit of the doubt. For now.

She entered the room, double-locked the door, and kicked off her shoes while she argued with herself over the short list of possible solutions if Gaspar failed.

Kim felt the Boss's burner cell phone vibrating in her pocket. She knew his call was no coincidence. He'd probably tapped the hotel's security system and watched her enter her room on the corridor cameras. Which meant that he'd been watching her since she'd entered the hotel. Didn't he have anything better to do? Was it just last month when being watched by the FBI made Kim feel protected instead of threatened? It felt like another lifetime.

"Yes?" she said, too tired to joust with him.

"Neagley's back in Chicago. She's been traveling, but she returned yesterday. She's due out again Sunday. Your flight from Kennedy won't give you much turnaround. You leave again from National at 9:30 a.m. Don't miss it."

"Good to know Neagley's still alive," Kim said.

A beat passed. Two.

He replied, "Is it?"

CHAPTER 8

Friday, November 12
4:55 p.m.
Chicago, IL

Neagley was the easiest member of Reacher's old team
to locate, probably because she wasn't afraid that psychos
might find her. She owned the top private security firm in
Chicago. According to her website advertising, her clients
were distributed around the country and the globe. Outwardly, at least, her professional life appeared somewhat
unremarkable.

Kim had discovered no evidence that Neagley had a personal life of any kind, normal or otherwise. Which worried
Kim because it meant Neagley remained detached and still
had nothing to lose. A woman with Neagley's talents who
had nothing to lose could be deadly.

Three high-rise offices in three cities with only one connection: each tenant had at one time been a member of
Reacher's special investigative unit.

Earlier today, they'd arrived unannounced in Neagley's

lobby twice, both times posing as potential clients. The first two visits had yielded nothing. Neagley wasn't in, her receptionist falsely claimed, simultaneously suggesting they make an appointment next month or with another member of Neagley's team.

"Third time's the charm, Sunshine," Gaspar said. "It's the rule of threes."

"And if it isn't?" she asked.

"Then we'll figure out something else." He pushed through the revolving door into the entrance lobby of the historic office building. The layout echoed every office building in every major US city. Another information desk, less imposing than Dixon's Manhattan building and manned not by an experienced military officer but a series of bored part-timers. This was today's third. He didn't look up from his crossword puzzle when they walked past him toward the elevator.

Again, they waited for the exceptionally slow elevator that would carry them to Neagley's office on the tenth floor. Kim could easily have run up the stairs. But Gaspar would have struggled and Kim worried about depleting his energy before they confronted Neagley. When they found Neagley, he would need all he had.

Eventually, the elevator arrived on the ground floor, its doors lumbered open, and a single unremarkable passenger emerged. Gaspar limped after her into the six-by-six-foot box and pressed the button for Neagley's floor. Eventually the doors closed. The elevator began its ascent.

What seemed like an eternity later, the doors lumbered open again and as Kim and Gaspar had done twice before, they emerged twenty feet left and across the corridor from Neagley's highly polished mahogany double entrance door.

The polish didn't stop there.

O'Donnell's office had been small and functional and fit for a solo investigator with one gal Friday. Dixon's office doubled as her home and was barely occupied.

Both had failed to prepare Kim for her first encounter with Neagley's State Street headquarters.

The same armed guard they'd seen this morning and again in the early afternoon stood formally at his post on one side of the door. He was a large black man, dressed in a navy blue business suit, a white shirt, and red tie. The high polish of his boss's digs extended to the blinding surfaces of the man's shoes, and he carried himself like he'd been a member of the Secret Service in another life, which he probably had. Those guys were unmistakable.

He nodded by way of greeting, perhaps acknowledging he remembered them.

Once again, Kim was struck by the excessive quiet in the corridor. Neagley's office must be hermetically sealed. Absolutely no audible sound escaped, which, in Kim's experience, was an exceptional feat for any office. She refused to wonder why Neagley needed offices more fortified than Fort Knox.

Gaspar turned the doorknob and pushed into the lobby. Kim followed and the door swung closed, perfecting a sound barrier between the lobby and the hallway. Four people were already seated within. Two men and two women. Aside from being present in Neagley's office, which meant they were in some kind of trouble, they seemed unremarkable.

Kim had lost the coin toss to decide who would ask for Neagley this time. Simply because they had to eat somewhere anyway, Kim accepted Gaspar's steak dinner at Morton's Steakhouse bet that she couldn't manage it this time, either.

She approached the sliding glass window partition separating the lobby from the receptionist's desk. The glass was heavy enough to be bulletproof. Based on what Kim had read in Neagley's file, she figured it probably was.

The desk chair was empty. Kim glanced at her Seiko. Just after five o'clock. Perhaps the uncooperative woman had left for the day. Could Kim be that lucky? She pressed what looked like a doorbell button recessed in the wall to the left of the glass and heard nothing in response. She waited.

Kim turned away from the frosted window when the door through which she and Gaspar had just entered opened behind them and Frances L. Neagley strode into the room.

Neagley looked unchanged from her official Army personnel photo. Her hair was long and dark and shampoo-ad shiny. Her eyes were dark and more alive than her photo had made them seem. Her body reflected a serious gym routine, which had not been evident in the official photograph but was consistently reflected in her combat record.

Neagley was older than Kim by maybe a decade, taller by several inches, equally slim and lithe. She wore a white T-shirt snugged up against her body under a tailored black suit jacket. Her slacks fell perfectly creased to skim the front of stylish oxfords that would serve equally well deployed as weapons or in a foot chase.

A younger, taller man, resembling Neagley closely enough to be her twin, followed closely. He was dressed casually in jeans, leather jacket, and sneakers. He seemed hyper-focused on reaching his destination. Whatever it was. Neither slowed stride before they reached the interior entrance, next to which Kim and Gaspar stood. Neagley opened the door and stood aside to allow the young man to precede her.

Kim sensed this was her one chance to accomplish something today. "Ms. Neagley?"

Neagley glanced toward Kim just long enough to allow Kim and Gaspar's approach. The three remained on the lobby side of the threshold while the young man stood a couple of feet inside the open doorway.

Kim lowered her voice and pulled out her badge.

"FBI Special Agents Otto and Gaspar," she said.

Gaspar displayed his badge wallet as well. Neagley stalled, perhaps by momentary indecision. No one offered to shake hands.

The young man started to fidget. "Frances. Frances. Frances," he said, uninflected, each repetition a smidge louder than the last. "Frances. Frances. Frances."

"Okay, Paul. Okay," Neagley said, seeming to make up her mind about something. "Agents, this way, please."

She waved Kim and Gaspar through the doorway and closed it solidly behind them.

Neagley led them along an interior passageway. Paul walked slightly behind her, intently focused on something, but Kim wasn't sure what. When they reached a private office, Neagley waved her left arm toward the room without stopping and said to them, "Take a seat. I'll be right back." Neagley continued along the passageway and Paul walked away behind her.

She'd ushered them into her personal office, though it took Kim a few seconds surveying its modest, characterless contents to be sure that's what it was. The walls were painted nondescript beige and bare of adornment. The furniture was reasonably fine in quality, but also unadorned. Her desk chair was a high-backed, black leather ergonomic design. Expensive. Sleek. Nothing remotely frivolous.

Unlike Dixon and O'Donnell, Neagley displayed no sentimental reminders of her Army days with Reacher's unit.

Gaspar was standing before the room's window. "What a great view of Lake Shore Drive she's got from here. I am absolutely in the wrong business. My office has a view of one the nastiest alleys in Miami. How about yours?"

"I don't even have a window," Kim said, mindful that Neagley's office was probably wired for cameras and audio inside. Probably had some sort of shield preventing inside conversations from being overheard, too.

Gaspar laughed. "Okay. You win."

Neagley entered the room just then, stealthily, like a feral cat wearing socks. She stood behind her chair, sensibly manicured nails displayed while her hands rested on the leather.

She said, "Win what?"

"The worst office view award," Kim said. "You might get the best view award, though. You must see some spectacular sunrises over Lake Michigan from here."

"I've got more clients to see before I can wrap up and they've been waiting a while already. Let's get to it, shall we? What does the FBI want today?"

She said "today" as if she routinely responded to the FBI. Maybe she did.

Kim replied, "We need information from you to complete a routine background check."

"A background check for what?" She wasn't hostile, exactly. More like detached.

"We're tasked by the FBI Special Personnel Task Force when the government is preparing to recruit a civilian."

"Why recruit civilians?"

"Although the government employs millions of people, we don't always have the expertise we need. From time to time, we hire that expertise outside the system," Kim replied, matching Neagley's no-nonsense tone. "We need to be sure the candidate is qualified. Mentally, physically, emotionally, and financially, as well as through his or her expertise."

Neagley nodded, as if the answer made sense. Maybe she was aware of the SPTF. Maybe she was just trying to get through the situation and move on with whatever her plans were for the rest of the day. She sat down and hid her hands from view, which made Kim nervous. She'd prefer to see Neagley's hands at all times.

Neagley asked, "What's the job?"

"That information requires a security clearance higher than ours," Gaspar said. "Or yours, I'm afraid."

His participation drew Neagley's attention from Kim for a moment, allowing Kim a chance to breathe again. Neagley looked directly at him. Maybe she wasn't testing him. But it felt like she was.

"Higher than your clearance, maybe. Not higher than mine." Neagley stated this without inflection of any kind. She turned her steady gaze back to Kim. "Who's the subject?"

Kim made a point of observing carefully. She'd seen a variety of reactions when she first mentioned Reacher's name to potential witnesses. She only had one opportunity to catch their immediate response. "You served with him in the Army."

Neagley folded her hands on the desk and continued looking steadily into Kim's eyes. "I served with a lot of people a long time ago. What's his name?"

Kim decided not to speak the name at all this time. Just handed over a copy of Reacher's last formal military photo and watched carefully for Neagley's involuntary reactions.

Kim's training in human lie detection was extensive and well internalized. She'd discovered an instinct for separating the liars from the rest of the herd that had saved her ass many times. The subject's body language was the most important indicator of truthfulness in response to surprise or threat, though it was easily missed.

Neagley displayed nothing. No physical reactions at all. Nor did she speak. There was no question on the floor. She waited until they supplied one. She was abnormally cold. Frigid, actually. Easily the coldest potential witness they'd pressed on the subject of Reacher thus far.

"When did you last see Reacher?" Gaspar asked.

Neagley said, "Years ago."

"Where did you see him?"

"California."

"How did that happen?"

"I was having lunch and he walked into the diner."

"Was he working at that time?"

"I didn't ask." Not exactly an answer.

"Do you have a current address for him?"

"He gets a pension, doesn't he? The Army would know where they send it. So would the IRS. Ask them. You federal types are supposed to cooperate with each other these days. So cooperate."

This was the longest answer Neagley had provided and wasn't even close to straight up. Kim wondered why.

Gaspar asked, "How about a last known address?"

Neagley grinned. The effect was not reassuring. "You can't

find him. That's the problem, isn't it?" She took a breath that Kim hadn't realized she'd been holding. "Don't waste your time, Agent Gaspar. You won't find Reacher unless he wants you to find him."

Kim replied, "We're not looking for Reacher at the moment. Whether we will be looking for him or not depends on what we learn during our background check. We're only interested in him if he's qualified, as we said."

Neagley's eyes narrowed and she looked at them as if she could see directly into their souls and divine absolutely everything about them through sheer force of will. Maybe she could.

After a couple of moments, she reached some sort of decision. She stood and folded her hands in front of her taut stomach. Her tone was friendlier than anything she'd used thus far.

"I haven't seen Reacher in years. I don't have any knowledge about his present qualifications. He's a pretty straightforward guy. Just find him and ask him whatever you want to know. He'll tell you or he won't. If he doesn't, then he's not qualified for the job. Problem solved." She stepped to the side of her desk and gestured toward the door. "Meanwhile, as I said, I've got clients waiting. Then I need to get my brother home and as you no doubt noticed, he's not very flexible in his routines. So if there's nothing else?"

Neither Kim nor Gaspar rose from their chairs. Neagley didn't seem at all flustered or bothered by their recalcitrance. She simply turned and moved to depart. Kim thought she'd leave them sitting in the office until they gave up and left.

Kim waited until the last possible moment before she said, "You know Dave O'Donnell was murdered in his office last week, don't you? Executed, in fact. Shot with a single bullet to the head and left to bleed out."

Neagley stopped. She turned her gaze toward Kim. Offered no response.

Kim watched Neagley carefully. "And do you also know that Karla Dixon is missing, probably also dead?"

Still, Neagley said nothing.

Kim lowered her voice, the better to hold Neagley's attention. "You probably know that Reacher was there. In DC. At the time O'Donnell was murdered. And in New York when Dixon disappeared. You knew that, didn't you?"

Neagley remained standing, but she didn't leave the room. Nor did she respond to Kim's questions.

Gaspar said, "No good cop believes in that kind of coincidence, Neagley. You know that, too."

"Is Reacher in Chicago?" Kim asked. "Has he been here? Or are you worried that he's on his way?"

Neagley glanced down at her watch and made some sort of assessment of the situation and the two agents. She returned to her desk, flipped through a neat stack of flat manila folders, pulled two and handed them to Gaspar, who was sitting closest to her. No wasted movement. No wasted words, either.

She remained standing. "Yes, I knew about O'Donnell and Dixon. The detective in charge of O'Donnell's case contacted me the day they found his body. I flew out to DC and evaluated the situation. I'm satisfied that they're doing a proper job."

"You don't seem very concerned about it," Kim said.

"O'Donnell handled private investigations for high profile politicians and their enemies, Agent Otto. His case files are full of potential suspects. It's likely there are more who haven't been identified yet. Seven days since he died. We all know the chances of solving the case diminish with time and it's unlikely that his killer will be found now. Fact is, O'Donnell lived a dangerous life and he'd survived more than his share of murder attempts. Everybody has to die sometime. Last Friday was his day."

Neagley was easily the coldest woman Kim had met in a very long time. Could her heart possibly be as icy as her words?

"What's in these two folders?" Gaspar asked.

"One contains a copy of the O'Donnell homicide file materials the detective shared with me."

"What about Dixon?" Kim asked.

"The second is a copy of materials I collected from a private investigator in New York when I went to Dixon's office the following day. He reports that Dixon had been gone for about two weeks before O'Donnell's death. She travels for work." Neagley moved to leave the room again. "There's no evidence to suggest she's dead. I've put a call in to her and when she has a chance, if she thinks it's important, she'll call me back."

"Why were you having Dixon investigated?" Gaspar asked.

Neagley said, "You may keep those copies. You'd get more information from the relevant investigators directly, maybe. But call me tomorrow or another time if you have anything else. Right now, I have to deal with my brother and finish my business so I can get him home. I don't have anything more to say to you tonight." With that, she started again for the door.

Kim managed to stop her progress one last time. "What about Reacher?"

Neagley paused on the threshold, looked back. "What about him?"

"If he killed O'Donnell and Dixon, and the rest of the members of your old unit, you're the only one left. He's on his way here next," Kim said. "We can keep you alive."

Neagley smirked and delivered her parting shot. "I can take care of myself, thanks."

"Okay, but take my card. If you can contact Reacher, do that. If he shows up here, let us know. We'll do as you suggested and ask him our questions directly."

"Sure," she said, in a way that meant, "A decade after the zombie apocalypse."

She headed toward wherever she'd parked her brother.

Gaspar shrugged, stood, stretched. Kim led. He followed.

Only two people remained in Neagley's lobby. It was late Friday afternoon and most of the working world had closed up shop already. At this hour, it would be almost full dark outside. Neagley's remaining clients were a man and a woman, seated together, not speaking. Something about them seemed vaguely familiar and made her more uneasy this time. But Kim felt she hadn't met the couple before.

He sat with his left leg crossed over his right knee. Shiny metal prostheses protruded below both pant hems. The woman betrayed damage of her own. Her face was creased by scars that she'd attempted to cover with heavy make-up. Deep cuts that might have been caused when she went through glass during a high-velocity car wreck.

Neagley's firm normally provided high-end security for influencers, government contractors, celebrities, and such. Why would she be working with accident victims?

CHAPTER 9

Friday, November 12
5:35 p.m.
Chicago, IL

State Street was winding down for the weekend. A few shops were open until 7:00 p.m., but most of the working crowd were already headed home on the train or otherwise. The wind off Lake Michigan was frigid against Kim's skin. Yesterday's ice storm had moved through Chicago a couple of days before and today's sunshine had melted the sidewalks well enough for walking but not for warmth. She felt the cold cement transfer through her shoes and wondered whether Neagley's client would be more or less comfortable on cold surfaces with his prostheses. Did those metal rods transfer heat and cold or insulate his stumps?

"Any chance Neagley told us what she knows about O'Donnell or Dixon or even Reacher?" Kim asked.

"That's a trick question, right?"

Gaspar led the way across the street to a still open coffee shop where they'd be warm enough. From this vantage point, they should be able to catch Neagley leaving after her meeting. Maybe they'd have a chance to interview her again after her clients left. Once they'd collected their coffee and found a small table with a view of Neagley's building entrance, he handed her one of Neagley's manila folders and opened the other.

"Did you notice the couple sitting in Neagley's lobby?" Kim asked.

Gaspar opened his slim folder to page through its contents.

"Did they look familiar to you?" Kim opened the second, thicker folder, but instead of examining it, she continued to see Neagley's clients in her mind. They'd been seated near each other, but not too close. They weren't speaking to or looking at one another. The woman had looked up, allowing Kim to see her face; he hadn't. Not overly friendly toward each other.

"Looked like they'd experienced some serious misfortune to me. I guess that's familiar, if that's what you mean," Gaspar said, preoccupied by the documents.

Kim gasped, snapped out of her reverie.

Her gasp pulled his gaze up from the pages.

"What?"

Gaspar's limp. The obvious pain. Constantly popping Tylenol. Was it possible she'd missed something so essential? Could he have a prosthesis instead of his right limb?

She couldn't stop her gaze from dipping to his leg.

He grinned.

"Oh man," he said gently. "It's okay, Kim. I'm fine. A little gimpy, maybe a little crotchety sometimes, but I still have my leg. Want to see it?" He stuck his right leg out into the aisle and pulled up his pant leg to reveal hairy shin above black crew sock. "God, my legs could use a shave, right? Bet that guy never has to worry about that."

As he'd intended, humor lifted Kim's tension. But unease lingered.

He returned to task, checking the entrance to Neagley's

building and continued his reading. "Dixon's file's pretty interesting. Do you want to hear about it now, or not until you're done with O'Donnell's?"

Message received. He didn't want to talk about what *was* wrong with his leg. But soon, they would. A decision had to be made.

"I'll have a look. Then we can swap. Then talk."

"Get to it, then. I'm almost done." He finished reading and set the folder on the table. Leaning back in the chair, legs crossed at the ankles, hands clasped over his flat belly, he closed his eyes in what she now recognized as his coping posture.

Keeping half an eye on Neagley's building, Kim finished her pass through the O'Donnell murder file and swapped it for the Dixon folder. "There you go, Cheech," she said. "Checking your eyelids for holes?"

Gaspar sat up and completed his scans while she thumbed through the Dixon documents. When they'd finished, the entire elapsed time from leaving Neagley's office was maybe fifteen minutes.

"How long do you think they'll be up there?" Gaspar asked.

"Neagley said they were new clients, didn't she? Even though she's in a hurry to get the kid home, it could be more than an hour. But we shouldn't count on it." She sat back in her chair. "In the meantime, we talk. Just the highlights now and we'll cover the minutia later," she said. "You start."

"The messenger at Dixon's building was not a messenger, as we suspected. He's a private investigator. Been watching Dixon for weeks. Why?"

Kim nodded. "And who hired him? Neagley?"

Gaspar considered it a moment. Shook his head. "Probably not. Because if she'd hired him, she'd have known Dixon wasn't home and had been gone for a couple of weeks before O'Donnell's murder and Neagley wouldn't have wasted her time going up there from DC."

"Agreed. Someone redacted the employer's information

from this file, though. Did the investigator do that before he gave Neagley the file? Or did she do it afterward? And why is someone watching Dixon anyway?"

Gaspar shrugged. "One more thing to ask her when we see her next."

"'Her' meaning Neagley or Dixon?" Kim asked.

Gaspar said nothing.

"Still no answer on whether Dixon is dead or involved or with Reacher. Agreed?" Kim asked.

"Right."

Kim gave the Dixon file a little shove on the tabletop. "And he's not much of an investigator if this is all the stuff he collected in more than a month." She glanced over to Neagley's building entrance to confirm the status quo and took a sip of her now-tepid coffee. "How about O'Donnell?"

"Nothing new or even remotely interesting in here that we didn't know already. But curiously, no mention of any surveillance on him."

"Because whoever was watching Dixon might have been watching him, too."

"Right."

Kim nodded. "Something else. Did you see it?"

Gaspar thought a minute. Came up empty. Shook his head.

"What private investigator with O'Donnell's experience and the kind of clientele Neagley says he had would fail to have full surveillance of his own operation? Yet there's not one word about cameras or security or anything else in this murder file."

"Meaning Neagley removed the references?" Gaspar asked.

"Makes no sense. She didn't know we were coming today so it's unlikely she'd taken anything out before we got there. And she handed the folder to us without removing anything from it." She waited a couple of beats while Gaspar thought it through.

"The equipment had to have been there before O'Donnell was killed," he said, "but this is a copy of the police investigation file and there's not a word about surveillance evidence."

"So?"

"So either the cops were idiots and didn't think to look for it, or . . . ."

Kim nodded. He was getting there. "Or?"

Both eyebrows converged at the top of his nose and his mouth set into a hard line. "Or Neagley beat them to it. And if they *were* too stupid to even look for it, she certainly was not. So either way, Neagley has the proof. She has the surveillance. She knows who killed O'Donnell and why. She's not going to let that go."

Gaspar sat up straight and thought some more. Kim waited for him to reach the only possible conclusions. Maybe he got there. But before she had a chance to ask him, sirens blaring outside caused her to look out the window for another spot check on the entrance to Neagley's building.

An ambulance pulled up out in front and two paramedics bolted out of the cab, ran around to pull a rolling gurney out of the boxy rear doors, and rushed inside.

CHAPTER 10

Friday, November 12
6:05 p.m.
Chicago, IL

After hustling across State Street, Kim and Gaspar reached the main lobby of Neagley's high-rise to find almost nothing remarkable. The last few people still heading home for the day appeared barely curious. Maybe paramedics in Chicago were nothing too far out of the ordinary in an office tower normally filled with hundreds of people, any of whom might need transport to a hospital.

Kim couldn't see the elevators from the entrance lobby. She approached the guy at the information desk, flashed her badge, and asked as if she had a right to ask, "Where did the paramedics go?"

The guy looked up from his sports page, startled, as if she was the first person who had spoken to him for hours. Maybe she was.

"Tenth floor," he said.

"Did you call in the request?" Gaspar asked.

"Nobody asked me to. Means it's probably nothing too serious."

"Why is that?" Kim asked.

"It's my job to call in first responders when anything serious happens. Figure they would have let me know if they needed me to make the call, you know?"

"Thanks," Gaspar said, turning away, leaving the guy to his newspaper.

At the elevator bank, Kim glanced up to see the poky car was only at the second floor. "Come on," she said, heading for the stairs.

Gaspar pulled open the heavy fire door at the base of the stairs, and Kim entered the stairwell ahead of him. She started a dash up the steps and made it up the third flight before she realized how far Gaspar was lagging behind.

Two businessmen heading home had passed her on the first flight of stairs and walked through the fire door into the lobby. Two more tenants had passed her on their way down afterward. She heard more footsteps on the flights above. The building's office workers didn't want to use the poky elevators, either. Walking was a lot faster exit at the end of a long work week. Or maybe this was a fitness thing. But a trickle of tenants passed as if the stairwell was their usual route. No one seemed alarmed, just tired after a long workday.

She waited at the third floor landing a second until Gaspar caught up so she wouldn't need to shout. "You think Reacher's up there?"

Gaspar said, "If he is, we need backup."

"By the time we got through the red tape, he'd already be in the wind."

Gaspar said, "I'm right behind you. Don't go in alone."

Kim started up the stairs again. Surely some sort of panic would have ensued if violence had exploded anywhere in the building. And then she remembered how unnaturally soundproofed Neagley's offices were. A gunshot like the one that killed O'Donnell exactly one week ago in a deserted office building could have gone unnoticed in this mostly vacant, soundproofed one.

Or, as the information desk guy said, it could have been nothing serious. Maybe a natural disaster of some sort rather than a Reacher-made one. She hoped.

Mid-flight between the sixth and seventh floors, after a group of five laughing women, Kim saw a familiar face coming down the stairs toward her. Neagley's client. The woman with the scars on her face. She was alone, which alarmed Kim for a moment until she remembered. Maybe her companion couldn't walk down the stairs on his prosthetics. He could have taken the elevator, instead, though it seemed unlikely that they'd split up.

When the woman got close enough, Kim would ask her if she knew why paramedics had been called to Neagley's floor. Kim turned to glance at Gaspar and inclined her head toward the stairway, signaling to pay attention to someone on the way down. He nodded understanding.

When Kim looked back, the woman noticed her and accidently met Kim's gaze.

The woman's scarred face seemed frozen, unable to form normal expressions. But her eyes rounded in recognition. She stopped, pivoted, turned and ran back up the few stairs she'd just covered and slipped through the first doorway she reached.

Kim quickened her pace, leaving Gaspar farther behind. She pushed past the five Friday night party girls and raced up to the fire door leading to the seventh floor.

She grabbed the handle, still warmed by the woman's grip, and pulled the heavy door open. The second she stepped across the threshold, one foot into the corridor, two quick, muffled gunshots propelled bullets into the steel doorjamb inches from Kim's head. She ducked back into the stairwell and behind the door. Subsonic bullets. The shooter had come prepared.

Kim pulled her gun and waited on the handle side of the door. Gaspar recognized the silenced gunfire and rushed up to Kim from the flight below. He positioned himself on the hinge side. On the count of three, Gaspar would open the door. Kim would enter low to minimize the target. A shooter would tend to aim high, where center mass was expected to be.

"Right behind you," he said to Kim's back as she went through the fire door again and entered the main corridor, shouting, "Stop! FBI!"

Instead of aiming high, another bullet slammed past Kim in a near miss. She dove into the nearest feeder hallway as she fired back.

Gaspar rolled through the fire door in a half-crouch, gun drawn, and slid into the feeder hallway across from Kim. They could see each other, but not the woman.

Where did she go?

Kim ducked her head around the corner in an effort to locate the shooter. The first shot had been too close for Kim to believe the woman was a lousy marksman. Twice more, the woman returned fire. But her shots hit wide of the mark and seemed to be wildly aimed. Maybe she was running away, but Kim couldn't see her in the dim corridor light.

And then the shooting stopped.

The woman had uttered not one sound, Kim thought. Her shoes and clothes had made no noise. She could be anywhere now.

Kim waited. She called out again. No response.

Gaspar stayed in place. Kim moved by sliding along the wall toward the elevator bank until she could see the digital elevator car progress sign. Both cars were in use. One had stopped on the tenth floor, Neagley's floor. The other car was moving down toward the fifth and eventually to the ground floor because the floors below were now mostly empty.

Where did the shooter go?

Had she entered the elevator?

Was she on her way down and out into the cold Chicago darkness?

There was another stairwell somewhere. Had she found it?

Or was she hiding somewhere on the floor or in the building, waiting for a cleaner shot?

CHAPTER 11

Friday, November 12
6:15 p.m.
Chicago, IL

Silence on the seventh floor lingered. If the woman was still there, Kim saw no evidence of her. The tenth floor situation pulled her even as seventh floor events held her captive.

Finally, Gaspar said from his vantage point a few feet away, "Your call."

They couldn't simply stay here, in limbo. She took a deep breath. Too many things could go wrong either way. But she sensed the woman was gone.

Probably.

Maybe.

Hopefully.

Kim carefully returned to Gaspar's covered position in the feeder hallway.

"Okay. I'll run up to Neagley's office and get someone to call Chicago PD, if they haven't already. Response time has got to be fairly quick here. Someone might have called in the gunfire already, with luck. If you don't find her in two minutes, give up. Meet me upstairs."

Before she went, she watched Gaspar's face to be sure he would follow orders, which would be unusual. Sternly, seriously, she said, "Don't make my first visit to your family be a condolence call, Chico."

He nodded. "You'll love Maria's *Tres Leches*, Sunshine."

Kim flashed him a quick, terse grin. Nodded. With no further delay, she turned, dashed back into the stairwell, and covered the remaining three flights to Neagley's floor two steps at a time.

When she reached the identical fire door on the tenth floor landing, Kim pulled the heavy steel slab open and rushed toward Neagley's security guard, still standing well-pressed and starched at the threshold as he had been all day.

He glanced down at her, grinned. "Heavy breathing AND a gun? Is this how the FBI answers the bell these days, Agent Otto?"

Kim spared barely half a moment to wonder how he'd learned her identity as she pushed past him through the open door to Neagley's interior lobby and tried to make sense of the discordant experience that instantly assaulted her senses.

The scent of recent gunshots and panic and death and medicine.

Paul highly agitated, babbling screams, hands held to his head. Left arm bleeding at the bicep. Frightened and frightening and every move volatile, extreme.

Neagley standing near her brother. She looks directly at Paul's face and speaks to him calmly, quietly. She offers no comforting touch.

Nothing she says makes a difference in Paul's behavior. Paul's screaming and incoherence consume every ounce of bandwidth in the room.

The double-amputee who had been waiting for Neagley earlier is laid out on the floor. Paramedics working on him. His eyes display the open stare of a dead man.

One paramedic closes the man's eyelids. The simple action

she'd seen too many times before triggered something in Kim's brain; it began to sort events properly again.

Kim watched as the paramedics placed the body on the gurney and his pant legs hiked up, flashing like shooting stars when overhead lighting bounced off the silver rods below his knees.

When the paramedics rolled the gurney toward her on their way out of the office, Kim stopped them and showed her badge. "What happened here?"

"No idea," one paramedic told her. "The young guy was acting just like that when we arrived. We tried to help with the arm, but he just went crazier when we tried to approach him. The woman told us to leave him alone." He glanced at the man on the gurney. "This man was dead already. Probably a heart attack."

Gaspar arrived in time to hear. He glanced into the office and must have seen Paul's bleeding arm and Neagley's odd behavior, along with the commotion, too. He displayed his badge briefly before he asked, "What makes you think he had a heart attack?"

The same paramedic replied, "You have any reason to believe otherwise? Because we don't see any."

"Where are you taking him?" Kim asked.

"Hospital. We don't have the authority to pronounce the obvious. Somebody with more liability insurance has to do that." The grim humor of someone coping with too much death in his line of work.

"Chicago PD on the way?" Kim asked.

"Not on our account. We don't call cops to heart attacks. Nothing else going on here beyond the young guy's nicked arm, is there?"

Gaspar looked toward Kim, who shook her head once before he said, "I just got here."

The paramedic nodded and joined his partner at the elevator. They tucked the gurney inside and the doors slowly reconnected before the car began its ponderous descent.

If the patient wasn't dead already, he would be by the time they made it to the hospital, Kim thought.

The woman who shot at them three floors below was already

gone. Kim needed to hear the facts about what happened here from Neagley as quickly as possible. Besides, surely *someone* else had been on the seventh floor during the firefight. Surely the cops had already been notified. Chicago PD was probably on the way. The last thing she needed was to be officially questioned. She didn't have much time to figure something out before the place was flooded with way more trouble than she wanted to be mired in.

Back in Neagley's lobby, Paul's tantrum continued unabated. Neagley continued efforts to calm him, with very little success. At least with the paramedics gone, a small slice of chaos subsided. Neagley managed to herd Paul through the heavy door and deeper into the interior offices. For a few moments, Kim barely heard Paul's muffled screaming, and then Neagley's lobby became eerily quiet, like the silence just before a tornado hits.

Kim knew they should move. Do something before Chicago PD arrived. But what?

She needed to reach Neagley, and fast. Neagley was the woman with all their answers. Neagley knew who the dead amputee was, knew what had happened to him. Neagley knew the scarred-faced woman, too. Probably knew why she shot at Kim and Gaspar, and maybe where she'd gone. Neagley knew O'Donnell and Dixon, too.

Neagley was at the center of it all.

Somehow, Reacher was, too.

And Neagley knew precisely how Reacher was involved. Kim was sure of it. But how to make Neagley confess was a knottier problem than Kim could solve based on what she'd learned so far, which was precisely nothing.

Only two people within immediate striking distance possessed more information than Kim already had. Neagley, who had disappeared inside her office fortress, unlikely to either emerge or cooperate when she eventually resurfaced.

And Neagley's standing guard, stationed fifteen feet away in the 10th floor corridor. Already moving in that direction, Kim glanced at Gaspar and said, "Let's go."

CHAPTER 12

Friday, November 12
6:37 p.m.
Chicago, IL

The security guard was still standing in the hallway at the exterior door to Neagley's offices, as he had been each time Kim had approached today. He appeared as unruffled and fresh as the first time she'd passed him this morning.

"You have the advantage. You know who we are," Kim said by way of opening.

The tall man said, "FBI Special Agents Otto and Gaspar, yes."

"What's your name?"

His lips turned up in a slight smile.

Kim waited a beat before she said, "Are you refusing to identify yourself to Federal agents?"

His smile broadened.

Gaspar said, "You aren't required to tell us your name."

He said, "I know."

Gaspar said, "But I'm suspicious about why you won't.

So suspicious, in fact, that you might be obstructing justice here, simply by refusing to cooperate in a federal investigation."

"Possibly," he said. "What is it you're investigating, exactly?"

"Murder. Kidnapping."

"Guess I didn't realize murder was the FBI's beat these days. Thought you folks were more interested in terrorism and such."

Kim said, "We're talking about your job, not ours. What exactly is your job?"

"You've observed me in the performance of my duties several times today, haven't you? My job is to remain stationed right here."

"Why?"

"You met Paul Neagley? He escapes. I'm the guy who finds him and brings him back."

"Not much of a job for a former member of the Secret Service," Kim said.

His eyes opened a little wider. He grinned, but didn't bother to deny she'd guessed correctly. "The pay is better and I don't have to take a bullet for politicians who can't find their butts with both hands."

"So what's your name? It won't take me long to find out."

"Probably not."

"And then I'll have to come back and have this conversation again."

"I'll be here."

"What happened in there? A guy is dead."

"Paramedics said heart attack." He shrugged. "That guy looked a little stressed when he came in, didn't he? If he needed to hire my boss, he already had big problems before he got here. Stress must have been too much for him."

"What about Paul's arm? Looked like a gunshot wound to me. I smelled a recently fired weapon, too."

"I didn't hear any gunshots."

"What was the dead man's name?"

"I don't know."

"What about the woman that was with him?"

"What about her?"

"Did you see her leave?"

"Of course. I was standing right here."

"Did she have a gun?"

"I didn't frisk her."

"What was her name?"

"I didn't ask. Look, my orders are to stand here. If Paul gets away, I'm to chase him down and bring him back. That's it. I'm not introduced to clients. I'm not tasked with identifying, scrutinizing, interrogating or remembering them."

"That's a little odd for a man with your training, isn't it?"

"Makes my job easier. Besides, visitors don't necessarily know my orders. Maybe they think my job is more expansive. So they don't mess with me much."

"What time does Frances Neagley normally leave for the day?

"Can't say. She leaves through the back. There's a secure parking garage attached to the building."

Kim turned and grabbed the knob to the entrance door only to realize it had locked automatically. "I left something inside. Do you have a key to this door?"

"No."

Kim pulled her smartphone out of her pocket and pressed the redial for Neagley's office. The phone rang repeatedly before a voice mail service picked up asking her to leave a message. She hung up.

"Office opens in the morning at nine," he said.

Kim pressed the camera button on her phone, lifted it to capture him in full face view and pressed the video record.

"You need facial recognition to identify me," he said. "You can't simply make a call, can you? Means you're not officially here, doesn't it?"

She closed her phone and walked away.

"We'll be back," Gaspar said, as he moved to follow Kim toward the elevator bank.

"I'll be here," he repeated.

When Gaspar reached Kim, he leaned against the wall where she stood waiting for the elevator.

"What do you suppose that guy is all about?" Gaspar asked.

"He's connected to Neagley. You expected cooperation? This has got to be the slowest elevator on the planet." She punched the call button again and glanced at her Seiko. "It's almost seven o'clock. Missed our plane."

"We could catch a cab to O'Hare and get a later flight. Or check in somewhere and grab dinner. Come back tomorrow. Try again with Neagley. Call the Boss in the meantime."

Kim said nothing.

"Want me to keep tossing out options, or are you going to pick one, Dragon Lady Boss?"

Before Kim could reply to his sarcasm, Neagley emerged from inside her office and strode purposefully past the door guard and then past them toward the stairwell. She offered no sign of recognition.

Gaspar noticed Neagley first. He went after her. His long stride covered ground quickly.

"Neagley!" Kim called out.

Neagley didn't alter her pace. She reached the heavy steel fire door, pushed it open and moved into the stairwell. She'd be down the entire ten flights and out into the night long before the elevator arrived.

Kim followed right behind Gaspar. Quickened her step to catch up.

Gaspar reached the stairwell entrance. He grabbed the knob and pushed against the closing fire door, pressed it wider and continued onto the landing.

Kim was a split second behind him.

She reached out to keep the fire door open after he passed through and followed him into the stairwell.

Before her eyes could adjust to the dim emergency lighting, Kim heard a heavy grunt three steps ahead.

In the dimness, she saw Gaspar's body crumpled on the

cement floor in front of her.

Her momentum carried her forward and she tripped over him.

She reached out, seeking the wall's solid, cool touch, and pivoted quickly away from his body.

But not quickly enough.

CHAPTER 13

Friday, November 12
3:00 a.m.
Chicago, IL

Kim felt relaxed and a little lazy. She hovered at the edge of consciousness in a state she sometimes attained through meditation. She felt no anxiety, no urgency. She seemed to be floating in a pool of delicious quiet. Her consciousness began to deepen into sleep once more and she willingly succumbed.

Until her pillow moved of its own accord, and her eyes jumped open. The only light came from weak emergency bulbs bolted to the wall, casting an eerie red patina.

The room was confusing. Not her bedroom. Not her hotel room. Where was she?

There was rough fabric under her cheek instead of the silk pillowcases she preferred. Her pillow was rigid, unforgiving. Something was wrong with her bed, too. Hard as cement and just as cold. How could that be?

Her pillow moved again. She bolted upright into a full sitting position, heart pounding, and blinked several times to clear the sleep fog from her vision.

What she could see in the dim light only ramped up her anxiety. Her pillow had been Gaspar's bony, trouser-clad shin. For a moment she thought he might be dead. But no. He'd moved a second ago. So not dead. But what? Drugged?

Somehow, understanding and returning awareness calmed her. Curious. But nothing frightening at the moment.

Her bed had been the concrete floor. The room appeared to be an enclosed stairwell. She'd seen similar stairwells not long ago, but where? She tried to remember. After a second or two, she gave up.

Yes. Drugged. But not dead. Why not? Odd.

Kim reached over and shook Gaspar's shoulder. He groaned, but didn't wake up. She shook him more vigorously until his eyelids popped open. She watched until he worked through the same initial disorientation and grogginess she'd felt.

"I have a slight headache, Chico. Got any Tylenol on you?" Her throat was parched and her voice sounded whispery.

Gaspar sat upright and said, in a slightly less croaky voice, "Probably."

She struggled to stand and offered him a hand, which he rejected. This reaction made her feel a little bit closer to normal, too. As if they were still the same selves as before. Comforting. But not true. A chunk of her mind was now gone. His, too, she figured.

Once on his feet, Gaspar reached into his pocket and pulled out four Tylenol and handed two to her. She put them in her dry mouth, tasted the bitter capsules, wrinkled her nose and swallowed them on the third try.

"How can you stand that stuff?" she croaked.

He rubbed his right shoulder near his neck—in precisely the same spot hers ached. "No choice," he said, looking around the gloom. "Where are we?"

She shook her head, then realized he probably couldn't

see her well enough to notice in the red dimness. "I'm not sure. It looks like the stairwell of an old building. Do you recognize it?"

"Kind of. They all look the same, don't they? How'd we get here?"

"What's your best guess?" she asked.

"Judging from the pain at the base of my neck, likely some kind of whack on the carotid sinus dropped me. Followed by a good-sized dose of roofies, probably."

Kim nodded again, noticed the low lighting anew, and replied, "Seems most likely to me, too. Which means our memories have been chemically erased. We won't get that back."

"What's the last thing you *do* remember?"

She'd been thinking about that for the past few seconds. Moving through her recall, backward from the moment her pillow first moved. She answered his question carefully, because pinpointing the last clear event was critical to defining the extent of the damage. "Maybe waiting for the elevator in Neagley's building? Not getting on the elevator, or even the elevator arriving on the tenth floor. Maybe I do remember that. I seem to. But then again, I don't." Her voice trailed off because she knew her speech was as garbled as her recall.

"We rode that elevator six times," Gaspar said. "Three up. Three down. Maybe your memory is confused as well as absent." He continued to massage the pain in his right shoulder. "It's hard to administer roofies precisely. They might have overdosed you a bit. I'm bigger than you are. More muscle mass. My dose probably metabolized quicker. You could be slower coming out of it."

Kim nodded. Realized yet again that he couldn't see her. Confusion was another hallmark; how bad would that be? "I feel like a slug. What's your last clear memory?"

He spoke slowly. "I'm not sure yet. I don't know how we ended up here. But I remember we climbed these stairs to Neagley's office before. I recognize the old-style tiles on the walls." He reached into his pocket, pulled out his car keys, and activated the tiny LED flashlight on his key ring. Its beam illuminated the stairwell brightly enough to locate the fire door. He walked over, turned the knob, and yanked the heavy steel slab open, but no fluorescent light flooded into the dark stairwell. "Follow me."

She remembered she had a key ring and LED light, too. She found hers a moment later. She used it first to illuminate the face of her Seiko.

"It's after three a.m.," she said, turning the beam into the dim corridor as she followed. Probably the building's lighting was on some sort of timer to save electricity or something. Not many office people would be around at 3:00 a.m. She checked her Seiko again, this time for the date. Saturday.

"Wonder how long we were knocked out."

"A few hours, maybe." He flashed his light on the double door entrance to Neagley's office as they walked past. "So we're on the tenth floor. The elevator is over here."

Kim wondered how he knew. Oh, right. He said they'd used the elevator six times before.

"If they've got only emergency energy turned on for the weekend, the elevator might not work," she said. Stood aside, still unsteady, watched him push the call button. The lumbering elevator car started up from the lobby and her lips turned up a bit when she realized she remembered the sound and stayed turned up while they rode the elevator slowly to the ground floor.

The lobby's information desk was unmanned. Maybe the building had surveillance cameras running during off hours. Maybe not. Maybe that's how O'Donnell's killer managed to get in and get out that Friday night in another building halfway across the country, Kim thought, aware that her thinking was improving, though still too fuzzy and jumbled to rely upon.

Once outside, the brisk cold further improved Kim's alertness. State Street was practically abandoned. Not many people wandered the business district at this hour. She faced the chill wind and let it bathe her face in welcome fresh air until Gaspar finally managed to flag a taxi.

"O'Hare, please," Gaspar told the driver when they were settled inside the warm cab.

Kim's mind felt thick, gelatinous. Too dense to conduct her usual state of high anxiety. She fished into her pocket and pulled out the Boss's cell phone. The screen reflected four missed calls over the past five hours. The last call was twenty minutes ago. She wondered whether the vibrating cell phone was the thing that had pulled her from the depths of unconsciousness. Thought about it. Maybe.

"Check yours, okay?" she said, holding the display screen out to Gaspar so that he could see what she meant.

He pulled his phone out of his pocket and showed her the display so she could confirm the same number of missed calls received at the same intervals. He asked, "What do you make of that?"

Slowly, she shook her head before stuffing the cell phone into her pocket. "I don't know. My mind is too foggy to sort it out. But I don't like it."

"Agreed."

She closed her eyes and let her head fall back against the seat. She felt exhausted, limp, drained of will. It was a foreign sensation. She was often tired, overworked, overwhelmed. But she hadn't been so demoralized since her divorce almost a decade ago. And she didn't like the feeling. Not at all.

Kim heard Gaspar calling ahead for reservations at the on-site airport hotel and she was glad. She could sleep off the rest of the drug's effects and begin again in the morning.

But begin what? Maybe she'd remember that when the drugs wore off, too. For now, she needed sleep. Followed by a long shower and a gallon of coffee. Then she'd get deep into the weeds of her data, including the bank records Gaspar had located. She'd figure things out and develop a better plan. She could do better tomorrow; she had to do better. They'd been lucky tonight. Their attacker had disabled but not killed them. They couldn't count on that level of luck next time. *Only one choice.*

CHAPTER 14

Saturday, November 13
7:30 a.m.
Chicago, IL

After a few hours sleep, a long shower, two pots of coffee and an extended session of thinking things through, Kim's body seemed almost restored, but her psyche had too many gaping black holes. She'd tried to fill them by studying her data, but failed. Her memory of those six hours had been chemically erased and it would never be restored.

There was only one reason anyone would do such a thing. Whatever memories had been erased were ones her attacker didn't want her to remember. But why?

The good news was that her memory gap was only six hours. It could have been much longer. Even so, she could muster no gratitude to replace her rage.

What was going on during those six hours that someone didn't want her to know?

The Boss's cell phone had vibrated twice this morning, but she hadn't answered. She wasn't sharp enough to deal with him yet. She was sure the Boss had located her by now. He knew she'd survived the night. He knew exactly where she'd awakened this morning.

But how much did he know about her experiences and other relevant events during the six missing hours? At least until she felt clearer on those events herself, she didn't trust herself to joust with him and win. Certainly, she wouldn't volunteer anything from this point forward. She would talk to the Boss on her terms, or not at all.

After the first pot of coffee, she'd figured the easy place to begin was with the guy who died in Neagley's office yesterday. At least find out who he was. Maybe discover why he'd been at Neagley's. Definitely determine why his companion had opened fire on her.

Kim had called the hospital identified by the paramedic as the body's destination, but got nowhere with the staff. Maybe she could do better in person, but she had more important leads to run down.

Maybe, when she'd exhausted every possible alternative, she'd surrender and put the Boss in charge of that task. He'd get the job done and, with luck, he'd also tell her what he found out. But she wouldn't do that yet.

The second-easiest starter was the first dead guy, O'Donnell. The DC homicide investigator should be easy enough to locate. But Neagley had collected and shared his entire file already, probably because there was nothing useful there. Kim, too, knew a complete homicide file when she saw one. It wasn't likely the homicide detective would have much to add. He could wait.

Which left only one good move. She made a thorough plan while mainlining the second pot of coffee. To make it work, she needed Gaspar fully on board.

Kim looked around the hotel room. Candid talk protected from eavesdroppers was essential and impossible. A large window overlooked the open runway. Glass was an open portal for eavesdroppers. Even cordless house phones broadcast conversations through glass. Windows were no match for the laziest listener, let alone the Boss or any three-letter agency.

She closed the heavy drapes and turned on the radio to add noise and confusion, then cranked up the fan on the room's air handler. Anything with a frequency she could find inside the room was switched on to its highest setting. Far from a perfect solution. The noise could be filtered out and conversations heard. But that would take time and a technician, which would slow listeners down. And it was the best she could do at the moment.

Kim took one last mental tour through her plan and a quick look around the room. She ordered a third pot of coffee and pastries to soak up the acid in her stomach. Then she called her partner. To start, he could fill her in with whatever memories he had recovered.

When she opened the hotel room door to Gaspar's knock, a flood of joyous *déjà vu* washed over her. She almost laughed out loud with relief. "Didn't we do this yesterday?"

He must have felt the same. Simply because they both remembered yesterday morning. He teased, "Don't tell my wife."

It was a start.

She put her index finger across her lips and gestured to the closed drapes and the rapping radio waves and the blasting fans. He nodded.

As was his habit, Gaspar poured coffee, added his usual excessive ration of sugar and cream, and snagged a cherry pastry from the room service cart. His tone was clear and firm and loud enough to be overheard when he said, "The last thing I remember clearly is standing outside of Neagley's office after the paramedics left. How about you?"

Speaking with more confidence than she felt, for the benefit of both Gaspar and whoever was listening, she said, "I remember flashes. I recall dashing up the stairs and running to Neagley's after leaving you to deal with the shooter. I remember the paramedics working on the victim. Paul Neagley's crazy freak-out seems to go on and on in my head."

All of this, Kim figured, was objectively verifiable, and therefore nothing their attacker should be overly worried about her remembering.

Kim moved closer to Gaspar and lowered her voice below the radio volume. "And his arm was bleeding, wasn't it?"

"Yes," Gaspar replied as quietly.

"What caused the bleeding?"

"Not sure. Gunshot grazed it, maybe. I think I smelled fresh gunfire at the time."

Kim nodded, considering. Did she remember smelling anything? Nothing came to her. "After entering Neagley's lobby, all I've got is a huge black hole where my mind should be." She cleared the emotion from her throat. "Catch me up."

Gallantly, he pretended he hadn't noticed how fragile she was, and threw her a bone to make her feel better. "I don't remember the important parts, either." He turned away to refill his coffee and to give her a chance to man up again. "After paramedics removed the victim, Neagley took her brother deeper inside her office. She never came back and we couldn't raise anybody else from inside, either."

He dusted sugar off his hands and began to pace the room. "We talked a little bit to the guard, who was some kind of wiseass and didn't tell us anything. Then we waited for the elevator. That's the last thing I recall."

Kim watched him. His familiar routine comforted her. He seemed exactly as she remembered. Everything that felt normal also felt welcome. She blinked, inhaled to fill her lungs, and stood to force down the panic that had rested on her chest since she'd ignored the Boss's first call this morning.

She had interviewed date rape victims and robbery victims who reported memory losses that varied in duration from thirty minutes to several hours after the drugs were administered. Memory of events prior to unconsciousness also varied and depended in part on the administered dosage.

"Since our drug-induced amnesia is probably permanent," she said, putting a deliberate edge in her voice, "we could try to investigate the attack to fill in the blanks. But it would be a waste of time."

"So, we move on, grateful that our attacker was an expert in the art of drugging victims?" Gaspar's tone let her know exactly what he thought about that suggestion. She felt the same way, but she knew they could chase their attacker until the end of time and would learn nothing. The evidence was gone as surely as her memory.

"The problem isn't the attack, Chico," she said, anger sharpening her response. "It's being hung out to dry."

He nodded. Said nothing.

An attack on two FBI agents should have caused swift, hard reaction from law enforcement. A backup team and additional agents should have flooded the building to apprehend their attacker. If he'd escaped, the full weight of the Agency should hunt him down for as long as it took to haul him to justice. Years, if necessary.

She and Gaspar were FBI agents on assignment. Every move they made was constantly monitored. Within seconds, the Boss had known, or could have known, that his two agents were down.

But no one came to their aid, either immediately or for several hours afterward. Or ever.

Only one conclusion possible. No agent in distress call was issued. No one was hunting their attacker. And no one would.

Kim and Gaspar were working under the radar. Kim knew that, had accepted it. But she had still expected the Boss to have her back. Now, she knew for sure that he didn't.

Toe-to-scalp shudders she couldn't halt threatened to escalate into something like convulsions.

She didn't trust herself to say more. Even as Gaspar watched, her anxiety refused to subside. He crossed the room and sat next to her, placing a firm hand on her shoulder.

After a few moments, he said, "The Boss didn't know,

Kim. He didn't know."

She nodded.

He spoke as if he were calming a frightened horse many times stronger than he was. "Think it through. If the Boss had known we'd been attacked and laid out, either he wouldn't have called last night at all, or he would have waited until we regained consciousness to call."

Kim nodded again, slowly, desperate to regain sufficient control over her central nervous system to speak without tremor.

Gaspar's tone remained quiet, but steady. And hard. "He kept calling because he *didn't* know. He didn't know where we were or what had happened." Gaspar flashed a sardonic grin. "He figured we were ignoring him."

Kim's shudders slowly dissipated as she listened to his calm logic reinforce the cold conclusions she'd already reached intellectually, even though her body hadn't quite metabolized them. If Gaspar believed the same evidence . . .

Maybe to show he'd already left Kim's fear behind, returning to business as usual, Gaspar talked tougher. "She must have disabled the surveillance cameras in the building corridor and in the stairwell before she attacked us."

"She?"

"Top of the list of the three most likely options." He raised his fingers one at a time as he ticked off the possibilities, like teaching a child to count. "The woman with the scars on her face. She shot at us shortly before we were attacked. Second choice, Neagley. Distant third, her security guy."

There were other options. Including an unknown subject. Hell, it could even have been Reacher. He was ahead of them all the way. He could have been waiting. Could have disabled the security guy. Kim liked the idea that it was Reacher better than Gaspar's three options. Reacher was more frightening, but at least he was twice her size and an experienced killer. She couldn't berate herself as much if Reacher had used stealth to overcome them both.

But Kim agreed Gaspar had named the three most likely suspects. She cleared her throat again. "We'll never prove it."

"We don't need to."

"Maybe *you* don't need to."

"We're not going to arrest any of them for laying us out. As far as the world is concerned, we weren't even there," Gaspar said.

Right.

"Look, he's a bastard," Gaspar said, referring to the Boss, whose name they both refused to speak. Safer not to, they'd decided. "But we've been doing this wrong."

"What do you mean?"

"We need to give him a vested interest in keeping us alive and on his team."

"It's pretty obvious he's not there yet, Chico," she said.

He grinned at the crack and she knew he was glad for the sign she'd come through her panic attack, even if neither of them would ever mention it. Just as she didn't ask about his injuries and frailties, he didn't ask about hers. Don't ask; don't tell. As if unacknowledged meant untrue.

That situation would have to change. But not now.

One thing at a time.

Gaspar paced the narrow hotel room, fueled by caffeine and sugar and something like outrage. "The Boss has enemies. Powerful people who'd love to destroy him. We've learned things the Boss never wanted anyone to know. As long as we keep the secrets, dead or alive, it's possible no one else will ever know. If we're killed in the course of this assignment, they'll offer some bullshit explanation and people will believe them."

"You're not making me feel safer, if that was your goal."

"But if we survive, we will always know them for what they are, always be a threat to them. Unless they're prepared to kill us, they won't dare to harm us. Don't you see that?" Gaspar's tone was triumphant.

"What I see is that the Boss and Neagley, and who knows how many others before we're done, are all involved with

Reacher somehow. The Boss doesn't want anybody to know about whatever it is."

"Exactly. Because if we *can* find out? Working in this straitjacket they've fitted around us? Then whatever *it* is, we'll prove that it's findable. And that's the very last thing they want. If it's findable, then they want to destroy *it* before anyone else finds out."

"Of course," she paused, "and destroy everyone who knows about it, too, don't you think?"

He stared straight into her face, heavy black brows pointed directly at the bridge of his nose, nostrils flared, tone determined. "First thing I learned in the Army: stop thinking like *you* and start thinking like *them*."

"Meaning what, exactly?"

"You're still struggling inside the upwardly-mobile-FBI-agent straitjacket. You still think you can pull your fat out of the fire and mine, too. That's what's crazy."

He stood a bit apart from her now—away from her, as if he could create distance from their situation, too. "The Boss and Reacher," he said, "and probably Neagley and the scar-faced woman and who knows how many others—they're all playing some game we don't even know. And their game has no rules at all." He turned his back to her and stuffed both hands into his pockets. "Follow your own advice, why don't you? Caffeinate and carry on, Susie Wong."

She laughed. The first time she'd really laughed since they were attacked. It felt good. And she didn't care who heard her. "Are you packed, Cheech? We've got a plane to catch as soon as we're done here."

"Done with what?" he asked.

CHAPTER 15

Saturday, November 13
9:30 a.m.
Chicago, IL

Kim stood, smoothed her suit, sucked in a deep breath. She reached for the radio and turned the volume a bit higher. She moved to the bathroom, flipped on the second overhead fan for more interference. Then, she sidled closer to Gaspar and lowered her voice.

"Yesterday, Neagley invited us to ask more questions after we reviewed those files she gave us on Dixon and O'Donnell. So I called her this morning. They said she's out of town. Return date open."

Gaspar snorted. "Three guesses where she went."

Kim shrugged. "Two options: Nowhere or somewhere, right? But we'll find her soon enough. I need to confirm something else quickly before we go."

She meant to tread carefully. Because they'd been ordered not to use official resources at all, every time they did so they were violating orders. Which was not great, but she felt it was justified under the circumstances—though putting their colleagues in harm's way *wasn't* justified. She wouldn't do it. So she'd use her personal connections inside the FBI and at other agencies sparingly, and with the utmost care.

This was doubly true with her partner and *his* connections.

Ultimately, Agents Otto and Gaspar would be forced to testify about this investigation when it went south, assuming they survived. The less they each knew about the other's extra-legal activities, the better.

"What about Reacher's bank records?" She phrased the question carefully, working around the minefield.

She didn't ask how Gaspar managed to get Reacher's bank records to begin with. Banks were hacked every day. Confidential information was leaked every day. Don't ask, do tell—they kept coming back to that. Certainly seemed like a good policy for the moment, where confidential sources were concerned.

Leaning in tight, Gaspar quietly reported the facts. "He's got one account. Branch in Virginia near the Pentagon. That's all. Army pension deposited once a month, always on the 5th. Early on he'd call to withdraw cash now and then. Never large amounts. Usually a few hundred dollars. The bank would wire the cash to a Western Union office of his choice. Always a different Western Union office. Withdrawals sporadic. Amounts varied. No pattern I could find."

"But he doesn't do that now?"

"After 9/11, Reacher started using an ATM card. Meaning the withdrawals are traceable. And there's likely photographs of his mug collecting the money at the machines, too."

"Only after the fact. You could go to the spot where he used the card last, but that doesn't tell you where to find him now."

But maybe it did explain how the Boss lost track of Reacher. Assuming he actually did lose track.

"No pattern at all to the banking?" she asked. "He's not

withdrawing regular amounts? Regular intervals? Nothing?"

Gaspar shook his head.

She couldn't wrap her mind around it. Reacher's habits seemed like complete idiocy to her. Could he really be wandering aimlessly from town to town? Taking a bit of cash here and there, and then moving on? It made no sense.

And even if it did make sense, in Reacher's world, maintaining that lifestyle would be too awkward to succeed for fifteen years, and flat out impossible to implement indefinitely. The more she thought about the idea, the more preposterous it seemed. Which meant her early-morning epiphany became more plausible by the second.

She reached for her coat and pointed from the face of her Seiko toward the door.

Gaspar didn't move. He said, "I see the wheels turning over there, Sunshine. What are you thinking?"

"I'm not sure. But we've got to go."

He grinned. "Another minute. Once we walk through that door, we can't talk about this again for a while. Give me something else to dream about while I sleep on the plane."

She scowled at him. Sleeping on an airplane was the height of idiocy, too. At least being awake gives you a fighting chance to save yourself during a fiery plane crash. Not a significant chance. But a better chance than if you slept through whatever fleeting opportunities might present themselves.

"Maybe it just happens that trouble finds Reacher wherever he lands," she said, "but generally people get what they ask for, don't they? Normal people don't find themselves in bar fights and fistfights and gunfights every day. Walks like a killer, talks like a killer, trained as a killer . . . ."

Gaspar shook his head. "Some guys are just trouble magnets," he insisted. He remained stubborn on this point, which Kim felt was so obvious even Stevie Wonder could see it.

She didn't have time to argue about this again, so said

nothing.

When she didn't relent, Gaspar said, "Suppose he is a mercenary of some sort. Let's say he gets paid for the work, too, because otherwise, why bother? Where does the money go? And what does he use it for?"

Kim shrugged. "Drugs. Women. Gambling. The list is endless."

"Back to his bank records. Slim, almost non-existent. For fifteen years, very few deposits other than his monthly pension. So he gets paid for these mercenary activities in cash?"

The best answer was another bank account. Given Reacher's friends in high and low places and the lack of information available about him, the likelihood of finding a second bank account, if it did exist, seemed remote and at the moment, she didn't have the time to spare.

She shrugged again, this time to convey something totally different. "You'll figure it out. Sleep on it." Kim gathered her equipment. "Collect your bags. We've got to go," she said, and left the room.

The Boss's cell phone began vibrating in her pocket again as she walked down the hall. Coincidence? Surely not. How much had he heard of their conversation? She ignored his summons for the third time today. Liberating, really, not to be tethered to his whims.

She worked through her plans for the next twelve hours, focused on the private investigator who had been watching Dixon.

The surveillance file Neagley gave to them yesterday was incomplete at best and probably had been scrubbed. After almost a month of watching Dixon, the investigator had to have accumulated more than Neagley had revealed. Maybe Neagley had scrubbed the file, but more likely someone else had done it. Could have been the investigator. Or his employer. Or someone else.

Regardless, there was more to know than what Neagley had shared. If Dixon could be located, Kim might be able to move on in her assignment and stop dealing with Neagley and O'Donnell and the rest. Let Reacher and his crew kill each other off if that's what they wanted to do. Kim didn't really care anymore.

She reached the elevator, turned, and saw Gaspar pulling his bag, limping toward her, and pushed the call button.

Inside the elevator, she said, "I want to see the surveillance video Colonel Silver used to grab the still-frame photos of Dixon's visitors."

Silver had already failed to mention Neagley's visit to Dixon last week. Old soldiers stick together, Kim knew, and this case overflowed with career Army veterans, most of them officers. Like any huge organization, the higher up the pyramid one climbed, the smaller the pool of pals. Officers of a certain vintage were likely to have at least a passing relationship with one another. At this point it would be foolish to assume Silver and Neagley didn't have a long history with each other. She needed to find out for sure.

As Gaspar said, it was long past time for Kim to think like *them*.

Kim glanced at her Seiko. She could feel her stomach already churning. Fifteen minutes until takeoff. "Someday, Chico, let's try getting on board our flight on time like normal passengers. What do you say?"

"You're my captain, Dragon Lady Boss. But you'd better hustle," he said. "Don't hold me back, okay?"

She hadn't planned to ask, but she did. "What did the Boss have to say when he called just now?"

"You think I talked to the bastard?" Gaspar laughed like a man watching a slapstick comedy gag over and over and over. Kim didn't understand slapstick comedy or why men found it funny. She only knew that they did. And when some dumb jackass comedy routine struck their fancy, they laughed as if God himself had tickled them into near hysteria. That was Gaspar's reaction.

When the elevator stopped at the gate level, he dashed out and she had to hustle to keep up.

CHAPTER 16

Saturday, November 13
12:54 p.m.
New York City

The flight had been blessedly uneventful, on time, as perfect as Kim could expect while being strapped to an explosive missile. She hoped it was an omen. Perhaps her luck had changed.

She spent the flight time reviewing and updating her files, as was her routine. She'd identified more open questions about Reacher than answers, but she could almost believe she'd been deployed on a cut-and-dry background check for the SPTF. Almost. If she ignored the six-hour gap in her memory and the soreness in her neck. And the end of her career, which for her would be the end of life as she'd planned it.

The moment she had Internet access again, she'd sent the materials to secure storage. They'd stashed their equipment in a locker and joined a short cab line. The cab was clean, the driver pleasant, and weekend traffic light. Elapsed time from their O'Hare hotel to the curb in front of Dixon's Manhattan apartment was under four hours. Not bad.

She waited on the sidewalk while Gaspar paid the cab driver. Unlike their prior visit only two days ago, the weather was crisp but fine and the city teemed with Saturday crowds. A Salvation Army volunteer stood on the sidewalk outside Dixon's building, vigorously ringing his bell beside the familiar red kettle. New Yorkers hustled along, loaded down with heavy shopping bags or lost in whatever coursed through their earbuds, but several stopped to slide coins and folded bills through the slot on the collection kettle's lid.

Kim's father served as a volunteer bell ringer after Thanksgiving every year. He and her mother would be expecting Kim home in Detroit for the long holiday weekend. Would she make it? She dropped a folded twenty into the kettle and made a wish like she always did. Kim wasn't superstitious. But her mother was and the wishing habit was ingrained from childhood. Today she wished to finish her assignment before Thanksgiving.

Kim could see through the revolving door that Dixon's building was busier today, too. Residents passed through the lobby, some coming, some going; most called out to Colonel Silver on their way. Kim saw no one she recognized. When Gaspar joined her at the entrance, she said, "You take the lead with Silver. He seems to relate better to you. Tell him we want to talk to him privately. Find out when his break is and how long it lasts."

"Ten-four." Gaspar waved his arm forward, palm up, and said, "After you."

She pushed through the door and waited for Gaspar on the inside before following him across the lobby. Seeing them before they reached him, a big grin lifted the corners of Silver's mouth. "Hey! Good thing you two came back."

Gaspar asked, "Why is that, Colonel?"

"Ms. Dixon came home last night. You still want to talk to her, right?"

"You've seen her?" Kim asked.

He wagged his head. "Not personally, no. But the night guy, he told me she'd arrived during the wee hours. She's probably still catching up on things. Jet lag and all, you know? You can go on up if you want."

Gaspar said, "Okay, thanks."

Kim followed, completely flummoxed, and reconsidering everything she thought she'd learned in the past three days. Finding the investigator, identifying the scar-faced woman and the dead man might be unnecessary now. Maybe Dixon would actually be helpful. A cooperative witness who knew Reacher and might have something worthwhile to add? Now that was a refreshing concept.

Unlike the elevator in Neagley's building, Kim remembered how this one zipped up the floors at light speed. They arrived on Dixon's floor in a hot New York minute and Gaspar led the way to her apartment.

He pressed the doorbell. They waited. He pressed again. No answer, just like their prior visit. Kim began to feel uneasy. Gaspar pressed one last time. Same result.

He turned to Kim, gestured toward the keypad, and said, "Your turn."

She spent a couple of moments in indecision before she stepped up and pressed the numeric keypad as if it were a cell phone, testing her hunch. 7-3-2-2-4-3-7.

Just as it had when Gaspar pressed the same entry code on their last visit, the door clicked open. "Good to have you back, Susie Wong," he teased, grinning. "How did you know Dixon's code?"

"I didn't. But I know you, Chico. And I know everything you know about Dixon. I just used the code you would have guessed first when you were trying to impress me."

"Which was?"

"The common denominator."

He laughed and she pushed through the door and they stood a moment to admire the breathtaking view of New York again before he called out, "Ms. Dixon? Karla Dixon? Are you here?"

Crickets.

Kim said, "I'll check the bedroom. You check the kitchen. Meet you back here."

Gaspar nodded and moved toward the kitchen, continuing to call out to Dixon. Kim did the same while moving in the opposite direction.

"Karla?" Kim called ahead to avoid the possibility of interrupting the woman in her own bedroom. She needn't have bothered.

Dixon's bed had not been slept in. Kim had left one pillow slightly askew on her last inspection, as a test, which remained as she had positioned it. The master bathroom's sinks and shower were dry. She lifted the toilet lid. The bowl had a full complement of water. After almost a month's disuse, some of the water should have evaporated. Maybe the toilet had been flushed since Dixon left, but when? No footprints on the carpets except her own size 5s and Gaspar's size 12s, made during their Thursday inspections. She looked inside the closets and found them unchanged. She stopped in Dixon's office again. Nothing out of place.

"No one back here," she called out to Gaspar as she rounded the entry to the dining room. "Find anything out front?"

She saw Gaspar through the kitchen door, facing her with his hands behind his back, leaning against the cold granite countertop. He tilted his head to the side, as if he was pointing toward the corner, outside Kim's visual range.

She felt every small hair stand up on the back of her neck. Alarm coursed through her venous system as she reached for her gun. But before she drew it, a woman's voice projected from that direction. An even, dispassionate voice she recognized.

"Hello, Otto," Neagley said.

Kim holstered her weapon and entered the kitchen. Neagley stood with her back to her, looking into the open refrigerator.

"Looking for lunch?" Kim asked.

"I was, actually," Neagley said, without turning.

My ass, Kim thought. "You might have answered when you heard us calling out."

"You called Dixon, not me." Neagley closed the refrigerator and moved to opening cupboard doors.

The woman was infuriating. "Is Dixon here?"

"You've been through the entire place. Did you see her?"

Kim's patience evaporated. "Why are you here?"

"Same reason you are, I suspect. I told you I'd left a message for Dixon. She got my message and left one in return. Said she was flying in last night and she'd be home today." Neagley returned to the refrigerator and grabbed a bottle of water. "No food in here." She offered a bottle to Kim, and closed the door again when Kim didn't accept.

"So you just hopped on a plane from Chicago this morning?" Kim demanded.

"Isn't that what you did?" Now Neagley was heating up too.

Gaspar interrupted. "Are we getting anywhere with this?"

"Where is Dixon?" Kim pressed.

Neagley said, "I don't know. It's obvious she hasn't been here. Do you know where she is?"

Gaspar said, "So we need to figure that out. Let's sit, okay? I'm tired of standing." He turned and walked into the dining room, pulled out a chair and waited.

Kim waved toward the archway and said, "After you."

Neagley volunteered nothing, but she sat across from Gaspar and Kim took the chair at the head of the table. Silence. Gaspar assumed his usual waiting pose. He extended both legs, crossed at the ankles, slouched in the chair, folded his hands over his stomach and closed his eyes. "Let me know what you want me to do, Boss."

Kim ignored him. Should she trust Neagley? She had no provable reason to distrust her, except that Neagley had been too close to Reacher once. Kim wasn't comfortable with that, even if Reacher wasn't orchestrating whatever was going on here. Which Kim still thought there was a better than decent chance he was.

"We were attacked in your office building last night," Kim said.

Neagley's eyes narrowed. "What do you mean?"

"We were knocked out and drugged. When we regained consciousness, we were lying in the stairwell outside your office."

"Do you have a suspect in custody?"

"We're working on that," she lied. No one was investigating the assault. Nor would they be. But Neagley didn't need to know that. Kim wanted Neagley to be worried about being arrested, but if she was, she did a damn fine job of hiding the fact. "We'd like to see the surveillance video from the corridor and the stairwell outside your office."

"So you don't know who attacked you? Surely you don't have so many enemies that you can't name them, Agent Otto." She'd amused herself there. "You'll need to ask the building security. I'm not responsible for those common areas."

"Why don't I believe you?" Kim already knew she couldn't get what she needed from building security. She'd tried. But she didn't argue. Neagley's refusal to cooperate was at least some evidence that she knew more than she let on.

Neagley said nothing.

"How long have you been waiting here for Dixon, Frances?" Gaspar asked without sitting up. He did open his eyes, though.

Neagley glared at him. "Don't call me that. About an hour. I figured she went out for food or something and she'll be back."

"Did you ask Silver?"

Neagley narrowed her gaze in his direction, but Kim could feel the frigid response emanating from her when she said, "No."

"Have you tried to call Dixon?"

"Of course. No answer." Neagley pushed her chair back and stood.

Kim wanted to shake that cold confidence. She chose a

different tack. "Is Dixon with Reacher?"

It worked. Neagley pushed her chair in and glared at her. "How would I know?" Then she turned and walked toward the exit. "When Dixon shows up, you can ask her."

"Where are you going?" Kim asked.

"Chicago."

Kim waited until she heard the front door close before she said, "Do you believe that?"

Gaspar shrugged, "Sure. She lives there. And her brother's a mess."

Kim would have punched him, but her arms were too short to reach him with enough force to matter. "There's no chance in hell anyone stayed here overnight. Dixon's bed hasn't been slept in, her shower and sinks are dry. Maybe the toilet's been flushed, but that could have been Neagley."

Gaspar said, "Yet Neagley believed Dixon would meet her here or she wouldn't have come. Which means Dixon did call Neagley and she was supposed to get home last night. Either she did get home and left again, or—"

"Or something, or someone, happened between her phone call to Neagley and now that sent her somewhere else."

"Reacher?" Gaspar sighed. "You're paranoid about that guy."

"Maybe. But it's not smart to ignore the common denominator."

Gaspar shrugged. "So where is Dixon now?"

If she could use FBI resources, she'd be checking airline passenger manifests to be sure Dixon had actually arrived last night. She'd find the cab Dixon took from the airport. She'd watch surveillance video and pull Dixon's phone records. And more. But those avenues were closed to her.

At the moment, her best choice was the private investigator who had been watching Dixon. He probably knew when and where she'd returned to New York. He might even know where she went when she deplaned and where she was now.

But Neagley would get to the investigator first and Neagley knew where to find him. Kim did not. She wasn't about to go chasing Neagley around New York City or anywhere else. Besides, she'd had more than enough of Neagley for a while. The next time she saw Neagley, she wanted to arrest her for attacking two Federal agents. In her gut, Kim knew Neagley was the one.

In response to Gaspar's question about Dixon's whereabouts, Kim glanced at her watch. "Maybe we can get ahead of Neagley. Let's stimulate Silver's recall, shall we?"

CHAPTER 17

Saturday, November 13
2:17 p.m.
New York City

Colonel Silver's security office was tiny, cramped, stifling, and smelled more than a bit ripe. Silver had pulled the surveillance video they'd requested and Kim scoured it as quickly as possible while she half-listened to Gaspar interview him. Kim occupied the only chair in the room. Gaspar and Silver stood in front of the door because there was nowhere else to stand. Kim hoped they wouldn't need to exit quickly.

"You didn't see Ms. Dixon at all, then?" Gaspar asked. Too gently, Kim thought, under the circumstances. They'd lost almost an hour upstairs with Neagley because they thought Dixon was here. Waste of time.

"She called from her cell phone and asked the night guy to send our car to Kennedy to pick her up at midnight. That's in the log right here." Silver pointed to the on-screen log reflecting Dixon's request on the computer screen next to the video monitor. The call had come at 9:00 p.m. Eastern time. She'd given him the flight number and airline. No indication of the departure city, but Kim could find that later. Pickup point was baggage claim, which meant Dixon had checked luggage, Silver said. Made sense, because she'd been gone almost a month.

"Is there an entry reflecting what time the driver got her back here?" Gaspar asked.

"We don't keep track of that. Just the dispatch requests and the destination and the time the car is supposed to be at the pick-up."

"What about the next pick-up after Dixon?" Gaspar asked. "Do you have that?

Silver pressed in next to Kim and flipped through a couple of pages on his computer monitor. "Looks like the car was done for the night after that. The next request was a pick-up at LaGuardia at 6:00 a.m. for another resident."

"Where was the car between midnight and 6:00 a.m.?"

"He takes it home," Silver said, stepping back by the door. Just as well, Kim thought. The man could stand an antiperspirant upgrade. "If we get another call, he'll go directly from home, which saves time. It's not a problem. We don't have a big party crowd living here; people are mostly home by midnight."

"What if Dixon didn't show up when he went to get her?" Gaspar asked. "What would he do?"

"Wait a while, I'd guess. Maybe try to reach her on her cell phone. He might call back here to see if we'd heard anything. You could ask him yourself, but he took a resident upstate this morning. He won't return until tomorrow."

"Unless we ask him to," Gaspar said, sternly.

"Right," Silver agreed. "Want me to call him and find out when he'll be back in the city? Just in case?"

Kim had gone back to the surveillance video. "It's not that important right now," she said without looking up from the screen. "We can follow up tomorrow if we need to. Don't bother him while he's on the road. Can you print that page of the log sheet for us so we'll have the flight information?"

"Sure. Anything else?"

Kim paused the video feed and turned around to face him. "Can you give me a copy of the video of these two visitors?"

Silver peered at the screen. "No problem. I can download it for you right now if you want."

"Please. I'll wait." Kim tapped the screen. "Did you see this woman's face when these two were here?"

Silver's eyes narrowed. His voice lowered and slowed. "Yes."

"What did she look like?"

He hesitated, as if the information was too personal to share. Quietly, he said, "Like she'd been on the losing end of a knife fight a few years ago."

"A knife fight?" Gaspar said, as if he hadn't considered the idea before now. But he should have. Knife fights had to be fairly common in Miami. Kim should have recognized the scars, too. They were common enough in Detroit.

Silver said, "A pretty nasty one, too, it looked like. Scars were bad, even under her makeup. A couple of keloid bumps. Dark lines." He swiped his palm across his sweaty face. "I felt sorry for her. She might have been a good-looking woman before that happened."

The room was quiet while they all considered what a woman's face, scarred and disfigured, might mean. Who would cut her like that? Why? And what might she do for revenge? Because the horrible scars they could see on her face were probably nothing compared to the wounds she carried on her psyche.

After a suitable time, Kim asked, "And what about him? Did you notice anything unusual about her companion?"

Silver bowed his head a moment. When he looked up, Kim noticed his eyes were glassy, as if the old soldier battled past emotions still. "At the time, I wasn't paying much attention to him because of her face, you know?"

Gaspar nodded. "I'm sure," he said, encouragingly.

"He walked . . . funny. That's what I noticed. Stiff. Jerky. I didn't connect his walk in my mind then." Silver stopped, cleared his throat, blinked. "But now I know he must have been a double amputee. I saw too many young men under my command end up like that, honestly." The old soldier pressed both closed eyelids with a gnarled left paw.

After giving Silver a moment to compose himself, Gaspar, absently rubbing his right side, said, "Thank you, Colonel. We appreciate it."

Kim got out of the man's way so he could squeeze himself in before the monitors, then handed him her flash drive. After a silent moment, Silver pulled the drive and handed it back to her. "Here you go. The video and the log, too. Maybe they'll help you find Ms. Dixon. I've known her a long time. She's an army vet, too, you know. Served with her. That's how I got this job. She was a fine soldier. Now you've got me worried about her."

What? What did he say? Kim felt like she'd been whacked with the stupid stick. How could she have missed that? "You served with Dixon in the Army?"

"That's right. Briefly," he said. A smile lifted his mouth in the way of an accomplished man reliving the glory days.

"Serve with Dave O'Donnell, too?" Gaspar asked.

"I knew him. He was around a while. Not as long as me, but long enough."

"How about Frances Neagley?" Kim asked.

His smile faded. He shifted against the door. "She wasn't an officer, but yes, I knew Neagley."

"You saw her today, then?" Kim asked.

"Yes."

"And you saw her earlier in the week, too?"

"Yes."

"Did you talk with her?"

"No."

"Why not?" Gaspar asked this time. It was a question Kim would not have uttered because the answer seemed obvious to her.

Silver seemed startled, too. "Neagley is . . . not a friendly person. She didn't stop to chat."

Kim nodded. She wondered briefly what had happened to his scarred left hand now. Silver had a good bead on Neagley, all right.

Kim took a deep breath. "Did you know Major Jack Reacher?"

Silver's lips all but disappeared in the hard, grim line. After a while, he filled the silence. "I'm sure you already know more about Neagley and Reacher than I do."

"When did you see Reacher last?" Gaspar asked.

"Just before the Army knocked him down to captain," Silver said. "He's damn lucky he's not in Leavenworth. Too bad, since you're looking for him. He'd be a lot easier to find if they'd put him behind bars where he belonged. Neagley, too, as far as I'm concerned. There's something not right about her. Watch your backs."

Kim said, "Reacher's never been here to visit Dixon?"

"Not that I'm aware of," Silver said. "I never asked her. But I've been here ten years and I haven't seen him." Silver's growl now was hard and strong and it was easy to believe he'd been a warrior once. "With any luck, I'll never see Jack Reacher again. If you can make that happen, you're better at your job than we were."

"What did Reacher do?"

"What didn't he do? That's all I'm going to say. There's files. You can read all about it. I've got work to do," Silver said.

Gaspar said, "And Neagley?"

He bristled again. Chose his words too carefully. "As far as I know, she and Ms. Dixon are not friends."

"Why do you say that?" Kim asked.

Silver hesitated again. Then he said, "Neagley isn't the kind of woman who has friends. Let's just put it that way."

"Weren't she and Reacher friends?" Kim asked.

This time, Silver's silence lasted a good while longer.

A loud rap on the security office door caused Gaspar to

jump aside. A man pushed the door open a crack and Kim felt a rush of welcome cool air from the hallway.

The guy stuck his head in. "Silver, are you coming back? I've got to go, man. Your break's been over for twenty minutes."

Silver said, "Of course. I'm sorry. I'm coming now." The man left and Silver said, "I can't leave you in here unsupervised."

"Okay," Kim said. "We've got everything we need for now. Thanks for helping us, Colonel."

She and Gaspar exited the room and Silver locked the door. They walked toward the exit together. He extended his good right hand and Gaspar shook. Kim did the same. "We'll let you know when we find out anything about Ms. Dixon."

"Thank you," he said, turning to leave.

"Colonel Silver?" Kim said.

"Yes?" He put his public smile back in place.

"Were they friends or not?" Kim asked. "Reacher and Neagley?"

His tone hardened enough to break steel. "All due respect, this is the last thing I'm going to say on the subject. They were co-dependent psychos. And my money says that's what they still are. You want to be very careful if that's where you're headed. Ma'am."

Silver left them standing in the hallway outside the security room door wondering what the hell Reacher had done in the Army to have lingered so long with the old warrior.

"Is that where we're headed, Ma'am?" Gaspar asked, mocking to lighten the mood, probably.

Kim said, "I'm open to any better ideas you've got. Right now, I want to look at this video and find that PI, don't you?"

CHAPTER 18

Saturday, November 13
3:56 p.m.
New York City

"So we watch the video, we find the investigator and talk to him, and then we get a bite to eat," Gaspar said.

"I guess."

"Once we're done with him, we can be done for tonight. If we stop now, I won't be interested in talking to this idiot at all."

"You're interested now, Chico?" Kim smiled, teasing him. She'd had even less sleep than he, and flying was always exhausting. She'd be as glad to call it a night as he was.

"Not really. But I know you won't quit until we do. So let's just get it over with. Unless the PI runs again. And if he does, this time don't chase him, okay?"

"What makes you think he'll be in his office?" Kim asked.

"Neagley just texted me the address. She said he wouldn't leave before we arrive."

"Seriously?"

He showed her the text.

They grabbed a cab. Ten minutes later, they were riding up in yet another elevator to another office, this time on the sixth floor. They walked down a dingy corridor to the very end, where an old-fashioned, half-frosted glass, half-wood door marked the office entrance. Gaspar turned the knob. The door was locked. He rapped hard on the scarred wood framing the frosted glass. A moment later, Neagley pulled the door open and stepped back inside.

They entered an office that might have served as a set for an ancient Humphrey Bogart film. Sam Spade surely worked in such a place in the last century. A single room, a battered desk, a thirty-inch door with frosted glass on top directly across from where they stood.

The place was trashed. Top to bottom, side to side. Not a single pencil was where it should have been. Given the size of the room, the search and destroy was completed in maybe five minutes. Ten max. Whatever they'd been looking for, Kim figured they hadn't found it. The entire room was destroyed. If they'd found what they came for, they'd have stopped searching while at least something remained intact.

"What took you so long?" Neagley asked when she'd re-closed the door.

"We thought you were going to Chicago," Kim said.

Neagley ignored the comment and replied, "I've got something to show you. Come on."

They followed her through the door into a tiny workspace smaller than Silver's security room. Again, someone had conducted a quick and very dirty search that left the room looking like an explosion's aftermath. A grimy window, a smaller, battered desk. The desk's top was adorned by gouged and scraped wood and dried brown blood, much of it obscured by the top half of the investigator's dead body, still dressed in his messenger outfit.

"Name David Downing," Neagley said. "And before you ask, yes he was dead when I got here. Gunshot wound to the back of the head. Just like O'Donnell." She took a deep breath. "Probably happened at least eight hours ago, judging by the blood."

"When was the last time you talked to him?" Kim asked.

"Meaning did talking to me and giving me that report get him killed?" Neagley replied. "I'd have to say it's likely, wouldn't you?"

"Yes," Kim said. Even though there were at least a zillion other possibilities, Neagley's was as good a working theory as any. And it could have the happy result that Neagley would be incarcerated for life, at least.

"Did you call NYPD?" Gaspar asked.

Neagley glared at him but didn't reply.

"Did you find anything useful when you searched his office?" Kim asked.

"What makes you think I searched?"

"Fairly obvious, isn't it?" Kim said. "Besides, whoever killed him would have forced him to turn over what they wanted before they did it instead of searching around after. Just in case he didn't have it stashed here."

Neagley raised her eyebrows and nodded as if to begrudgingly acknowledge that Kim might be slightly smarter than a fifth grader after all. "He had no office surveillance installed. Strictly a low-rent amateur operation."

"Low-rent operation is probably why he was chosen," Gaspar said. This time, Neagley turned her condescension his way. He grinned. "You can't possibly think we just fell off the turnip truck, Frances."

"I told you not to call me that," she fairly growled.

Gaspar smirked. It made Kim feel better. Maybe that's why he did it.

Kim said, "What were they looking for?"

Neagley said, "Something small. But vital."

Kim said, "Such as?"

Neagley replied, "Dunno. A key, a flash drive, a note, a photo. Could be anything."

"What about the original copy of the man's report on Dixon? Did you find that?" Gaspar asked.

Neagley glared at him again. "No. Unfortunately."

"So we still don't know who hired him?" Gaspar asked.

"We know," Neagley said, "but we don't have time to go over that now. I wanted you to see this for yourselves. Now we can go. We'll call 911 from a pay phone on the street if we can find one. Come on."

Neagley waited in the dingy corridor while Kim and Gaspar took a fast but better look around. Kim used her smartphone to video the rooms in less than a minute. There was very little to record. She collected a business card from the holder on the desk and made sure she got a still photo of his license hanging on the wall.

Neagley stuck her head into the room. "Come on. We've got to go."

Kim ignored the prod, pulled a pair of latex gloves from her pocket and stretched them on. Then she patted him down looking for his cell phone. When she found it, she dropped it into an evidence bag, sealed it, and slipped it into her pocket. Gaspar watched without comment.

After that, she ran quickly through the desk drawers, which were mostly empty. Whatever the PI's clientele expected of him, they rarely came to this office. His was an I'll-meet-you-anywhere operation, from the looks of things.

Kim stood briefly beside the investigator's body, putting herself in his field of vision. What had he seen? What had gotten him killed? Where had he hidden whatever the killer searched for and didn't find?

Gaspar said, "Let's go, Sunshine. Now."

They joined Neagley in the corridor and made their way to the elevator. Neagley said, "I came up the stairs, so I'll go back that way. You two should go up a few floors and get off the elevator and wait a few minutes and then come back down. When you're asked, you can say who you were visiting up there and describe it accurately. I'll meet you down the block, out front."

What Neagley suggested made sense, so that's what they did. But when they got outside, Gaspar opened his untraceable cell and called the Boss.

"We need interference," he said again, for the second time in the past three days. While Gaspar finished his call, Kim saw Neagley half a block down. She'd hailed a cab and stood waiting for Kim and Gaspar with the door open.

CHAPTER 19

Saturday, November 13
6:06 p.m.
New York City

When they approached the cab, Neagley said, "Get in."

"Just hold on," Kim objected. "We need to find Dixon before she ends up like the PI back there, don't you think?"

"You won't find Dixon."

"Why not?"

"Because I've already looked and I know her better than you do. If I can't find her, you can't find her," Neagley said.

Gaspar just shrugged and entered the cab, leaving Kim standing on the sidewalk facing Neagley.

Neagley sighed. "You two have some sort of beacons on you, right? Tracking devices? It's not like your boss won't know where you are."

"True," Kim said, although she didn't feel as confident that the Boss knew her every move as she had before the stairwell attack. "Why should we trust you?"

"You shouldn't," Neagley replied. "God knows I don't

trust you. We can still be useful to each other. Up to you."

Kim nodded, followed Gaspar into the cab. Neagley tucked in beside her and slammed the door. "Kennedy, please," she told the driver. "United."

Clearly, Neagley was a woman used to being in charge. Kim waited to see what she would do next. This was Neagley's party. For the moment.

Gaspar said nothing. Maybe he was waiting, too.

Neagley turned slightly in the seat to face them. She studied them as if she had some sort of machine in her head that would evaluate them. Maybe she did.

"I've got a flight to Chicago," Neagley said. "I'd like to talk before I go."

Kim said, "Did you contact Reacher like we asked you to?"

"I tried."

Gaspar said, "That's true."

Kim tried to cover her surprise, but knew she didn't do it as well as Neagley covered hers. How could Gaspar possibly know Neagley had tried to contact Reacher?

Kim would ask that question when they were alone. Now, she needed to get what she could from Neagley. "Where's Dixon?"

"That's what I want to talk to you about," Neagley said. "When we reach a quiet place for conversation."

Kim understood that she meant a place free of eavesdroppers and metadata collection. *Good luck with that.* Perhaps there were such places somewhere in the country, but Kim thought not.

Neagley settled back into her seat. Nothing else was said for the remainder of the drive. When the cab pulled up in front of the United terminal, Neagley opened the door and stepped out. She handed the driver a bill and said to them, "Are you coming?"

They scrambled out of the lumpy back seat and followed as Neagley strode through the airport without regard for Kim's comfort or Gaspar's limp. Both agents kept up with her. They followed her down what looked like a service corridor and through an unmarked door into a small, white-walled conference room. Maybe she reserved it while she waited outside the investigator's office.

She waved them to sit at the conference table and then they watched as she pulled two small objects from the overnight bag she'd been carrying—a sleek portable device clearly designed to detect surveillance equipment, and a small black box Kim decided must emit interference at high decibels which would, presumably, prevent eavesdropping and perhaps block the tracking devices contained in their cell phones.

Kim didn't mention that FBI equipment was designed to penetrate such devices. Neagley should have known that. Otherwise, Kim would be carrying a couple herself.

When Neagley had everything set up to her satisfaction, she retrieved a smartphone from her jacket, located a photograph, and showed it first to Kim and then to Gaspar.

"Five years ago, this man claimed to be a rocket scientist. He used the name Edward Dean."

Kim knew a few rocket scientists and this guy looked more like a coach at some third-rate high school. He had a shock of sandy hair. Maybe forty years old in the grainy photograph. He looked like he'd just been rudely awakened from a sound sleep. The photo was cropped about mid-chest, meaning Kim couldn't judge his height or weight. He wore a wrinkled grey T-shirt. Kim imagined he was wearing jeans or sweats. Maybe no shoes, if he'd been sleeping when Neagley shot him.

Neagley found and displayed a second photograph. "Yesterday, as you know, this woman showed up at my office. Five years ago, she claimed to be a human resources director. She used the name Margaret Berenson."

The photo seemed to be some sort of publicity shot. She wore a tailored black jacket and white blouse. Her hair was brown, cut in a style popular back then. Berenson, too, looked to be about forty. For the publicity shot, the scars on her face were maybe airbrushed or something. But they were visible under her makeup. Her photo was cropped like Dean's, but Kim had seen this woman yesterday. She was still slim enough, medium height, medium build. Bigger than Kim and Neagley but smaller than Gaspar.

Neagley pulled back the smartphone, located a third photograph and displayed it. "Fifteen years ago, this man was U.S. Army Major Jorge Sanchez."

This was the third photo Kim had seen of Jorge Sanchez. The first was his official personnel file headshot. And the second was the casual group photo she'd seen hanging in two places, O'Donnell's office and Dixon's home. Like those photos, the Sanchez grinning at her in this one looked durable. His eyes were narrowed. He showed a hint of smile that revealed a gold tooth. He looked almost content, Kim thought.

Finally, Neagley found and displayed a fourth photo. This one Kim recognized as a still shot edited from a video of some sort. Unmistakably the dead guy on the gurney in Neagley's office.

As if they didn't already know, Neagley said, "Yesterday, this man, also claiming to be Jorge Sanchez, arrived with Margaret Berenson and died in my office."

In this photo, a decimated Sanchez looked nothing like the Army officer in the other photos, Kim thought. Neagley finished: "And then Berenson ran away. But before she left the building, she tried to kill you."

Was Neagley saying that Berenson had attacked them in the stairwell? How could Neagley know that?

Neagley slipped the smartphone into her pocket, placed both palms on the table and leaned forward. "I know who and what you are. I know you're working off the books for Charles Cooper, one of the meanest snakes that ever lived. And he's watching you the way a hawk watches a field mouse."

She stopped talking for a moment, maybe giving them a chance to argue.

When they said nothing, Neagley continued. "But what I want to know, Agents Otto and Gaspar, is why you are sniffing around my team. I want to know why Dave O'Donnell is dead and where Karla Dixon is and why you're asking about Reacher. I want to know what you've done to piss Berenson and Dean off and why they want to kill you."

Neagley waited a beat. Her voice lowered half an octave, slowed, and quieted. "This is your last chance to tell me what the hell is going on here."

Kim was trained in interrogation techniques and she had a savant-like talent for profiling, all of which led to the inescapable conclusion that Neagley must be crazy if she thought Kim would tell her anything.

But she didn't look crazy.

She looked, what? Determined. Serious. Her words were angry, but her demeanor was dead calm. Maybe that *was* crazy.

How far could Neagley be pushed before she did something psychotic?

"I'd like to know all of those things, too," Kim said, in the same tone she'd have used to persuade a jumper not to leap off a skyscraper. "And I have a few other questions as well. Beginning with how you know Berenson and Dean, because we've never heard of either one until just now. We've never seen Dean before."

Neagley's pupils widened and then narrowed. The effect was eerily like a camera lens, opening to capture the truth and closing after reality was ensnared.

Kim's tone hardened, "And I have no idea why Berenson was shooting at us, but I'd bet every last dollar in my retirement fund that it has something to do with you. Just like I'm pretty sure I have you to thank for this pain in my shoulder and about seven hours of missing memory."

Neagley didn't reply to any of Kim's comments. Instead, she looked at Gaspar. "What about you? You're following her lead, even if it gets you killed in the process? You've got kids and a wife who are gonna miss your paycheck, don't you think?"

Gaspar's jaw clenched, nostrils flared. Kim knew Neagley had done the wrong thing by mentioning his family. But he drew himself in, just that quickly, and hoisted the customary Gaspar flippancy into place.

"My family is resourceful and they don't eat much." Then he went very still, and said very softly, "I'd worry about your brother, Paul, though. He doesn't look like he can fend for himself very well."

Neagley's expression calmed. It was chilling to witness. Gaspar had clearly crossed a line of some kind, himself. Now he'd planted himself firmly on the other side as far as Neagley was concerned.

The acid churned in Kim's stomach. Whatever line Gaspar had crossed, he'd made a deadly enemy. Another one. When they already had more enemies than they needed.

Neagley picked up her equipment. Turned them off. Returned them to her bag.

"We won't see each other again." She turned and left the room.

When the door had shut behind her, Gaspar rose. "That went well, don't you think, Susie Wong?"

"You're not happy unless everybody you meet wants to kill you, Cheech?" She didn't mention the glaring omission in Neagley's outburst. Sanchez. Neagley hadn't asked why he was dead or how that happened. Which probably meant she knew the answers and Kim could take a pretty accurate guess, too. But she didn't want to speculate aloud just yet.

Gaspar shrugged. "She's too controlled. Too cool. We need her to make a few mistakes. She won't do that as long as she thinks she's in charge. And until she screws something up, we don't have a chance in hell of getting anything useful out of her."

"All true," Kim replied. She pulled out the Boss's untraceable cell phone. Pressed redial. "But I'm sure glad it's your guts she hates and not mine."

Gaspar smirked. "Don't feel left out, Sunshine. Neagley

can kill you without hating you first."

The Boss picked up before the first ring completed, confirming her suspicion that he'd been following along with events as they unfolded, as usual.

Kim said, "What the hell is she talking about? And what do we do now?"

"I'll do some checking," he said. "Meanwhile, you need to hustle or you'll lose her. They're holding your flight to O'Hare on American. I sent your boarding passes to your smartphones. She's arriving thirty minutes ahead of you on United."

He paused briefly.

"Otto? Answer your damn phone when I call you, not just when you feel like it. I'll call you as soon as I know anything useful. Until then, stay out of her way."

Before Kim could retort, he'd disconnected. She jammed the phone into her pocket and told Gaspar, "Time to go."

CHAPTER 20

Saturday, November 13
8:56 p.m.
Chicago, IL

When the wheels touched the tarmac in Chicago, Kim felt the Boss's cell phone vibrate in her pocket. She checked the screen. He'd sent two texts while she was in flight, unable to retrieve anything. The first message said, "Files available for download." The second was, "Vehicle arranged as usual."

They'd crossed into the Central time zone when they'd flown over Lake Michigan, but Kim's body clock registered an hour later. She collected her equipment and nudged Gaspar awake as she trudged out past his seat. She waited at the jetway exit.

When he joined her, they made their way to the special reservation counter and identified their vehicle's location, which, due to Gaspar's requirements, took longer than it should have on a Sunday night.

Kim had lost every debate and given up arguing about transportation with Gaspar after the first day they worked together. He was persuaded that no vehicle on the planet was suitable for their purposes except the Crown Vic Police Interceptor. He liked the powerful V-8 engine and tough, body-on-frame construction. Rear-wheel drive was better for rough driving over curbs and potholes and other urban road hazards. Reduced spin-outs, too. Problem was, Ford had stopped production in 2012 and the big tanks were a challenge to procure. As usual, the Boss could do what mere mortal FBI Special Agents could not. Which meant Kim could look forward to riding in a giant-sized vehicle with severe duty shock absorbers that tossed her lightweight frame around like a rag doll. After fifty miles, she always felt like she'd gone ten rounds with an Olympic champion heavyweight.

Finally, bags stashed, Gaspar behind the wheel, they were on the road headed toward Lake Forest and the address contained in the Boss's text. Neagley's house. The GPS estimated thirty-four minutes to travel 25.5 miles, mostly North along I-294, to the tony Chicago suburb.

Kim had been to Lake Forest before. The area reminded her of Grosse Pointe, Michigan. She knew what they'd find before they arrived. Winding tarmac along Lake Michigan. Stately homes. Grass and gardens and brick pavers galore. She wondered how Neagley could afford to live there and why she'd want to. It seemed much more upscale than a retired soldier would be able to support or feel comfortable living in.

She set up the laptop and connected to the secure server to download the Boss's encrypted file, which was larger than she'd expected. When she opened the zipped contents, she saw three individual files. One labeled "Berenson," one "Dean," and one "New Age Defense Systems."

"Talk to me, Sunshine," Gaspar said. "Otherwise, I'm gonna take a nap."

"Just so you keep this bus between the ditches, Cheech."

"You're never going to get that Cheech Marin is Mexican and I'm Cuban, are you?"

"Susie Wong was Chinese and I'm only half-Vietnamese. Doesn't seem to bother you."

He grinned. "What have you got over there?"

"I'm scanning now. Looks like the important part is a defunct California defense contractor called New Age Defense Systems."

"What kind of a name is that for a defense contractor? What do they do, hold hands and meditate before they develop bio-weapons? Sounds like something even Gandhi would hate."

Kim barely listened to his babble as she scanned the information on the screen. "Highly classified. Went out of business five years ago. Suspected of trading with the enemy, it says here. Berenson and Dean both worked there. The suggestion was they maybe were part owners or held significant stock or something."

"What were they suspected of trading with what enemy, exactly?"

"Looks like the only thing New Age developed and manufactured were missiles. Chiefly something called Little Wing, which is now obsolete. It was a man-portable, shoulder-launched, surface-to-air missile."

"Five years ago, we had plenty of enemies interested in those. Still do."

"Right," Kim said, scanning down the reports. "Dean was the R&D guy. Berenson was in HR. Nothing about Sanchez or O'Donnell that I can see." She stopped talking and read more quickly.

After a while, Gaspar said, "What?"

"Head of security at New Age was Tony Swan," she said.

"One of Reacher's team, now dead."

"Right."

"What else?"

"New Age was the sole source of Little Wing. The project was discontinued after two years when countermeasures were designed to defeat Little Wing. And everything else in the file about Little Wing was classified. Which could mean that the Boss saw it and decided not to send it along." Kim closed the laptop for a moment and rubbed her eyes. She was running low on every one of her standard triple A's: ambition, anxiety and adrenaline. Caffeine would give her a temporary recharge until she could get some much-needed sleep. "Is there anywhere we can stop for coffee?"

"Might be some all-night diners around here somewhere. But it is Sunday night, so maybe not. I'll keep a look out. What happened to Dean and Berenson when New Age went OOB?"

"The file doesn't say. Presumably they lost their jobs, maybe their investments."

"Lots of people lose their jobs. Doesn't make 'em homicidal," he said.

"It feels like everything's all connected, though. Swan and the other members of Reacher's team died five years ago. Sanchez went missing, presumed dead, five years ago. New Age went belly up five years ago. Neagley hasn't seen Reacher for years, she said. I'm guessing about five years, don't you think? But I don't see anything in this file to give us a clue."

"You think Neagley knows whatever the connection is?" he asked.

"She knows a lot more about the situation than we do. For sure. I'm only sorry we can't arrest her for obstruction. Or treason. Or even murder. I'd take robbing candy from a little old lady if it meant I could slap the cuffs on her and lock her up."

Gaspar laughed. "Frances really got under your skin, didn't she, Susie Wong?"

Kim frowned, but he ignored her. "If I could prove she's the one who assaulted us, she'd be sitting in a cell already."

"The Boss wouldn't like that."

"Who cares what the Boss likes? You?"

Gaspar said nothing and Kim couldn't see him very well in the dim interior of the Crown Vic. He'd been the one who'd distrusted the Boss from the start. Kim had been more gullible initially. But not anymore.

After a while, Gaspar said, "Let's recap. This is one of those assignments where missing the smallest detail could be, well, not good for our health, right?"

"Exactly."

"So we know that the point of connection is New Age. We know the time frame was five years ago."

"We know Sanchez and Swan were involved," Kim contributed. "Because Orozco and Franz died around the same time, it's reasonable to assume the rest of Reacher's unit was involved, too. Including the big guy."

Gaspar didn't argue. But he didn't say he agreed, either. He'd flipped on his turn signal and moved into the exit lane. Kim glanced up to see a sign indicating an all-night truck stop ahead. Her nostrils quivered. Coffee.

He said, "The question is what the hell kind of 'trading with the enemy' they were involved in that got them all not arrested, tried, and convicted, but maimed or killed. Some at the time. Some years later. Any clue?"

Kim sighed, ran her hand over the sleek cap of black hair that she'd pulled back and twisted into a chignon hours ago. She felt so weary of it all. Even six hours of uninterrupted sleep seemed like the holy grail. Something she could forever seek but never find.

She sighed again. "Oh, it has to be money, doesn't it? Money and maybe ego. Everything else is too perishable to have gotten them killed so many years later. It's hard to sustain any sort of rage for five years, in my experience. Cold, hard, hatred is another matter."

Gaspar's eyebrows jumped up. "Missiles aren't perishable."

"Sure they are. They're a strategic weapon. And they've pretty much been replaced by drones and newer missiles, haven't they?"

Gaspar pulled the Crown Vic perpendicular to the curb in front of the truck stop. It was one of those all-in-one places where truckers could sleep or get a donut for breakfast or a beer before bed to go with their sandwich. Kim didn't speculate about what else might be available for the right price. All she cared about was a caffeine jolt, which, for her, was the second best alternative to solid shuteye. She unlatched her seatbelt and rooted around in her pockets for the necessary cash.

"Let's say you're right that the missiles themselves are not the current motivator, at least," he said. "I agree about the rage thing and nothing says this is a vengeance thing to me, either. So let's focus on your best guess. Who has the money? And who wants it?"

Kim opened her door and stepped out into the cold dark. Gaspar did the same. Their gazes met over the hood. "Excellent questions. I'll think about that. And you think about why you agreed with Neagley when she said she'd tried to contact Reacher for us. After I make a pit stop and buy a quart of stiff black caffeine, you can talk first."

CHAPTER 21

Saturday, November 13
10:21 p.m.
Chicago, IL

The coffee cup Kim returned to the Crown Vic with was at least a quart-sized one. She also had collected a nutritious dinner: a bag of donuts and a large pouch of peanut M&Ms. She settled into the Crown Vic's seat, pulled out the alligator clamp she kept in her pocket and anchored it firmly to the shoulder harness to keep it from cutting her head off at her neck. She inhaled the coffee's aroma like a coonhound sniffing prey and tore the M&Ms open with her teeth.

"Protein first. Then dessert," she said.

"*Bon appetit!*" Gaspar hoisted his cold cola and sleeve of chocolate cookies in a one-hand salute. With the other, he slid the key into the ignition, buckled his own belt, and reached down to start the engine.

"Hold on a minute," Kim said. "I want to know the answer to my question. When Neagley said she'd tried to contact Reacher, you confirmed. Why?"

Gaspar stretched, yawned, delayed. "I was just trying to make peace between you two."

"No you weren't. You believed her." Kim continued to munch on her candy as if his answer didn't matter. But they both knew it did.

He shrugged. "We've got to find out what she's up to, don't we? Maybe she lied. Maybe not. Either way, why not say we believe her? Makes her feel a little less confident in her privacy methods and at the same time, suggests we know more about her actions than she thought. Diabolical, hmm?"

Kim reached over and pulled the keys from the ignition before he realized what she intended to do. The heavy V-8 engine died without so much as an extra whimper. "The woman's a whack-job. She's dangerous. And maybe crazy. I'm not going any further until I know what you know."

He looked down at the steering wheel and then returned his gaze to hers, some decision reached, she figured. He said, "Remember I told you that Reacher's bank records showed very few deposits except for his pension?"

She realized they were on treacherous ground whenever the bank records were mentioned, and that their conversation was being monitored, as always. Still, she was a little afraid of Neagley. Her gut told her she needed to know, even if the Boss overheard. She trusted Gaspar to protect whatever he needed to protect.

She sipped to delay her final decision a moment more. The coffee was strong and hot and hit her stomach like a jolt of nauseous energy added to the sugar from the candy. She was starting to feel wired.

Kim nodded. "I remember."

"Well, I found four deposits," he said, quietly. "The first three happened five years ago. The first was $1,030.00. Five weeks later, two more deposits made on the same day, $101,810.18 and $10,012. The first one came from a bank in Chicago. The last two from a bank in New York."

She thought about it. Obviously, if the bank deposits were somehow used to contact Reacher back when he collected money from Western Union offices, people close to him might know about the arrangement. Maybe Neagley and Dixon improvised, or maybe Reacher suggested the covert connection. Either way, Gaspar was probably right. They'd found no other way to locate Reacher. Follow the money. Always the best plan, in Kim's experience.

She sipped, munched, considered carefully. She returned the keys to the ignition and Gaspar started the engine. She punched the on button for the radio and turned up the volume, then looked at Gaspar and mouthed, "And the fourth was Tuesday?"

He nodded, "The same amount as the first. $1,030.00." He shifted the car into reverse, turned the radio volume down. "Geez! Even my kids don't blast my eardrums like that!"

"What do you make of the deposits?" Kim asked between thoughtful crunches.

"Dunno. You?"

They returned to the expressway and continued toward Lake Forest, while Kim considered what would likely happen when and if Reacher got Neagley's message, whatever the message was.

Kim tried to think about the deposit numbers, but she was too tired to hold them in her head, so made a quick note of the amounts and then she focused on the circumstances. She could usually see the hidden relationships others missed.

Two deposits of the same amount, five years apart. If the second was a signal from Neagley, did that mean the first was a signal from Neagley, too? Probably.

Or at least it meant the deposit amount was a signal and Neagley knew about the signal and what it meant and she duplicated it now because it had worked five years ago to get Reacher's attention.

But what about the other two deposits? Were they signals as well? From whom? Neagley? Or Dixon? Or someone else?

A hundred-and-one grand was one hell of a signal, if that was the case.

Maybe if she finished the coffee and chocolate, her synapses would fire correctly again and she could figure things out.

Gaspar said, "We're close to Neagley's. Let's talk about your money theory. Suppose this is all about money. Which is as good a guess as any."

"High praise, Chico."

He grinned. "So if this is about money, you figure it's what? Somebody got cheated back in the day?"

"Makes sense."

"Who has the money? And who wants it?"

"I figure that's what we'll ask Neagley when we get there. If nothing else, it'll be fun to watch her squirm."

"Assuming you're doing the teasing, not me. And from an assured clear distance," he said, as he turned the Crown Vic onto Neagley's street. Her address was two dark and silent blocks ahead.

They could see Neagley's home clearly in the distance.

While most of the homes in the sleepy neighborhood were closed up for the night, Neagley's was flooded with bright lights and three local police cruisers were parked out front. The newer, reengineered versions of the Interceptors. No match for the Crown Vic, should it come to a challenge. Which Kim hoped it wouldn't.

"What the hell do you suppose is going on here?" Gaspar said, as if he was asking no one but himself.

Kim turned on the police scanner inside the Crown Vic. She heard the usual radio calls between dispatch and patrol units.

"Ten-forty-three, please," the dispatcher requested. Polite.

"Ten-eighty-five; ten-sixteen; ten-ninety-six," an officer responded.

"Ten-sixty-nine," she said.

"Say what?" Gaspar asked.

Kim easily located the Illinois State Police 10-codes list on her laptop and translated. "Dispatcher wants information. He says he's delayed due to a domestic problem involving a mentally disturbed subject." She looked up from the screen.

"I told you Neagley was crazy, but you didn't believe me."

"Yeah, yeah," he replied. "Though her brother can get a little agitated, too, don't you agree? What else?"

"The dispatcher says ten-sixty-nine, message received."

Gaspar scowled. "How wacky is that? Who could remember all those 10-codes? We only had fifty in the Army."

"Soldiers have notoriously bad memories. They didn't want to over-tax your systems." Kim's caffeine high had finally kicked in. She felt buzzed with energy.

Most agencies had abandoned the old 10-codes in favor of plain words because 10-codes varied too much from one jurisdiction to the next. But here in Illinois, where they were invented back in 1937, not only did they remain in use, but the locals had devised quite a few extras in the past seventy-five years.

"Well, 50 ten-codes should be enough for anybody," Gaspar groused. "In the Army, we never had a situation that didn't fit somewhere."

Kim turned the scanner's volume down. Before she could formulate a snappy reply, the answer to an earlier brain-teaser gobsmacked her. She grinned. "I know what those deposits to Reacher's bank account mean."

"You do?"

"Ten-twenty-eight."

"In Army-speak, that means loud and clear," Gaspar said. "Ten-four."

"Wrecker requested? What the hell is that?"

Kim laughed out loud. "Okay, Chico, okay. Ten-four means okay."

Her mirth only annoyed Gaspar further. "No, it doesn't. In the Army it means 'wrecker requested.' In the civilian world, it means 'acknowledged.' What's acknowledged?"

Still chuckling, Kim replied, "Think about the deposits. You're good with numbers. Meanwhile, park the car. Let's go see what's going on here."

CHAPTER 22

Sunday, November 14
12:13 a.m.
Chicago, IL

As instructed, Gaspar parked the Crown Vic along the curb behind one of the cruisers, making sure to leave enough room for an easy exit. They left the vehicle unlocked and walked down the tree-lined sidewalk toward Neagley's home, which looked like it had been owned by a railroad baron once upon a time.

The house was set back from the road and surrounded by at least an acre of green all around. Lots of doors and roofs and huge windows and giant garages. The brick pavers alone would have cost Kim a year's pay.

The first uniformed officer they reached stood leaning against his patrol car which, upon closer inspection, was a private security service vehicle, not Lake Forest PD. Kim pulled out her badge wallet and showed it. Gaspar did the same.

But before she could introduce herself, probably because

of his assumptions about their jurisdiction, the guard said, "No need for the FBI. We've called the locals. The kid's run away a dozen times before. We'll probably find him in the next hour."

The former secret service agent Kim remembered standing guard at Neagley's office came out the front door and hustled down the long and winding sidewalk toward the police vehicles ahead on the street.

Kim called out. He turned, saw them, and waited for their approach.

"What's your name, anyway?" Gaspar asked when they were within hailing distance.

"Never give up, do you?" he said. "We didn't report a kidnapping. Why are you here?"

"Is Ms. Neagley inside?" Kim asked.

"She is."

"I'll meet you there," she said to Gaspar, leaving him to interrogate Nameless as well as possible while she traveled the sidewalk he'd used to reach the curb.

The air smelled like home to Kim. This Chicago suburb was a long way from the Michigan farm town she grew up in, but Midwestern fall smelled clean and cold here, too.

The wide-open space around Neagley's house allowed cold wind to blow through her lightweight overcoat. She hugged her arms to her body and thought about how cold Paul would be now, and much colder he'd be as the night wore on, if he'd run out without a good warm fleece and knit cap, at least.

The front door of the house stood open and every light on the lower level was ablaze, spilling brightness onto the front pavers and lawns like outdoor floodlights.

Wearing the same clothes she'd worn in New York earlier, Neagley stood just inside the entrance, talking with two uniformed officers, her back to the door. Which allowed Kim to approach the group unnoticed.

Kim listened to the conversation while forcing herself not to gape at the home's spacious open floor plan and pricey interior decor. She couldn't remember the last time she'd seen as many wing chairs collected in one place. She counted fifteen from her vantage point at the entrance. Not to mention the artwork she recognized and the sheer volume of high-end stuff everywhere. Several heavy wood pieces were tall and dark and solid enough to require a forklift simply to rearrange the furniture. Could this possibly be Neagley's taste? She'd seemed much more practical up until now.

Neagley was explaining the situation to the officers as if she were dictating a police report. "He was in bed by nine, like always. Morrie was here the entire time. I got home late and when I went in to check on him, he was gone. We inspected all of his usual hiding places before we called you. He likes to hitchhike. So get a BOLO out and do the best you can until daylight."

So the former Secret Service guy's name was Morrie. Wonder why he didn't want to reveal it? One small mystery solved, anyway.

Kim's pocket vibrated and she considered ignoring it. Under the circumstances, perhaps the Boss had something positive to offer. She turned her back and pulled out the phone.

She could feel Neagley's eyes burning holes in her back. "Yes?"

He said, "Berenson snatched the kid. Found him outside, a couple of blocks down. I'm working on video. Should have it soon. Show Neagley alone."

"Okay," she said and was about to disconnect when she realized he was still talking.

"And Otto?"

"Yes."

"Dean has Dixon. Intercepted her at Kennedy when she deplaned. Working on that video, too. No mistake."

"Current locations?"

"Unknown. Still checking."

"Anything else?"

"Reacher's on the way. Might be there already. Stay alert," he said and terminated the call.

Before she could slide the phone back into her pocket, Kim looked up into Neagley's bottomless gaze. She felt the woman's anger pulsing off her like sonic waves.

Neagley's hand shot out, grabbed the phone from her hand and dropped it into her own pocket before Kim had time to blink.

Neagley dismissed the officers and they left, promising to promptly report anything they found.

"What did he want?" she said, glaring at Kim and referencing the phone call.

"You make it hard to tolerate you, you know that?" Kim snapped. "Give me my phone."

Neagley stood like a sentry at the gates of hell, which was probably where she wished she could send Kim right about now.

"Fine. Keep it. I hate the thing anyway."

Neagley said nothing.

A moment ago, Kim might have tried to deliver the news kindly, but Neagley wouldn't appreciate kindness and Kim didn't have the patience. "He said Berenson has your brother."

Neagley showed no response at all. "What else?"

Briefly, Kim considered mentioning the Boss's promise to send video of the kidnapping, but instinctively held back. She didn't trust Neagley. She'd wait to receive the video, watch it first, and then decide when or if to reveal it to Neagley. The Boss was looking for the missing and he had superior resources; Neagley couldn't do more. Kim would learn more about the situation and show her the video before daylight.

"Dean has Dixon."

"And?"

"We don't know where they are."

"Like hell he doesn't," Neagley said, nostrils flared half a second.

Will you look at that. The ice queen feels something.

"Get Gaspar in here and follow me." Neagley turned and strode toward the back of the house.

CHAPTER 23

Sunday, November 14
1:43 a.m.
Chicago, IL

Gaspar and Kim were seated at Neagley's oversized kitchen table at the back of the mansion. She'd made coffee and poured large mugs full and the aroma wafted enticingly. Kim's nerves were humming and her skin felt too tight on her frame. Gaspar had assumed his usual slouch, but his eyelids were open, which was about as anxious as he normally allowed himself to appear.

Neagley's cool demeanor had returned as quickly as her anger had flashed, leaving Kim to wonder whether she'd seen any anger at all. Neagley requested and received Gaspar's cell phone, disabled it, and stuffed it with Kim's inside a signal-shield box.

Kim couldn't retrieve the Boss's encrypted video of the kidnapping using the phone even if she'd wanted to. And if she couldn't talk to the Boss for a while, Neagley could hardly blame Kim for holding back when the video was finally shared.

"Cooper can't hear you or see you," Neagley said when they'd settled in. "My home is a bug-free zone. You can speak freely. So let's get to it."

"You first," Kim said, not believing Neagley's boast. Even if the Boss's sophisticated equipment was temporarily thwarted, Neagley's home was probably more wired than the Pentagon. Someone was always eavesdropping. To assume otherwise was foolish and Kim was not a fool. "Where's Reacher?"

Neagley replied, "I told you, I sent him a message—"

"Yeah. Days ago," Gaspar said. "How long does it take for him to pick up?"

Neagley continued as if he'd never spoken. "I wish to hell he was here because we could use some help. But we can't wait for him."

"How do you contact him?" Gaspar asked.

"You found my message, so you should know that." She smirked. "Can't figure it out?"

The woman was too smug and Kim was tired of taking her crap.

"You told him 10-30. 'Request assistance, non-emergency.' Why not 10-19? If you'd asked, he might have contacted or called," Kim revealed, even though it might not have been the best time to play that card and she hadn't explained her hunch to Gaspar or told him about the Boss's warning yet.

Neagley shrugged. "He knows what to do."

"What happened with your brother?" Kim asked.

Neagley looked away briefly. Then she turned a steady gaze toward Kim and said, "Paul is autistic. We never leave him alone, even to sleep. He's a good kid in many ways. But he's very clever and he's sly. He was upset about what happened in my office yesterday and he was angry about his arm wound and who knows what else goes on inside his head? Somehow, he got away from Morrie tonight and ran outside. Morrie and I discovered him missing when I got home from New York, and we looked for about half an hour before we called for help. I guess we know now why we couldn't find him."

"It's not your fault," Kim said, automatically, as she would have said to any kidnapping victim's family. But Neagley wasn't just a normal sister.

"The hell it isn't. If I'd been here, he might still have run out, but Berenson wouldn't have been able to take him. I thought she'd be in New York going after Dixon. That's why I went there. But I screwed up. And Paul's paying the price. I didn't count on her working with Dean."

"Why not?"

"Because she was petrified of him five years ago. I figured she'd be as far away from Dean as possible. Didn't see that one coming. Not even remotely."

"You never see the bullet that gets you, Neagley. If you'd seen it coming, you'd have moved him out of harm's way. Get over it. We've got to deal with where we are."

"She had to sedate him somehow and she knew that," Neagley said. "She'd been watching him for days. She knew there's no way she could have gotten close to him, let alone grabbed him and taken him somewhere against his will unless she drugged him first."

Gaspar said, "Then there's a good chance she's still close by, unless she's driving. And if she is driving, we'll find her. She can't get on an airplane with an unconscious man. Not undetected, anyway."

"Is Cooper even looking for them?" Neagley asked.

Kim replied, "He suggested he was."

"Bastard," Neagley said. "And Dixon. Did he say how Dean managed to abduct her? She's pretty good at taking care of herself."

"Didn't say that, either," Kim said. "But would she have been worried about being abducted, though? Could Dean have tricked her somehow? You didn't suspect Dean and Berenson were working together. Maybe Dixon didn't suspect that, either."

Kim could almost see the gears turning in Neagley's head.

"Maybe," Neagley finally said. "We thought Dean and Berenson were victims back then. Thought they were co-workers, not connected in any way we could see. Maybe Dixon didn't see that one coming, either." The thought seemed to make Neagley relax slightly. Maybe telling herself, if Dixon screwing up didn't mean Dixon was an idiot, maybe her own screw-up didn't mean she was incompetent, either.

Gaspar cleared his throat. Apologetically, he said, "It's possible they're already both dead."

"Not likely," Neagley said, unconcerned. "Neither Paul nor Dixon have any value to Berenson and Dean if they're dead. More likely they wanted hostages."

"Hostages?" Kim asked. "It's about time you told us what the hell is going on here, isn't it?"

Neagley rose and grabbed her coffee cup. "Nothing more we can do right now for Paul or Dixon. Come with me."

She walked swiftly down a long corridor to another wing of the house. She stopped in front of what appeared to be a solid, wood-paneled wall. She reached for a small framed watercolor, which opened on hinges to reveal a wall-mounted keypad. She punched a security code and the solid panel slid open. Neagley led them into what looked like a high-tech security office.

The room was empty, but someone had been here recently. At least one man, from the slight male scent Kim detected. She saw dirty coffee cups and scuff marks made by large and small boots on the carpet. Maybe Neagley and Morrie had been working here earlier.

There were multiple television screens on the walls and a control board for operating electronics. Neagley picked up a remote and turned on one of the screens. A twenty-four minute video had ended. She selected a shorter one.

"This is two minutes. Watch first. Then talk," she ordered.

Kim recognized the location. It was Dave O'Donnell's personal office. Two men were talking, but there was no sound. One was O'Donnell. The other was the dead man she'd seen in Neagley's office yesterday. The one Neagley claimed was Jorge Sanchez. The effect was a little eerie because both men onscreen were now dead and Kim had never known either of them. She felt detached from the scene, attracted and repelled at the same time. Whatever Neagley felt, if anything, she kept well concealed.

The video was surprisingly clear for office surveillance equipment. Kim had seen too many such recordings. O'Donnell's stuff was top notch. Which didn't keep him alive. But it might help identify his killer.

After the first run-through, Neagley cued it up again and they asked questions.

Gaspar said, "You were watching O'Donnell?"

"No."

"So you removed relevant evidence from a murder scene, then."

Neagley said nothing.

"When and how did you get this video?" Kim asked.

"The DC homicide cop called me and asked me to come over. I did. By the time I got there, he still hadn't found O'Donnell's surveillance equipment. I found it on my second visit. After I saw it, I figured Sanchez would go after Dixon and me, so I went to New York, hoping to get there first."

"Have you shared this with DC?" Kim asked.

"They'll close their homicide investigation shortly. Sanchez is dead now. What's the point?"

"And if you did give the evidence to DC, someone would get in the way of your own plans," Gaspar said.

Neagley said, "Yours, too. Not helpful to either of us, is it?"

Kim watched as Sanchez paced around O'Donnell's office behind O'Donnell's chair. O'Donnell must have trusted him. Otherwise, why let Sanchez get behind him? Sanchez's gait was awkward—the prostheses. He pulled the gun and shot O'Donnell in the back of the head, stood there for a few moments in the silence, then disconnected the speaker, stepped around O'Donnell's body and left the room.

Kim remembered the fingerprint on the speakerphone on O'Donnell's desk. So it was Sanchez who put it there. DC crime techs found it, which was why the residue was visible when Kim was there. Sanchez's print should have come up in the databases. He had been a military cop. His prints would have been on file so they could be excluded from his many investigations, if for no other reason. But he also had concealed weapons permits and a private investigator's license in Nevada awhile back, which should have required prints. There may have been other sets as well. Yet Sanchez wasn't mentioned in the homicide file at all, which probably meant the DC cops didn't run the military databases. Or maybe Sanchez's prints were no longer there, either. Whoever had been eliminating all of Reacher's paper trail could also be eliminating others.

"Who were they talking to on the speakerphone?" Kim asked.

"We weren't able to trace the call and the listener never speaks, unfortunately," Neagley said. "I thought it was you."

"What?"

"Think about it, Otto. You come on the scene, asking questions about all of us, especially about Reacher. Sanchez comes back from the dead, working together with someone, too. Reasonable to assume he's looking for Reacher. Sanchez shoots O'Donnell in cold blood, which is way beyond the pale, wouldn't you say? Then Berenson tries to kill you. And you know what I think of your boss. All in all, you and Gaspar here were not a bad working hypothesis."

Neagley was right. Not that Kim would ever admit it.

Gaspar spoke up. "But now you know Sanchez was not working with us because we didn't even know he existed until you told us, and we're sitting here trying to help you find Paul and Dixon. So who was listening on the speakerphone?"

"I figure either Berenson or Dean, or both, or someone working with them. They had a couple of kids who would be adults now. They had a crew. Or it could still be you,"

Neagley said. "Seems most likely at this point."

"Why isn't there any sound on this video?" Gaspar asked, ignoring her accusations as she ignored his.

Neagley said, "It's not helpful."

"Let's hear it anyway," Kim said. "I want to hear the conversation. Does Sanchez say why he's doing this?"

"He does. But that's not helpful, either. And it won't make any sense to you at all."

"You can explain it to us, then."

Neagley shrugged, pushed the restart button. The video opened with Sanchez standing behind O'Donnell, but Kim figured there had to be more footage prior to this point. Sanchez was pacing. His voice was agitated. Whiny. Distraught.

"They've got my *kids*, Dave. My *wife*. You have any idea what that's like? Knowing it's your fault? Knowing you let it happen and you've only got one very slim chance to fix it? Knowing you're playing beat the clock and time is running out?"

"What are you talking about?" O'Donnell asked. "When did you get married?"

Sanchez waved the Glock in the air. O'Donnell didn't seem at all concerned. Sanchez executed his friend and watched him die.

You never see the bullet that gets you, Kim thought again.

CHAPTER 24

Sunday, November 14
4:13 a.m.
Chicago, IL

They'd watched the full twenty-four minute O'Donnell video twice and the short murder scene several more times. Sanchez's story was grim and heartbreaking and Kim could easily see how Berenson and Dean drove him to the edge of madness, if not beyond it.

Hindsight being what it is, Kim identified a number of tactical mistakes O'Donnell had made which led to his death. Like watching a horror movie, Kim wanted to shout out a warning several times, but O'Donnell could not hear or heed warnings, then or now.

The video opened with a vital, attractive Dave O'Donnell seated at his desk. He was movie-star handsome, dressed in a dark suit, blue shirt, and a designer brand tie Kim often noticed around the necks of successful stockbrokers. Perhaps he'd rushed in from another event, because he seemed slightly breathless.

He began with an establishing statement for the video. "Scheduled conference with Jorge Sanchez's brother, Jose. Friday night, November 5, 11:10 p.m. Jose called earlier today and requested the late meeting because he's traveling through town and only has a short layover. He didn't want to meet in a public place, so we could talk. He said he had something to discuss about Jorge's share of the money. Wouldn't say any more. I've never met Sanchez's brother. Didn't know he had a brother, actually. We weren't close enough for that, I guess. Never saw Sanchez either, after we left the Army. He was killed by the scum who murdered the others back in California—"

He was interrupted by the buzzer Kim remembered, indicating a visitor had pushed the call button in the corridor. Kim wondered about O'Donnell's choice of words. The "we" who had been so mistaken about Sanchez? The likely culprits were Neagley, Dixon and Reacher. And who were the "scum"? Did he mean Dean and Berenson?

O'Donnell stood, smoothed his hair with the flat of his palm, left the room and the next action was the two returning to O'Donnell's office less than a minute later. O'Donnell was taller, fairer, and a thousand times more handsome than the leathery, gaunt Sanchez.

Maybe Sanchez identified himself or maybe O'Donnell recognized him. Either way, they walked into the frame laughing and seemed genuinely pleased to be together. Which was jarring because Sanchez would kill O'Donnell within the next fifty-one minutes, as cold-bloodedly as any murderer Kim had ever witnessed.

After the backslapping and pleased-to-see-you-vertical-and-above-ground guy stuff, O'Donnell suggested that Sanchez take a seat, but he declined. He said, "I've been sitting awhile and my legs get stiff and I've got another flight tonight. Okay if I walk around? I'm getting permission in case you still have that switchblade in your pocket."

They chuckled and O'Donnell consented, but he didn't deny the switchblade.

"Man, Sanchez," O'Donnell said, "I can't tell you how great it is to see you're alive. I know we served only a short time together. And it was a long time ago. But you guys were closer to me than my own family, man. Too many of us are dead now. We'll get the unit together. Have a few beers. Let's really do it, okay?"

Sanchez coughed a little. "Could I get some water? My throat is parched. Room temperature, not chilled, if you have it."

"Absolutely," O'Donnell said as he hurried out. In the few seconds he was gone, Sanchez reached over and pressed the speakerphone button. The call connected but no words were spoken.

Kim pressed the pause button on the remote and turned to Neagley. "Can you identify the phone number?"

"It was a burner. We are working on identifying the location. No luck yet."

Kim restarted the video.

O'Donnell returned with a plastic bottle of water and handed it to Sanchez, who opened it, took a swig, and dropped it into his jacket pocket.

If O'Donnell found the water bottle stashing odd, he didn't mention it. Instead, he asked, "Where've you been? We were in California and we were trying to find out what happened to you guys. And the news was bad, man. We found Franz and Orozco. They were dropped out of a helicopter onto the desert floor. While they were still alive, Sanchez. Can you imagine? We never found Swan. Or you. We looked, but we failed."

Sanchez said nothing.

O'Donnell swiped his sweaty face with his palm, forehead to chin, and ran both hands, fingers splayed, through his hair. "We made them pay, Sanchez. You know we did. And we did what we could for the families. We collected some spoils and Dixon converted them and we shared it, with extra for the families, not so much for the rest of us." He smiled at Sanchez, shook his head. "I can't believe you made it out alive. How'd you do it? You're one tough bastard, aren't you? Reacher always said that about you."

Sanchez seemed more agitated the more O'Donnell talked. His pacing was jerky, and deteriorated as O'Donnell continued. Sanchez's lips pressed into a hard line and his brow furrowed into deep horizontal lines. Nostrils flexed.

When O'Donnell finally wound down, Sanchez seemed to have a little trouble getting started. But once he began, his words flowed nonstop. Even the third time she heard it, Kim felt punched by an opener that was almost as shocking as his close.

"I'm confused, Dave. I thought you'd feel a little bit guilty, at least."

"What are you talking about, man?"

Where Sanchez had halted his circuit of the room, he was looking right into the camera. His expression was chilling. Wrong. "You left me for dead," he said, quietly, almost pleasantly. "Never even tried to find me. Can you imagine what it's like to be out of your mind with pain because some goons beat your shins to bone meal with iron rods? And then you're laying on a pile of rotting garbage in a desert landfill for three days, when the summer heat reaches 110 degrees, watching the circling buzzards just waiting to pick your carcass clean?"

O'Donnell's face was ashen now. Maybe he'd started to pick up on the fact that Sanchez was clearly mentally unbalanced. Maybe he remembered he was sitting in a deserted building, too late at night, too late in the week. Maybe he just figured out that this could go bad very quickly.

To his credit, O'Donnell remained seated and calm. "That's not how it went, Sanchez. We looked, and we looked hard. Came up empty." Sanchez had started his circuit again, so when O'Donnell next spoke, he had to crane his neck to find him. "Do you need money? Because I'm doing okay now. I can help. Dixon and Neagley, too. They'd help us out."

Sanchez flashed a tight grin that revealed a gold tooth. "How about Reacher? Does he have money? Is he going to help out?"

"If we can find him, he might. The guy's a drifter now. No address. But Neagley found him once. She might be able to do it again. How much do you need?" O'Donnell talked like a hostage negotiator. He didn't seem afraid, but he should have been. Maybe he was.

"I need $65 million, Dave," Sanchez said quietly. "How long will it take you to get that together?"

"What in hell are you talking about? You think we got $65 million? That's cra—" He stopped himself. Took a breath. "We didn't get $65 million. Not even close. I got about a hundred grand. Like I said, I really needed it. Spent it probably in the first ten days."

"What happened to the rest of the money?" Sanchez sounded encouraging, almost reasonable again.

"Some of it was in a Swiss bank. We couldn't touch it. Dixon had to liquidate the rest. Like I said, we took care of the families. We repaid Neagley's expenses. Then we all got equal shares," O'Donnell said, matter-of-factly. If he suspected Sanchez was reaching the breaking point, he didn't show any concern.

"Where'd you stash the rest of the money? Reacher? Swiss banks? What?" Sanchez asked.

"I told you, man. We divided it up, just like I said."

And then the final two minutes replayed again, no less shocking than the first time.

When the video stopped, Kim asked Neagley. "Does his story track?"

Neagley looked tired now. As tired as the rest of them. She had dark circles under her eyes. Her clothes had long ago lost their starch, but she was as stiff as ever.

"Not that it can possibly matter at this point, but yes. We found the paper trail. We talked to witnesses. Confirmed. Sanchez was tortured and his legs were broken and he was left for dead by the same New Age guys who killed the rest of our team: Franz and Snow and Orozco. But Sanchez was the first one they tried to kill and they hadn't figured out the helicopter technique yet. They tossed him in a landfill, maybe thinking the crime techs would never sort out all the trace evidence because his body would be so contaminated and decomposed by the time it was discovered." She raked her hands through her hair. Drew a breath. "He was eventually found and eventually completed surgery and rehab. And eventually he moved to Mexico and married Orozco's widow and adopted her kids. By all accounts, they were living their version of happily-ever-after when this started."

Even Neagley's dry recital of Sanchez's ordeal sounded horrific to Kim. Sanchez's story in his own words was that much worse. Kim had watched the video several times, partly hoping that the retelling would blunt its impact, but it did not. She vacillated between wanting to know the rest of Sanchez's story and avoiding it as long as possible.

She could only guess how Gaspar must be feeling. Maybe he'd had enough, too. His next words were professional and detached.

"So Dean and Berenson figure Reacher has $65 million," Gaspar said. "That's why and how he lives off the grid."

Kim was more than ready to detach, too. "Dean and Berenson want the money. They figure Reacher's team has some of it or knows where it is. They figure it belongs to them." Kim looked at Neagley. "Where did the money come from? New Age?"

Neagley shrugged. Flipped off the screen. Stood and poured herself a drink. Said nothing.

Kim tried again. "Five years ago, four members of Reacher's team were tortured. Three were killed. Sanchez almost dead. Berenson and Dean did all that? And Reacher let them get away?" she asked, unable to hide her incredulity. "Sounds like a monumental screw-up, doesn't it?"

CHAPTER 25

Sunday, November 14
5:53 a.m.
Chicago, IL

"Exactly," Neagley said, tossing back the whiskey and pouring another.

Kim kept pressing. "In the mix, Reacher stole the $65 million Sanchez now wants. Did Reacher cut the rest of you out? O'Donnell said he got $100,000. That doesn't seem like a very big share."

Neagley said nothing.

"Berenson and Dean have been, what? Hunting Reacher for five years?" Gaspar asked.

"Doubtful," Neagley said. "Reacher lives off the grid, but he's not invisible. If they'd been looking for him all that time, he'd have heard about it, done something about it."

Maybe Neagley wasn't issuing a warning, but Kim's body felt it that way. "Why surface now, then?" Kim asked. "What kicked this thing off?"

Neagley said, "When I found out about Sanchez four

days ago, I put my team on him. We've been running down his backstory. Like I said, he was hospitalized a while. Did a long stint in rehab. And about two years ago, he moved to Mexico. Married Tammy Orozco."

"Manny Orozco's wife," Gaspar said. "Another member of your old unit. How convenient. Were they having an affair? Somehow caused all this?"

"No," Neagley said. "All that happened afterward."

"Where is she now?" Kim asked. "Mrs. Sanchez?"

"We haven't found her. Or her kids. Or her elderly mother, who lived with them in Mexico."

Kim thought about the video again. Sanchez's desperation. A man who had lost everything, including half his body and most of his life. Finds something to live for. And years later he goes berserk. Most likely cause? Probably not $65 million, although Kim had seen people go berserk for less.

As always, Kim's mind circled back to the Boss. He'd been leading them on this grim chase. What was his involvement? He at least suspected something. Otherwise, why task her with finding out about Reacher from these people?

Gaspar said, "So we go on the assumption that Berenson and Dean do have Sanchez's family, like he said. He knows firsthand they're capable of torture and murder. Sanchez freaks out and kills O'Donnell when O'Donnell doesn't have the money. That how you see it?"

Neagley swallowed the second whiskey and set the class down softly. "Sanchez looked steady as hell to me when he pulled that trigger. Stood there afterward, over Dave's body, watching the blood pulsing out of his head wound. Then, presses the off button on the speakerphone. Walks out. Shows up at Dixon's place the next day." Neagley shook her head twice. "Sanchez was cool. Deliberate. He either killed Dave on orders—"

"Orders from whom?"

"—or he improvised in the moment for a solid tactical reason."

"Such as?"

"Such as he believed O'Donnell didn't have the money," Neagley said. "He believed O'Donnell didn't know where Reacher was."

"Meaning O'Donnell was of no further use to Sanchez," Gaspar said.

"And that O'Donnell might actually get in the way of Sanchez's mission," Kim said.

"What mission?" Gaspar asked.

"Dixon. Neagley. Reacher," Kim replied. After a few moments, Kim asked Neagley, "Franz had a wife and kid, didn't he?"

Neagley said, "She's remarried. Moved somewhere. But we should have contact shortly."

"How did you find her?"

"I can usually find things," Neagley said.

Which is why it was frightening that she hadn't found Dixon or Paul or Sanchez's family, Kim thought. Or Reacher, for that matter. If she really hadn't located him, which, given all the things she said she'd already accomplished since O'Donnell's murder, seemed even more unlikely. The Boss said Reacher was on his way. Maybe he knew that because he'd tapped Neagley's phones.

"How much of all this does the Boss know?" Gaspar asked.

"Cooper usually knows things," Neagley replied.

"Where is Reacher?" Kim asked.

"Hard to say," Neagley said. Not an answer.

The house phone rang before Kim could ask again. Neagley picked up. Listened. Her body language revealed nothing. She hung up the phone softly.

"Berenson?" Kim asked.

Neagley nodded.

"What does she want?"

"Reacher."

Gaspar said, "Who doesn't?"

Neagley smiled. "Berenson should be careful what she

wishes for, Gaspar. And so should you."

"Meaning what?" Gaspar demanded.

A fight with Neagley right now would not be helpful. Kim didn't have the patience for it. Better to move forward.

"Speaking of Berenson and Dean," Kim said, figuring that she could trust Neagley enough at this point to follow the Boss's orders, "the Boss said he was sending encrypted video. It should be available by now. I need my laptop to download it. I'll go get it."

Kim walked toward the exit. Before she reached it, a fast rap on the panel by a beefy-knuckled paw preceded Morrie slipping his body into the room before the panel opened completely. He moved stealthily for such a big man, Kim noticed.

"All set," he said.

Neagley told Kim, "We've already collected your equipment and your luggage and moved your car into one of the garages."

Kim's controlled tone was deceptive. "You held us in here while you invaded my equipment? Seriously?"

Neagley's whiskey-weary voice said, "We tried. Unfortunately, your encryption was beyond the reach of my onsite hacker. We can't spend any more time on it. You're going to have to show us what you've got. Morrie, take Otto and Gaspar to their rooms."

Kim's body quivered with anger. She didn't trust herself to speak.

Neagley said, "I'll have your equipment brought in and set up while you're gone. See you back here in ten."

"Good plan," Kim said, exercising control beyond what she thought she could muster. "Bring our cell phones and car keys, too. You can prepare to tell us exactly where that $65 million is and how you plan to get it back."

"Why waste time on that? It's history," Neagley replied.

"Because we're going to need ransom money if you expect to see Paul or Dixon alive again. Unless you have it hidden in your basement or decorated this castle with it, we'll need to collect the money from wherever it is now." Kim glanced at her Seiko. It was already after seven. Paul had been a hostage for almost ten hours. Dixon had been held for thirty-one. Long enough for Berenson and Dean to have met up and made a plan. "It's likely we'll be hearing from them very soon, don't you think?"

The scowl that tortured Neagley's face felt like a small but significant victory. Kim savored it as she followed behind Morrie and Gaspar all the way upstairs to her room, where she planned to take a long, hot shower and change into clean clothes before she came back. Neagley could just cool her jets.

When she closed the door behind her she opened her travel bag. It had been rifled. Nothing seemed to be missing, but everything was slightly rearranged. The bag contained nothing sensitive or confidential. Still, she felt violated. And confused. Was Neagley friend or enemy? Either way, Neagley would answer for this and everything else she'd done soon enough.

CHAPTER 26

Sunday, November 14
7:26 a.m.
Chicago, IL

Twenty minutes later, Kim was showered, dressed and ready to return to the battle of wits with Neagley that seemed a constant tug-of-war between Neagley's insistence on controlling everything and Kim's desire to get out before she and Gaspar got sucked in beyond the point of no return.

Whatever was going on between Reacher's team and the Berenson/Dean gang, Kim didn't see any benefit to standing in the line of fire. Her job was to build Reacher's file, not to stand between him and every criminal he'd wronged.

Gaspar knocked twice on her door. Kim opened it and said, "I'd like to be on the road by nine." She wanted to tell him what the Boss had said about Reacher, but Neagley would no doubt be listening here and everywhere.

"Works for me," he replied as they began retracing their route to the security room. "Marion Morrison. The former secret service guy. That's his real name. I asked the security guard outside."

"I guess 'Morrie' is a better guy's name. I can see why he'd want to ditch 'Marion.' Good thing he's a big fellow. How'd you like to have to defend that one in the schoolyard?"

"Did the Boss say anything about what's on the video he sent?"

"You're worried Neagley's guy was able to hack in? Don't be. The Boss would have planned countermeasures for that."

"They do have full and mutual admiration for each other's skill sets, don't they?"

Kim replied, "That's only one of the things that worries me."

"Agreed."

His answer surprised Kim. Gaspar rarely admitted to worrying about anything. Given the likelihood that Neagley's house was fully monitored, Kim didn't ask what else Gaspar was concerned about.

They'd traveled the full distance back to Neagley's security room. Now, they stood outside the heavy door panel. Kim raised her fist to knock, but the panel slid open smoothly, as if it sensed her presence, which it probably did.

Neagley and Morrie were inside. Both had showered and changed into clean duds, too. Kim's laptop rested on the conference table in the corner of the room. Four cell phones she recognized as theirs were placed adjacent to the laptop. Nearby stood a wheeled table laden with breakfast foods and coffee.

Kim accepted Neagley's peace offering graciously, but not because she thought for a moment that Neagley was capitulating in their war of wills.

Nor would she win.

Gaspar collected his usual ration of sugar-laden goodies from the cart. Kim snagged a cup of black coffee, sat down at the laptop and powered up. Entered her security codes. And waited for the Boss's video file to download. The entire process consumed ninety-four seconds.

Neagley noticed how simply Kim completed the task

Neagley's team couldn't. She said, "Everything's easy once you know it, Otto."

Kim smiled, sipped, said nothing.

After the file was downloaded, she opened the first of two videos, but hesitated before starting it. She didn't like the set-up. She couldn't watch Neagley and the video simultaneously. And the Boss had told her to show the video to Neagley alone, not with Morrie in the room.

The moment's indecision resolved—she had no options—she pushed the play button.

Instead of everyone gathering around her laptop as she'd expected, the video popped up on the big television screen where they'd watched O'Donnell's murder. Neagley may not have been able to hack into the Boss's encrypted file, but she'd invaded the laptop in other, insidious ways.

Never let them see you sweat, Kim heard her mother whispering in her brain.

The video's first scene was a grainy aerial shot. Could have been a satellite, but more likely, a drone. An irregular intersection of two curved, oak-lined streets, bordered by wide lawns. No traffic signs visible. Night-time. Full dark. Generously spaced, dim gaslights illuminated little. No people. No vehicles.

No clock or timer in the frame.

"Do you recognize the place?" Gaspar asked.

"Looks like about four blocks west of here," Neagley said, watching, never taking her gaze from the oversized screen.

"How can you tell?" Gaspar asked.

"Streets in this neighborhood are distinctive. No two intersections the same."

A panel van arced into the frame along one of the curved avenues, moving slowly and without headlights. It stopped between two gaslights and in the deep shadow of the adjacent oak tree. No audio, so Kim couldn't tell if the van's engine remained running. If it had a license plate, it wasn't visible.

Neagley reached over and pressed the remote's pause button. She squinted at the screen. Kim saw, perhaps, a man's shadow in the lower right edge of the frame. Neagley restarted the video. The shadow grew larger and the man casting it followed behind.

"Where's the light coming from?" Kim asked.

Morrie said, "We had a bright moon last night. There's no streetlights behind him that would throw a shadow like that."

As the man's silhouette grew larger on the screen, Neagley said, "It's Paul."

"You're sure?" Gaspar asked.

"Yes."

Paul moved quickly, but he wasn't running.

"Where's he headed?" Gaspar asked.

Morrie replied, "Toward the highway. He likes to hitchhike. Truckers will pick him up on the highway. Around here, people are more cautious. He knows that."

Paul crossed the sidewalk, the narrow blacktop, and loped up onto the opposite curb. As soon as his body reached the other side, he crumpled as if he'd been shot, and lay twitching on the ground.

Neagley didn't react at all, as far as Kim could see. She continued to watch intently, as if the video might evaporate after she'd seen it once.

A few moments after Paul went down, he stopped twitching. He lay perfectly still. He might have been dead.

Less than two minutes later, a figure emerged from the shadowed van nearby. The video zoomed in closer. The Boss said it was Berenson, but the figure was dressed in a heavy, coverall-style jumpsuit that made its sex difficult to determine.

The figure pushed Paul with the toe of a heavy work boot and he flopped with the pressure but otherwise didn't move.

Seeming satisfied that he was not a threat, she—Kim decided to give the Boss the benefit of the doubt—returned to the darkness where the van was parked and came back with a four-wheeled hand cart that she lowered to a few inches above the level of the ground. She stooped and with significant effort managed to work Paul's limp body up onto the cart.

She stood, pumped a lever near the handle with her foot a few times, and the cart rose up. She must have been overheated with the exertion because she wiped her face with a gloved hand and then lifted her face to a refreshingly cool breeze that had begun to ruffle the oak leaves on the nearby trees.

That's when the camera zoomed in on her face. Even in the dim light, her scars cast a complex roadmap over her complexion—a gruesome tangle of distinctive intersections, Kim thought. She remembered the scars, the keloids near her eye. Definitely Berenson.

After a moment or two, she wheeled the cart into the shadows. Maybe a minute more and the van pulled away from the curb and traveled further along the street until it came to a corner, turned, and disappeared.

The first video ended. A few empty frames came next. And the next video began.

This one was footage from an exterior airport security camera. The scene was LaGuardia in New York, according to the signs out front of the well-lit terminal at baggage claim. The frame counter said 12:13 a.m. Saturday, November 13. Busy airport sounds had been left intact.

Karla Dixon walked out of the terminal pulling her travel bag and lugging a laptop case and an oversized designer handbag. She was dressed in slacks, a blazer and an unbuttoned overcoat.

A uniformed driver approached her. He wore a hat, dark blazer, dark trousers and heavy soled shoes. He said, "Ms. Dixon? This way, please."

"Where's Harry?" Dixon asked.

"Home sick, they said. Asked me to fill in for him."

"Pause it," Neagley said. She cocked her head slightly to one side, narrowed her eyes. "The driver. Dean."

"You're sure?" Kim asked, but had to accept Neagley's silence for an answer. The Boss said Dean abducted Dixon. Neagley recognized him. Nothing more was needed. She hit play.

Dixon followed Dean as if she'd never seen him before and he was no threat to her. Maybe she never had. The two reached the black sedan. Dean opened the back passenger door and said, "Luggage in the trunk?"

"Sure," Dixon responded.

He took her travel bag and stashed it while she tossed her laptop and purse into the back seat and tucked into the cabin. Dean shut the trunk, then moved purposefully to the driver's seat.

The video switched to the interior of the vehicle, a fish-eye lens mounted above the rearview, by the looks of things.

"Neat trick," Gaspar said.

Dixon was snugged into her seatbelt in the back. Dean started the engine. "Good to go back there?" he asked.

She laid her head back on the headrest and closed her eyes. "Ten-four," she said. "Wake me up when we get there."

"Will do," he replied and then pulled away from the curb. Just like that.

Back to the exterior view. The video grabbed a shot of the car's rear license plate as it pulled away. New York, it said.

The next scene was time stamped 12:56 p.m. The big sedan was parked along the curb on a vaguely familiar city side street. Dixon was asleep or passed out or maybe sedated in the back seat. Dean had left the vehicle but was now returning. He used the remote to open the trunk. He pulled off bloody coveralls, bloody paper booties, bloody latex gloves and a bloody paper shower cap and tossed them all inside the trunk.

He returned to the driver's seat and departed. As he pulled away, the video panned to the building's exterior address. The office of David Downing, recently deceased private investigator.

The video cut again to the final six seconds. 2:24 a.m. The vehicle was abandoned in a multi level parking garage.

Neagley said, "Now we know who murdered Downing."

"Indeed," Kim replied. Not Reacher. The Boss's cell phone began vibrating on the conference table. Kim picked up the call. "Yes."

"Neagley's seen the video?" he asked.

"Yes."

"Let me talk to her."

Kim held out the phone. Neagley brought it to her ear. Her tone was far from respectful when she asked, "What do you want, Cooper?"

"You know I can't help you with this," he said loudly enough for Kim to hear.

"No surprise there," Neagley replied, coldly. "Where is Dixon now?"

"Still looking," he said.

"And Paul?"

"The same," he said.

Neagley's eyes were as dead as marbles and her tone frigid. "Just stay out of the way, Cooper. See if you can manage that. Because if you screw this up any more than you already have, I promise you, you'll live to regret it."

"You've always been a woman of your word, Neagley," he replied.

She disconnected and tossed the phone back. Then she leveled a steady gaze first at Gaspar and then at Kim. Maybe she was making up her mind or maybe she was playing another kind of game. Impossible to tell.

Neagley said, "We don't have time to screw around. The ransom call came in while you were upstairs. The exchange happens in less than six hours. We could use a couple of extra hands to get Paul back alive, but you heard what Cooper said. He's refused to assist us. Are you two in or out?"

Kim replied, "Are you asking because you want to piss off Cooper? Or do you really need the help?"

Neagley said, "Does it matter?"

Of course it did. Two trained agents could make the difference between success and failure in what was bound to be a tricky hostage-for-ransom exchange. Kim could think of only one reason Neagley needed help before and now seemed not to care one way or the other: Reacher.

CHAPTER 27

Sunday, November 14
1:36 p.m.
Chicago, IL

Sunday afternoon, the area around Neagley's mansion was deserted except for Neagley's strategically placed team. Outdoor temperatures were cold, weak sunlight provided minimum atmospheric warmth, but the adrenaline coursing under Kim's Kevlar supplied sufficient body heat.

Kim and Gaspar were stationed inside the front great room, ten feet from a dark grey hard-shell Samsonite containing bearer bonds printed by Neagley's ink-jet in the security room, two drawstring pouches containing cheap cubic zirconias she'd bought at the local drug store, and a single page of fake Swiss bank access codes they'd downloaded off the Internet. The total value of the contents of the Samsonite was about $6.50. But the Samsonite was real and the weight was okay. It might fool Berenson for a second or two, if she just flashed to its contents then lifted it.

Neagley's Secret Service guy Morrie was stationed outside in one of the garages, assigned to direct the team to monitor Berenson and Paul when they arrived and capture Berenson after she left Paul at the mansion. Neagley shuttled back and forth, confirming.

Kim would have preferred a larger, more expert team. Fifteen FBI agents would have been enough, maybe. Reacher might have helped to level the playing field, had he not ignored Neagley's summons.

As it was, they had a total of six Neagley personnel in addition to Neagley, Gaspar and Kim. Nine in all. Which was at least six guns, twelve eyes, twelve ears, and six brains short. Kim had not supervised their training, and she remained wary of Neagley's team. She felt fairly confident in Gaspar only. In every arena, Neagley's procedures had proved unpredictable at best. Had Marion Morrison done the job he'd been trained by the Secret Service to do, Paul wouldn't be missing and in Berenson's clutches to start with. And fatigue levels were too high.

All of which meant Kim was far from comfortable with the plan, the team, and the probable outcome. But Neagley had made it clear that she was running the operation and Kim could participate or go.

"How would you do it?" Gaspar asked, probably as uncomfortable with Neagley's plan as Kim was.

"Exchange my hostage for $65 million in ransom right now? I wouldn't," she said. "Not in Neagley's home, for sure. Not even in Chicago. It's Neagley's backyard. I'd want a better opportunity somewhere else. Preferably on terrain and under conditions I controlled."

"Me, too," he said, thinking aloud. "But Paul is not easy to handle if he's awake. Drugged is another set of problems. They have Dixon now, too. That's a lot to manage if it's just the two of them. Maybe Berenson and Dean have more help and maybe they don't. They're better off getting rid of Paul as soon as possible. Then they'll be able to move more effectively."

Kim looked at him as if he'd lost his grip on reality. "You

do know they're going to kill him, right?"

"I know they're going to try. Neagley knows that too, don't forget."

Kim said, "I read her file. I know she's formidable. But she's going into this thing blind, too. We don't know where they are or how many people they have with them or what kind of training they've got."

"My money's on Neagley," he said, rubbing his shoulder.

Kim felt the same pain in hers but said nothing because, as she watched through the great room's large plate glass windows, Neagley was walking toward the house from the garage office. Neagley closed the main doors quickly enough, but a blast of cold air still rolled through the great room—the big front doors opened right into it. She stood and scanned the room again as if something might have changed in the past few minutes. Nothing had.

"Any doubt at all, act first and think later. Okay?" Neagley checked her watch. "Ten minutes to go. Are you ready?"

"As ready as we were going to get," Kim replied, which wasn't exactly affirmative.

"You worry too much," Neagley said.

"It's not possible to worry too much in my line of work," Kim replied. "You should understand that. Or don't you deal with as many lethal people now as you did in the military police?"

"Different kind of lethal now, I guess. Back then, I couldn't shoot them. Now, I can." Neagley's lips slashed in what for her might have been a smile. "You are wearing your vests, right? No point in taking unnecessary chances."

Kim didn't say again that Neagley's entire plan was one big unnecessary chance. She wanted to pace because she was nervous, thinking through the last minute checks for the hundredth time and worrying about everything she knew could go wrong as well as the thousand things she didn't know about. *You never see the bullet that gets you.*

She listened for vehicles but heard none. She listened for footsteps and heard none of those either.

While they waited, Kim again attempted to find out something Neagley had refused to discuss. "What happened to Paul on Friday? In your office before we got there, before Sanchez died?"

Neagley frowned. As if she was creating an official report, again without emotion, she delivered the facts. "Paul lives in a group home during the week and here on weekends. A year ago, we found him a job working in a local office. We never leave him alone. He's escorted everywhere. But he walks to work—with his detail, of course. And he stops off on the way home to get a strawberry milkshake every day."

Neagley sat there, perfectly relaxed. Her cold competence was unnerving. Maybe Colonel Silver was right. Maybe she was some sort of psychopath.

Kim said, "And?"

Neagley picked up where she'd left off. "On Wednesday, when Paul stopped for his strawberry shake, Berenson was there. He didn't know her, but when he described her to me, I knew who he meant. She approached him and touched his arm—"

"Wait," Kim said. "Why didn't the detail step in?"

"The detail was waiting outside."

Kim stared at her. So did Gaspar. Finally Kim said, "The detail was waiting outside? What kind of security—"

"Paul likes to go in alone. It makes him happy."

"Well that might be, but—"

"Not much makes Paul happy."

Neagley's expression was implacable. No advantage to be gained in pressing. Maybe she simply loved her brother.

Which meant Frances Neagley was capable of love.

Was that possible? A moment ago, Kim would have bet against it.

Kim said. "So Berenson touched his arm and then what?"

"You can't do that with Paul. His kind of autism makes physical touching painful for him."

Kim remembered that Neagley tried to talk to her brother and calm him down when he freaked out in her office, but she never touched him. It had seemed odd at the time. Still did, even explained.

"Berenson backed off, but it took quite a while to get Paul to calm down." Neagley took a deep breath and released a thin smile. "His detail had to come inside."

"And Berenson?"

"Slipped away in the disturbance."

Kim nodded.

Neagley went on. "So when Berenson walked toward Paul in my lobby on Friday afternoon, he just lost it. And his behavior can be quite frightening, as you saw. Sanchez had his gun out, kind of waved it around. Maybe he felt threatened, or he thought a gunshot would stop Paul's outburst. Or maybe he was just unhinged. Who knows? You saw the video. For whatever reason, he didn't shoot to kill, but he discharged his weapon. And the bullet grazed Paul's arm. And then Paul turned it up a dozen notches."

After a couple of seconds of thinking about it, Gaspar shook his head. "Too convenient."

"What?" Neagley asked. Matter-of-factly.

"You already knew Sanchez killed O'Donnell by Friday afternoon because you've seen O'Donnell's surveillance."

"So?"

"Sanchez shows up in your office and approaches you at gunpoint. Paul freaks out. Sanchez shoots and the bullet grazes Paul's arm."

"That's right."

"And then Sanchez has a heart attack and dies? And Berenson bugs out and gets away?" Gaspar said. "Damned convenient."

Neagley snorted. "Not even close to convenient, Gaspar. Paul had to be sedated after that. Sanchez—a man I had worked closely with and at one time considered to be part of my family—was dead. Berenson escaped. O'Donnell is dead. We can't find Dixon or Franz's widow and son. Doesn't sound the least bit convenient to me." Neagley checked her watch. "Stay alert. I'm going for a last check on the team outside."

After she left, Gaspar said, "She could have told us that about the lobby before. You believe her?"

"Not at all," Kim said. "She killed Sanchez. There's too many stories just like that in her Army file. Guys who were standing too close to her one minute and flat out on the ground the next."

"How'd she do it?"

Kim shrugged. "She's exceptionally proficient at unarmed combat, according to the Army. Probably a heel kick to the heart muscle. Maybe an elbow. Anything hard enough and placed correctly would do it."

Thoughtfully, Gaspar said, "The autopsy wouldn't show a bruise over the heart. Bruising requires blood flow, and there wouldn't have been any after his heart stopped."

"Makes you feel lucky to be alive with nothing but a sore neck, doesn't it?" Kim glanced at her Seiko. "Stay sharp. Berenson and Paul are supposed to be here in five minutes."

Kim felt the familiar blast of cold air when Neagley opened the wide front door. Then she sensed a dull chalky impact nearby and something stung her on the left cheek. From the corner of her eye she saw a puff of dust around a small, cratered chip on the surface of the plaster wall.

Once again, she heard no sound at all.

Instantaneously, she thought: *Bullet. Silencer.* She watched another puff slightly below the first. She hit the deck and rolled under one of Neagley's huge Spanish tables.

"Gun!" she screamed.

A line of puffs and craters raced toward Gaspar. He ducked behind a heavy chair and fell onto the floor below the line of fire and landed with a millisecond to spare.

Kim belly-crawled to the front wall and peered out the bottom corner of the nine-foot glass windows. Paul was running for the house along the sidewalk, flashing in and out of the pockets of gloom created by the heavy canopy of oaks.

"Frances! Frances!" he shouted.

He was in a total, frothing panic. Must've broken free of Berenson, and now the peaceful exchange had exploded.

Craning her neck, Kim could see Neagley crouched behind a heavy Spanish armoire hugging the side wall just inside the front entrance, scanning for the shooter's location.

"Paul! Get down!" Neagley screamed.

Paul kept running.

A volley of shots rang out from a second gun.

Neagley fired back, but didn't have a clear sightline to the shooters. Kim and Gaspar repositioned to provide cover fire through the broad open front door. Team members outside must have released a bullet-wall, too. Front windows shattered, spraying glass everywhere. The noise was deafening.

Paul was still coming, all pumping arms and knees, zig-zagging wildly. Half a dozen feet shy of the threshold, he launched himself like a baseball player diving head-first for home plate just at the moment Neagley moved and he landed square on his sister's upper chest where she crouched near the armoire. The impact blasted her off her feet and the two of them crashed backward to the floor while the bullet storm never let up.

Returning fire along with the outside team toward the invisible shooters, Kim saw Neagley trying to struggle out from under her brother. Too much blood spurted—from Paul, she guessed. A *lot* of blood. A major artery hit. His or hers?

Then only Neagley's outside team was firing—the shooters had pulled back. Kim glanced out the window and saw the slope of a body loping fast toward what might have been a dark van parked down the block moments before the vehicle sped off. Neagley's team charged off in pursuit. Gaspar dashed outside.

Kim rushed to help Neagley and Paul, but Morrie got there first, dragging him off Neagley. Neagley only shoved Morrie aside, slipping through the lake of blood to pull Paul to her and cradle his head in her arms.

It was the first time Kim had seen Neagley touch her

brother. Kim wondered how many years it had been since she or anyone else had done so. Paul could bear it now. He was completely limp and still, like his clothes were empty. His eyes were wide open, moving slowly, searching side to side.

"Frances?" he whispered. His voice was very quiet, but alert. "Are you okay?"

Kim's eyes welled up. She hard-blinked to clear them. But no tears streamed down his sister's face.

Neagley's voice was strong. "I'm fine, Paul," she said.

She slid her hand under his neck, where the blood was pulsing out in a warm, hard jet. Neagley's hands were strong. She applied pressure as she'd been trained to, directly to the wound, attempting to stop the blood flow.

"Medic," Neagley called softly. A soldier's reflex.

Paul's chin fell to his chest. Blood flooded between the folds of his skin and soaked his shirt. Pooled on the ground around Neagley's legs and soaked into the plush carpet.

"Medic!" she called again, louder.

"On the way." Kim watched helplessly because she knew they'd be too late. Paul weighed about one-sixty-five, which meant he had about ten to twelve pints of blood in him. Most of them were already gone. His heart was doing its job, valiantly pumping his life straight out onto the carpet around his sister's lap.

"Medic!" Neagley screamed it this time. Nobody came.

Paul looked straight into his sister's face. "Remember?" he whispered.

Neagley bent closer.

"I love you, Sissy," he whispered. "Remember?"

"I remember, Paulie," she said.

Paul smiled weakly, like her answer satisfied totally. He was very pale now. Blood soaked everything in a widening pool. It was warm and slick. His eyes settled on her face.

Neagley held him until he bled out and died in her arms.

Paramedics had arrived and helped Neagley to her feet. Neagley laid Paul's head gently on the blood-soaked carpet and moved away while the paramedics handled the rest.

Official vehicles had been steadily arriving since the van sped off. Gaspar returned from a swift canvass of Neagley's team and the outdoor stations. He had conferred with the first responders and now met Kim and Neagley at the front entrance as the paramedics removed the gurney.

Neagley looked down at her blood-coated hands. Her clothes were soaked in Paul's blood and clung to her lithe body. She smelled of a mix of coppery blood and gunshots.

"It wasn't your fault," Kim said.

"Of course it was," Neagley said, matter-of-factly. "That bullet was meant for me. Subsonic bullet. It would have bounced right off my vest."

"Yes and no."

Neagley looked at her.

Gaspar's right eyebrow inquired.

Kim said, "The bullet wasn't meant for you. They don't want you dead. Yet. They want their money back first."

"Dixon is the one who can help them with that, and they already have her." She sounded weary, almost beaten. Kim's heart went out to her, even knowing she wouldn't be pleased to know it. "I'll get cleaned up. Meet me in the security office in ten minutes."

Remembering Sanchez's tortured body, Kim shuddered to think about Dixon and the other hostages in Dean and Berenson's hands. If the same memories concerned Neagley, she didn't show it. Her self-control was nothing short of robotic.

Kim watched her back as she headed to her room upstairs.

Then, she turned to Gaspar and asked, "They had a lot of firepower going. Any evidence that Reacher was helping them outside?"

CHAPTER 28

Sunday, November 14
3:36 p.m.
Chicago, IL

Law enforcement vehicles continued to flood Neagley's driveway and the street. Personnel worked the crime scene inch by inch outside. Kim watched, saw nothing amiss in their procedures from her vantage point inside the house. She saw Morrie deep in conversation with the officer who appeared to be in charge. Neagley's team had not returned since they dashed after the surviving shooters and experience said the longer they were gone, the less likely they'd return alive.

Gaspar tilted his head closer to report on his brief crime scene inspection for her ears only. "Two dead—one ours, one theirs."

Kim nodded. Waited for something worse, which she sensed was coming.

"Berenson's dead crew member sported visible gang tattoos on his neck and chest. The Las Olas Mexican cartel," he said. "You know them?"

"By reputation. I've seen the FBI estimates they've killed more than two thousand of their enemies, using our guns and ordnance fighting over drug distribution in Mexico and the U.S. No personal experience. They don't reach all the way to Detroit."

"Lucky you. They also specialize in kidnapping for ransom and home invasions. The full menu. They've been involved in a turf war with a rival gang for about six years. Last time I had a case involving Las Olas was back in the summer. The cartel targeted Miami law enforcement vehicles to steal firearms, vests, ammo, ID. Never recovered any of it. We lost two good agents and never made an arrest."

"Terrific," Kim replied. "If we were old enough to be nostalgic for the Mafia, Las Olas might get us there."

A second officer joined Morrie and the officer in charge. Morrie might have been describing the Las Olas attack and Paul's murder, but she couldn't hear the content of their conversation.

Neagley's team had been in pursuit for too long. Kim guessed they'd been overtaken somewhere shortly after they left Neagley's home and more bodies would be discovered very soon. With any luck, at least a few of those bodies would be Las Olas, too, though in Kim's experience, cartel members had nine lives.

"It gets worse," Gaspar said.

"Of course it does."

"The cartels have been recruiting in prisons all over the country, as you know. So the crew members shooting at us could theoretically have been locals. Except the Illinois State Police officers outside didn't recognize the tats."

"Means Las Olas has no presence here. Berenson must have imported her own crew for the job." Kim ran a weary hand over her still-tight, sleek chignon and rolled her shoulders. She was bone tired. She'd been awake almost 36 hours. Gallons of coffee could only carry her so far. Very soon now, she'd require sleep. "Which means Berenson and Dean are long gone. Probably back in Mexico by now. If they haven't already killed her, they've taken Dixon with them."

"And we're damned unlikely to get her back alive," Gaspar said. He held something in his closed fist and dropped it into her palm. Kim recognized it from FBI anti-terrorism training. A polymer cartridge subsonic bullet, military prototype. "Picked it up off the ground near the first body. There's plenty more out there, so don't worry about evidence. Not that anyone will ever be charged with killing Paul, regardless."

Kim caressed the bullet, said nothing. The cartels were frighteningly adept at acquiring U.S. weapons and ordnance. Possible sources for these prototypes were endless. Still, she'd ask the Boss and Neagley for answers.

Gaspar said, "Neagley had to know Berenson's crew were Las Olas."

"No way she'd have missed that," Kim agreed as she turned and headed toward the coffee pot first and then Neagley's security office. Neagley shed no tears for her only brother, but Kim had brothers, too. Brothers she loved like crazy. She told herself it was exhaustion, but she could barely hold it together. She had to think about something else. She cleared her throat. "Come on, Chico. Daylight's fading fast out there. It's about time we figure out what's really going on here and whether Neagley's on our team, don't you think?"

"We might only get good intel from her at gunpoint," Gaspar said.

"Fine by me," she said, but her heart wasn't in it.

CHAPTER 29

Sunday, November 14
5:36 p.m.
Chicago, IL

When Neagley returned to the security room, she was dressed in a black suit and crisp white shirt. Her hair was wet from the shower and combed straight to her shoulders. She had collected coffee from the kitchen as well. She looked resigned, perhaps.

"We are very sorry for your loss, Frances," Kim said. "I can't imagine how devastated I would be to lose one of my brothers."

"Don't imagine you and I are anything alike, Otto. And don't imagine my brother was anything like yours, either." Her words were harsh, but her tone was flat, lacking affect, as the psychologists say. She drank the coffee and stared at the blank television screens, as if she was considering a weighty decision.

Kim knew Neagley was hurting. Paul was a difficult kid, to be sure. But a brother is a brother and Kim had seen

Neagley's loyalty in action already. She was loyal to her Army unit, loyal to her team, and loyal to Reacher. No way she was untouched by her only brother's death, whether she showed her grief outwardly or not. No way.

Neagley needed action.

"Let's get to work," Kim said. "Start by telling us the rest of the story. There's a dead Las Olas outside. You knew Berenson and Dean were associated with Las Olas, didn't you? Were Sanchez and O'Donnell involved, too?"

Neagley's response was devoid of denials or excuses. "O'Donnell, probably not. Sanchez is possible. We have no evidence either way so far."

Gaspar allowed his anger to surface. "You knew Berenson and Dean were Las Olas-connected and you didn't tell us that before we agreed to help you get Paul back. That's a lot of gall, Neagley, even for you."

"Quit whining," Neagley said, without rancor. "You didn't die, did you?"

"You think you can take credit for that?" Gaspar snapped.

Neagley looked unruffled, but Kim sensed she was exercising a level of control that could easily snap at any moment like breaking brittle steel. Kim wasn't afraid of Neagley, exactly. But getting her off-track and angry couldn't help.

Kim interjected before full-on combat broke out between them. "You must have located Berenson and Dean's Mexico headquarters. Where is it? We can start with that and move forward."

"Sanchez was living openly with his family in a small town called Colina near Camargo City, three hundred and forty miles south of New Mexico. Berenson and Dean were headquartered hundreds of miles away, southwest of Matamoros, near Valle Hermoso. Across the Rio Grande from Brownsville, Texas. The entire Sanchez family is missing. Sanchez seemed to believe they'd be killed if he failed in his mission to recover the money. So my best guess is that Tammy and the kids, and her mother, were kidnapped and taken to the Las Olas compound in Valle Alto about two weeks ago. Doubtful they're all still alive."

"Is there a way to confirm?" Kim asked. "And can we find out if Dixon is there now?"

"Probably."

"Not that it helps to know the answers to those questions," Gaspar said. "Mexico wouldn't extradite Berenson or Dean or any of the Las Olas cartel even if we could get the paperwork, which we can't. The Boss isn't going to send troops or a Seal team into Mexico to collect a few civilians. And there's no way the three of us can get them out of there without half a dozen M1A1 tanks."

Neagley actually smiled at the image of traveling with half a dozen tanks. Kim took that as a good sign.

Kim noticed Gaspar didn't say anything about the extensive multi-agency investigation of Las Olas. The FBI had been involved in the deep undercover project for two years. ATF and IRS and Homeland Security and others had been working longer. The man-hours already devoted to bringing Las Olas down would prevent Cooper from helping Neagley, even if Cooper and Neagley were best buddies. Under the circumstances, elephants were more likely to appear on the moon.

"You've got intel on this Valle Alto compound, right?" Kim asked.

"Of course."

"Then let's see it," Gaspar fairly growled.

Neagley didn't move so much as an eyelash before the panel slid open again and Morrie entered the security room alone. "What's the status out there?" she asked him.

"Locals are directing evidence collection and crime scene. Paramedics are gone with Paul's body to the hospital and then the morgue for autopsy."

"News on the rest of our team?"

Morrie hesitated a split second. "Found both vehicles torched two miles north at the landfill. All five dead by gunshots to the head."

Neagley's lips pressed into a strong line. Eyes narrowed.

She placed the coffee cup on a nearby table and folded her hands together as if she might otherwise attack something. Her self-mastery was amazing to behold. Kim might have kicked something, at least.

Morrie continued to stand in his formal at-ease posture, waiting.

"Something else?" Neagley asked.

He reached into his pocket and pulled out a glassine evidence bag containing a brown envelope. He handed the envelope to Neagley, who turned it over a couple of times and pressed through the glassine bag to feel its contents before passing the bag to Kim.

Kim first looked at all sides of the contents through the evidence bag. The brown envelope was two inches by four inches. An unbroken Las Olas wax seal sprawled across the longer lip on the back side. The smaller lip had been glued by the manufacturer. She flipped the evidence bag over. The front side of the brown envelope contained flowing cursive script in black ink: *Frances L. Neagley*. She felt the small, padded envelope through the glassine bag as Neagley had done.

When she finished, Kim passed the bag along to Gaspar who repeated the same steps before he returned it to Morrie asking, "Where'd you get this?"

"Found it in the pocket of the dead Las Olas guy," Morrie replied.

Gaspar said, "So they either planted it on him after he died or they intended to leave his body here and probably killed him to make sure we found this."

"That's how I figure it," Morrie replied and, turning to Neagley, said, "I'm turning this over to them. They'll be outside a bit longer and then they'll be processing in the house. They've got probably three or four hours of work yet tonight. They've been asking to interview you, but I put them off. I told them you were too distraught tonight and you'd contact the chief personally. Call me if you need anything."

Neagley said nothing. Morrie turned to depart. When he

reached the panel, it slid open of its own accord.

Before he stepped through and the panel secured the room from observers again, Kim called to him. "Morrie?"

He turned his big body a bit to enable eye contact. "Yes?"

"Where's the copy you made of the drive before you put it in that evidence bag?"

"Already uploaded for you, Agent Otto," he replied on his way out.

Neagley picked up the remote, pushed a couple of buttons, and the screen they'd watched earlier came to life once more, this time with images unfamiliar but no less disturbing.

CHAPTER 30

Sunday, November 14
6:52 p.m.
Chicago, IL

The room is dimly lit. Like a decades-old hospital ward, five single cots are lined up in a vertical row, headboards against the cinderblock wall and footboards ten feet in front of the videographer.

On each cot a patient lies flat, covered to the chin with a lightweight blanket. Three children and two women. Each patient's left arm lies outside the blanket and is connected by a clear tube running from the inside of the elbow to a medicinal-looking bag filled with clear fluid hanging on a hook next to each bed.

After a few moments of determined staring at the crude proof-of-life, Kim felt her own breath synchronize to each patient's chest, rising and falling with unassisted but frighteningly shallow breaths.

The camera's eye approaches each cot and lingers several moments on each patient's face.

First, a woman about 45 years old. Wild black hair, slight frame, eyes closed. In the second bed, a dark-haired girl, maybe 14 years old. On the third and fourth beds, younger dark-haired boys rest as peacefully as angels. In the fifth, another woman, maybe 70 or more. Grey wiry hair, pulled back tight. Sunbaked complexion reflecting a lifetime lived close to the equator. The camera zooms in. On her chest is a copy of a Spanish Language newspaper, dated today.

Kim didn't need DNA to confirm the five were related. None of the patients moved even slightly except for the gentle rise and fall of breathing. But human bodies were not meant to be in medically induced comas for weeks on end. Kim worried about the level of supervision. Could they wake up unharmed?

The camera backs away from the beds and pans the room, perhaps to display the bleak conditions, because there is nothing more in the room to see. Nothing at all. No window, no television, no sentient beings. And absolutely no sound of any kind on the audio.

Less than two seconds displaying the nothingness. The video abruptly jump cuts to another scene.

Another room similar to the first, but this one is only dark around the edges. In the center stands a plastic floor lamp illuminating the single straight wooden chair beside it. A woman is affixed to the chair's sturdy arms and legs at her wrists and ankles with black plastic cable ties cinched tight enough to cause swelling.

The woman is not much larger than Kim, judging by how little space she takes up in the chair. She is dressed in dark, dusty slacks and a grimy yellow blouse, sleeves torn above the elbows. Feet bare and filthy. The camera tightens in on her lap to a neatly folded New York Times front page, dated yesterday.

The camera rises. Her head is bent forward on her neck, chin touching her chest. Dark, stylishly cut hair falls forward to obscure her face.

No matter, Kim thought. The woman had to be Karla Dixon.

Kim stared without blinking. When she saw the now familiar life signs she'd observed in the five patients, she realized she'd been holding her own breath and exhaled slowly through slightly parted lips.

As before, the camera pulls away as if establishing the emptiness of Dixon's prison for a full second. The video abruptly jumps to the next scene.

This segment is a slideshow, sets of images moving smoothly from one to the next, showing the story, each set offering a separate warning that is always the same: Death is nigh.

First, the Spanish language newspaper dated two weeks ago, followed by a photo of the five now-comatose patients enjoying lunch at an outdoor cantina along with a smiling Jorge Sanchez. Then, the same newspaper dated today, followed by a photo of the five comatose patients. Next, the front page of the Chicago Tribune dated Friday, followed by a photo of Sanchez's body lying in what could have been the morgue.

The women and children, too, can die now.

The second set of images is the New York Times front page dated yesterday, followed by a photo of Dixon coming out of the terminal at Kennedy airport. Then, the New York Times front page dated today followed by a photo of Dixon bound and unconscious in the chair.

She can die now.

The third set begins with The Chicago Tribune front page dated last week, followed by a photo of Paul Neagley standing happily in the ice cream shop where he bought his strawberry milkshake every afternoon on the way home from work. Then, the Chicago Tribune front page dated today followed by another photo of Paul splayed on top of his sister after he'd been shot, both lying bloody and still. Only Paul is dead, but the photo shows they might both have died.

After that, a short recap: Today's New York Times front page, followed by photos of the five patients, Dixon bound and unconscious in the chair, and Paul's body on the gurney being loaded into the ambulance in Neagley's driveway.

Finally, like any good film, the director reveals his climax:

the front page of the Houston Chronicle, dated today, followed by a long, lingering photo of a happy family enjoying lunch at another outdoor cafe. The parents are maybe forty. Fair, handsome man, wearing a wedding ring, holding his wife's hand. She looks Scandinavian. Tall, rail thin, white-blonde hair, icy blue eyes. She wears an open collared shirt that shows the bones on the front of her chest.

Kim's breath caught. The boy was maybe nine years old. Short legs. Low waist. Long arms. But it was the eyes that captured and held her. Uncanny. Dark, reassuring, like the child knew, like he was saying, *Don't worry. Everything will turn out fine.*

For Neagley, Kim realized something else took her breath away: The boy was Charlie Franz. He looked precisely like a miniature version of his father, Calvin—Neagley and Reacher's team member, dead years now after being beaten senseless and pitched to the desert floor from a helicopter by Berenson and Dean.

When the director was sure they'd had a good long look at the boy and plenty demonstrations showing his message, he finished his masterpiece with the very last slide.

A simple graphic completes the video. It contains only three words: Return My Money.

Kim got the message loud and clear: Or they will all die. Before she had a chance to say anything about the proof-of-life or the ransom demand, Neagley had pressed the speed dial on the house speakerphone. The connection was swift and crystal clear.

Morrie said, "Yes."

Neagley asked, "Have we authenticated the video?"

"Affirmative."

"Where are they holding Dixon?"

"Unknown."

"Sanchez's family?"

"Also unknown."

"Franz's family?"

"Unclear."

Neagley disconnected the call. She turned to Kim and demanded, "Call Cooper."

Kim asked, "Why?"

"Because we're out of time for flailing around on our own. We need higher level assistance. Cooper's the quickest option. He's already involved and he's got the resources at his fingertips. Get him on the line."

"What do you think he can do that you can't?"

"Locate the hostages within a two-mile radius in less than thirty minutes."

"And then what?" Gaspar demanded.

Neagley shrugged. "We go get them."

Kim said, "Easier if we had the $65 million ransom."

Neagley seemed to consider this briefly. She neither admitted nor denied guilty knowledge. Instead, she pushed the speakerphone button again and quickly dialed ten digits. They heard one ring begin to chime before the call was accepted.

"What do you want?" the all too familiar voice challenged.

"You owe me, Cooper," she said.

"If there was anything I could do, I'd have already done it. My hands are tied."

CHAPTER 31

Monday, November 15
3:50 a.m.
Houston, TX

Neagley had said she could usually find things and she had proved it by finding Franz's family home with dispatch. Three quick phone calls were all it took. Neagley had connected with a source at the Pentagon she refused to name to get the address, arranged a private jet to Houston, and extricated herself from Chicago without participating in the official investigation of the Las Olas attack on her home and murder of her brother. She was some sort of mutant superwoman, it seemed.

Neagley's private security business was far more extensive even than Kim had imagined, and she felt a little jealous, actually. She was an FBI Special Agent, a member of the most elite law enforcement agency in the world. Yet she worked the Reacher file with none of Neagley's privately available resources. The seething anger Kim had felt when she awakened on Neagley's stairwell Saturday was like a fire seed in her belly; it flamed hotter every time she matched herself against Neagley and came up wanting. Like now.

"Check your watches," Neagley had said. "We'll go in at four o'clock. No one expects you to arrive at four o'clock. It's the best time to catch them unprepared."

"Reacher teach you that?" Kim asked.

"Among other things."

"Such as?"

"Such as the best way to figure out what someone else is going to do is to think like them, *be* them," Neagley said. "You should try it sometime. It works."

Kim ignored her condescension. Now was not the time to take Neagley on. But that time was coming. And Kim was looking forward to it.

Now it was ten minutes to four. The moonless night sky felt brisk against her skin. The cloud ceiling was more than a mile high. She knew the Boss was watching and he'd be able to see and hear outside activities clearly. Whether he'd help if this went south in a hurry was unclear. He'd made no promises.

So Kim, Neagley, Gaspar, Morrie, and two private security personnel Morrie had recruited locally were stationed outside the darkened Houston condo where the former Mrs. Calvin Franz now lived with her son, Charlie, and her new husband. The husband worked for an oil company as a junior executive of some sort. Neagley's contacts said he'd been sent on a six-week work assignment to Alaska three hours after the family outing recorded in the proof-of-life video. Which was already too many hours ago.

The husband's absence presented an easier opportunity for Berenson and Dean to kidnap Angela and Charlie Franz. Phone calls to the home and to Angela's cell phone had been unanswered. All other location efforts were unsuccessful.

What they didn't know for sure was whether Angela and Charlie were home asleep or had voluntarily left or, worst case, were already taken.

"Cooper could answer this question, you know," Neagley

said. "He has the ability to pinpoint their heartbeats inside this building. Assuming they're still here. One call to the Pentagon. That's all he had to do. You might want to ask yourself why the heartless bastard is unwilling to make that call, Otto."

Kim didn't have to ask; she already knew. Sure, the request to use military surveillance on domestic citizens was illegal. But he wouldn't have let that stop him. The Boss wanted the Reacher File assignment off the books. Each time he intervened on their behalf, and the more sophisticated his actions were, he increased his risk of exposure. He wanted plausible deniability and he would sacrifice Angela and Charlie Franz to get it. Neagley, too, for that matter. Kim figured she and Gaspar were slightly less expendable because the Reacher file was not complete. He'd prefer not to lose them and start over with a new team. Maybe.

Gaspar rubbed his hands together and shuffled his feet. "Damn, it's cold out here."

"Be a lot hotter in Mexico when we get there," Neagley replied.

"Can't wait," he said.

Kim looked around again. Once more, she saw no indication that anything was amiss here. No cars traveled the residential street. No lights flickered in any of the homes. Night sounds were almost nonexistent, too. No barking dogs or meowing cats or distant traffic noise. Even the wind was still.

Nestled between Washington Avenue and Memorial Drive on Croft Street, the area could charitably be described as a neighborhood in transition. Angela Franz's abode was one half of an upscale duplex. But the home on the other side of Franz's was a ramshackle one-story frame house, 1950s vintage, and the vacant houses across Croft would have been improved by a good fire.

Angela's three-story condo resembled a saltine box, deeper than it was wide or high. Online real estate records claimed 3,191 square feet on three floors of living space.

Four bedrooms and four bathrooms, inside any one of which Las Olas killers could be waiting. Windowless two-car garage on the main level at the Croft Street side meant Kim couldn't see whether Angela's car or any other vehicles were parked inside. The condo had a market value of $700,000 or so, which meant the decor was likely to be upscale, too. In Houston, that meant hardwood and tile floors in most of the rooms, which would make it impossible to move with stealth.

Morrie had disabled the house alarm and then stationed himself and the two private security personnel at the east side entrance to the fenced patio, Morrie and one man inside the fence near the back entrance of the home, and the other man behind the fence, in case someone climbed over and landed in the empty lot adjacent on the south side.

Gaspar would remain out front. Kim and Neagley would enter through the side garage entrance and, hopefully, find Angela and Charlie Franz blissfully unaware, sleeping in their beds, precisely where mothers and children should be in a quiet residential neighborhood at precisely 4:00 a.m.

"Time to go, Neagley," Kim said. "Ready?"

"Always," Neagley replied.

They crouched, guns drawn, and crept quickly, close to the building, until they reached the garage entrance. Kim picked the lock rapidly. She held her breath as she opened the door, listening for another alarm or a screaming child or whatever might come to a home invader at 4:00 a.m.

She heard nothing.

She pushed the door open and slid inside the blacker-than-black garage, feeling Neagley enter immediately behind her and gently close the door. Kim settled night vision goggles onto her face and relaxed into the soft green glow that eliminated the darkness.

Only one vehicle in the garage. A silver Volvo station wagon of indeterminate age. The other parking slot was empty. This would normally hold the husband's car, which was now parked at the airport. Against the wall was a mess of kid stuff. A bike, a skateboard, a scooter, a few balls of various shapes and matching bats and gear to go with them. Across the back was a workbench, neatly organized; hand tools hung on a pegboard, several rolls of duct tape rested on the shelf. Under the bench were gardening tools and supplies.

To the left of the bench was the entrance door to the home's interior. There was an alarm pad next to it. The red "armed" light glowed. Above the door was a security camera. Kim saw the red "recording" light steady on, too. Had Morrie screwed up? Were the security measures disabled or not?

She grabbed the doorknob. It held fast. Unlike most homeowners, Angela Franz evidently realized the vulnerability of her security system at the interior garage entrance. Kim picked the flimsy lock quickly, turned the knob, held her breath and opened the door. No warning beeps. No sirens. If a silent alarm fed directly to the police department, there was nothing they could do about that now. Get in, get out, hope no one got hurt.

Neagley followed Kim through a laundry room and into a hallway that led to the back of the house on the right, or upstairs to the other living areas. They both went to the back patio door and opened it to let Morrie inside. Then the three split up to search the rest of the house.

According to the online records, the second floor contained an open floor plan of common rooms and one guest suite. Along the back, French doors opened onto a second floor balcony. A total of four areas to search. The third floor contained the remaining three bedrooms and three bathrooms, and another balcony. Seven more possible hiding places.

They worked swiftly. Kim searched the second floor. Neagley and Morrie took the third. Within five minutes they knew Angela and Charlie Franz were gone. They saw no signs of violence or that the home had been ransacked. To the extent that any home invasion could be peaceful, it seemed they came and took only what they wanted: the two hostages. In exchange, they left only one obvious piece of evidence.

The three rejoined Gaspar out front, recalled the two freelancers, and piled back into the van Morrie had procured. One of the freelancers drove. When they were on the road, Kim pulled from her pocket the two-by-four inch Las Olas sealed brown envelope she'd collected in Angela's kitchen. She hadn't opened it, but she could feel the flash drive inside. And on the front it said: *Agent K. L. Otto.*

She knew what it was. Proof-of-life on Angela and Charley. Or proof-of-death on another of the hostages. Either way, not good. She held onto the envelope a few moments more before she said, "Gaspar, take a look at this and pass it over to Neagley."

When Neagley received it, she handed the envelope to Morrie. Because there were no official law enforcement personnel present, no one needed to pretend chain of custody for the evidence was important this time. But still, maybe DNA could be lifted off the envelope's seal at some point.

He pulled out a small pocket knife and, as Kim noticed he'd done with the previous envelope, carefully separated the factory applied adhesive on the bottom lip from the envelope to get inside but avoid breaking the Las Olas seal. He poured the shiny silver flash drive out into his hand.

They couldn't view the drive's content. No one had a laptop. They'd left their equipment in the jet.

Morrie looked at his watch. "ETA twelve minutes," he said.

Kim estimated twenty minutes more to reach Houston Executive Airport, board the private jet they'd arrived in and plug the flash drive into the laptop. Twenty-two minutes before they learned what Berenson and Dean wanted them to know. Her stomach had already been pumping acid into her system in anticipation of the flight. What she felt now was sharp, unrelenting pain in her belly.

CHAPTER 32

Monday, November 15
5:35 a.m.
Houston, TX

Parked at HEA, the freelance security waited in the car while Kim and the others boarded the jet, located a laptop and crowded around it to watch the flash drive's short and pointed contents.

The video began with an establishing shot of the front of the Franz condo. There was no time or date stamp, but the footage probably was recorded only two or three hours before, given the all-enveloping nighttime. As when Neagley's team had been there, the building was dark and quiet and no activity in the immediate vicinity.

After the establishing shot, the next few frames showed Charlie sleeping in a bed that looked like a race car from an animated movie. His room was decorated in primary colors bold enough to be recognizable even in the dim nightlight's glow. The car was bright red, the sheets were bold red stripes, and the pillowcase was blue.

The next brief scene was Angela sleeping alone in a pricey, wrought iron, king-sized bed. She was covered with an ivory damask comforter. Her hair fanned the pillow and blended with the shiny white pillowcase so that she almost looked bald.

The next scene was half a second of Charlie's empty bed followed by a shorter view of Angela's empty bed.

"Subtle, aren't they?" Gaspar deadpanned.

"They put Agent Otto's name on the envelope," Morrie said. "How did they know she would collect the envelope and the message?"

Kim said nothing. Neagley said nothing.

Next was the hospital ward again. Five cots. Five patients. Five IV lines feeding who-knew-what into their veins.

Once again, the cameraman approached the elderly woman. Again, today's Spanish language newspaper was placed on her chest, which rose and fell with her shallow breathing.

After the video lingered long enough to establish she was still alive, the cameraman's straight right arm raised from his side into the viewfinder. He wore a black long-sleeved shirt and a black glove so that not even a slice of skin was showing. He held a black gun in his hand. Glock 19, Gen 4. Utilitarian, tough, reliable. Comfortable grip, controllable recoil, easily concealed. Used by law enforcement because of its stopping power. The same perfect choice Sanchez had made to kill O'Donnell. Probably the same choice the killer had made to eliminate Downing, the New York PI.

Kim knew what was about to happen, but she was powerless to stop it. She glanced briefly at her companions. Gaspar's eyebrows pointed toward his nose and his mouth set into a hard line. Hands clasped, Morrie seemed to be holding his breath as his nostrils flared. Only Neagley seemed clear-eyed and unconcerned.

The cameraman pointed the Glock directly at the woman's head and waited a moment, as if he thought they might not be watching closely and he didn't want them to miss anything. The film was morbidly mesmerizing. At this point, Kim couldn't have torn her gaze away if she, herself, had been forced at gunpoint to do so.

After he'd waited long enough, he slowly pulled the trigger once, twice, three times. Kim heard the deafening noise of the gunshots in her mind, but the audio remained silent even as the woman's head flew apart like a melon. Blood splashed everywhere.

He lowered his arm out of the camera's eye but left the video feed running for a few moments more. Then, as before, he left the camera running and panned the room as he retreated to the exit. So deep were their medically induced comas that the patients in the remaining four cots never stirred.

The video ended with two single slides delivering a clear, unmistakable message.

The first slide was a graphic depicting a digital clock with the date and time reflected: Monday, November 15, 6:00 a.m. CST.

The second slide was similar to the one that had ended the prior flash drive video, but the graphic was slightly altered. It said: *24 Hours Left to Return My Money.*

Kim automatically checked her Seiko. 6:02 a.m. Only 24 hours to find and recover the hostages.

Neagley said, "How long will it take us to fly to Valle Alto?"

Morrie replied, "Doesn't matter. We can't do it. The pilot won't fly his equipment into Mexico. Period."

"Buy the jet," Neagley said.

"The jet doesn't belong to the pilot. And even if it did, he told me when we hired him back in Houston that he wouldn't fly into Mexico," Morrie insisted. "The security guys won't go, either. Nobody is interesting in dying down there. Or spending any quality time in a Mexican prison."

"What's your idea? Let seven more hostages be slaughtered in their sleep?"

It was the first time Kim had heard Morrie refuse Neagley anything. She didn't respond well when thwarted. Kim watched the scene unfold to see how far the two would go. What would Neagley do?

"Of course not. But we don't know where they are. Shouldn't we confirm the location first?" Morrie's suggestion was reasonable, but Neagley was a woman of action. Her instincts were to strike first, declare victory, and sort it out much later, if at all.

CHAPTER 33

Monday, November 15
10:00 a.m.
Valle Alto, Mexico

The Las Olas compound was located fifty-two miles inside Mexico. As with almost everything in life, getting in promised to be much simpler than getting out. Neagley had made the arrangements. Morrie executed them. They'd picked up the armored panel van in Houston and now the four traveled in silence, Morrie at the wheel, Neagley in the navigator seat.

Gaspar had been sleeping since they left Houston. He'd slept on the jet to Brownsville and slept since then in the back seat behind Neagley. Kim was bone tired and Morrie seemed more subdued than usual. Great, Kim thought. When we launch our plan, Morrie will be sleep-deprived beyond safety levels, Neagley will charge the place as if she commanded an entire battalion, and Gaspar will be rested and looking for breakfast.

Kim sipped stiff coffee and munched the candy bar she'd

collected at the airport vending machine and drew her mind from fatigue by rehashing what she'd learned and the plan they'd made, hoping rote memorization and mental rehearsal would serve well enough when the time came. Not likely.

The compound was not as far from civilization as Kim might have expected, but still remote from the modern world. Satellite images rarely lie and the ones Kim pored over were retrieved from secure government sites. Which meant they were reliable if not reassuring.

Kim's research exposed a near-perfect fortress surrounded by nothingness. Had Neagley managed to persuade Cooper to deploy a predator drone, rank amateurs inside the Las Olas compound would have plenty of time to defend themselves. Dean had been a rocket scientist for New Age Defense Systems. He knew all about missiles. Smart money would bet he'd developed a missile with an error margin sufficient to down drones well before they launched a payload.

Breaching that security would be a challenge, even for Neagley. Retrieving hostages and removing them as short a distance as fifty-two miles across flat terrain was certain to produce collateral damage. But the effort had to be made. Kim would feel like she'd pulled the trigger on Sanchez's family if she failed to try.

From Brownsville, they'd traveled the Veterans International Bridge and crossed the border into Mexico through the larger city of Matamoros and headed further south along Carr/Federal 101. Every mile south of Matamoros revealed more open space while the population steadily declined. At Valle Hermoso, population 48,918, they turned west on highway TAM 12 and covered exactly what the satellite images reflected: miles of nothing but farmland. The last reasonably-sized hamlet before their destination was El Riolito, population 3,208.

Twelve miles west of El Riolito was the village of Valle Alto, population 273, according to the sign at the village limits. Four miles beyond the village, Morrie stopped the panel van where a mile-long northbound private road intersected with TAM 12. The overhead sign crossed through blue sky above the single lane blacktop and proudly proclaimed it: Las Olas Boulevard.

Under different circumstances, Kim might have laughed at the word "Boulevard," but she was too tired to even grin. Neagley betrayed no such fatigue. She seemed hard-wired for constant action. Maybe she was fueled by anger over her brother's murder. Maybe she felt duped by Dean and Berenson because she'd set them free five years ago when she shouldn't have. Probably she was ticked at Reacher because he hadn't responded to her call for assistance when she felt she could have used the help. Whatever kept Neagley going, she demonstrated an abundance of energy and battle readiness Kim had rarely felt. Watching Neagley was unnerving.

The single lane blacktop road led straight north from TAM 12 to the compound and stopped. One way in. One way out. Not ideal.

On the south side of TAM 12, and on every side of the Las Olas compound, was two miles of nothing but open farmland.

They'd checked the satellite feed the Boss had supplied. Although details were less clear than she liked, the clarity was sufficient to survey the compound, determine how many Las Olas members were on the property. Maybe figure out which of the outbuildings were holding cells for hostages.

The Boss had supplied thermal images of the buildings. Several showed interior heat signatures consistent with human occupation. Meaning there were people in at least six of the buildings. But were they hostages or cartel?

The compound had seven large buildings and at least four smaller structures, any one of which could house the hospital ward where Berenson and Dean were holding the hostages.

The buildings were arranged like a rectangle with an open space inside, maybe 100 yards wide and 130 yards long. The perimeter of the open space was surrounded by stadium lights, as if work often continued late into the night. Perhaps it did.

The main house reflected an earlier era. Two-story, painted wood construction, metal roof, rambling style. It faced east on Las Olas Boulevard. A wide paved driveway, large enough to accommodate semis, ran along the north side of the house and through the center of the yard beyond the far west edge of the property.

Four similar buildings, two on the north side and two on the south, flanked the house. Each was cement block construction, one-story, no windows, and shingled roofs. They might have housed equipment or livestock. Or hostages.

Opposite the main house across the open yard, the sixth building closed the rectangle. A seventh building aligned behind the sixth. Kim guessed these two contained the Las Olas cartel drug inventory and perhaps some portion of its revenue. Both buildings were enormous open warehouses surrounded by a chain link fence with a spiral of barbed wire around the top and an electronic gate across the east side.

Kim felt if they had any chance of succeeding here on the Las Olas compound, the cover of darkness was the only time it might happen. Unless they could be sure the compound was unoccupied during daylight. Even from the undetailed satellite photos, Kim had concluded a daylight raid was a suicide mission that would get them all killed. The only joy in that prospect was knowing that Dean and Berenson would never retrieve their money. Somehow, that knowledge didn't lighten Kim's mood.

Neagley wasn't always right, but she was rarely wrong. Maybe they should have gone into Angela Franz's condo before four o'clock in the morning, but Neagley had insisted. Something about the old Army way, she'd said. If they'd arrived an hour earlier, they might not be sitting here in the hot panel van now. Maybe that mistake would make her slightly more willing to listen to reason now.

Kim checked her Seiko. "We've got time. It's 11:32 now. We've got nineteen hours left before Las Olas kills another hostage. We go back to Matamoros, as we planned. We check into the hotel. We get some sleep. And we come back after dark. We'll be well inside our deadline if we get here by six o'clock. It's the only way we've got a chance in hell of completing this mission," Kim said.

For once, Neagley didn't challenge her.

Morrie made a U-turn at the foot of Las Olas Boulevard and returned along the TAM 12 route they'd traveled inbound. The countryside began to take on familiar markers. Kim recognized the towns, the road signs. She could find her way along the route in the dark. Probably.

On the outskirts of Matamoros, Morrie pulled into a traveler's hotel. They checked into separate rooms under false names and paid in advance and agreed to meet in the diner on the main floor at five o'clock to go over the plan one more time.

Less than five minutes after she entered her room, Kim fell onto the bed and into the deepest sleep she'd experienced since the morning she discovered Dave O'Donnell's murder. Was that only five nights ago? It seemed like a lifetime.

CHAPTER 34

Monday, November 15
5:00 p.m.
Matamoros, Mexico

Gaspar and Morrie were seated in the diner when Kim arrived. Two pots of coffee and two extra coffee mugs were on the table in front of the two empty chairs. This diner was like every diner. Open floor plan, no privacy, brightly lit, inexpensively furnished, kid friendly. Breakfast served all day, sandwiches for lunch and dinner. No alcohol. Constant coffee. Which was the only attribute that mattered to Kim at the moment.

After she'd poured her first cup and sipped, Neagley arrived and did the same. Gaspar said, "So let's order, now you're finally here."

Neagley scowled. "Cheap motels don't do it for me anymore. Haven't for a long time."

The waitress took their orders. Pancakes with eggs on the top and bacon on the side for Neagley and the guys. Kim ordered a breakfast burrito, which was identified on the menu as the specialty of the house. She figured if it was the specialty, maybe it would be cooked well done and not swimming in grease. Always best to eat when you can; you never know when you'll get the next chance. Although if this was to be her last meal, Kim would have preferred a good steak and a gallon of Brunello.

The waitress left and they moved on to business.

Kim said, "I downloaded more satellite images an hour ago, while we still had good daylight. Looks like the number of people at the compound has diminished. Two of the buildings could be what we're interested in."

"Which two?" Neagley asked.

"The main house, and a block building north and west of the main house—probably a bunkhouse a couple of decades ago, when the compound was a working farm."

Gaspar said, "The bunkhouse would provide seclusion. Shooting a Glock in an enclosed space like that had to be loud. Anyone inside either of those buildings would definitely have heard. Questions would have been asked. Especially in the main house."

Neagley shrugged. "Maybe. But these cartel members shoot off guns all the time. The murder rate down here is higher than the body count on a Civil War battlefield."

"Still," Morrie replied, "it makes sense that they'd want to keep the hostages away from the main building. We've seen dozens of people coming and going from the compound, based on the satellite and thermal images. Stands to reason that not all of them would think shooting a comatose old lady in the head or keeping kids sedated for weeks is okay."

Silence.

"We have to pick a target," Kim said. "Logic says it's the bunkhouse. Anybody disagree?"

Silence again.

The waitress returned with the hot food. Aromas flooded their senses and all four dug in like they were loading up for a hundred-mile bike race. The food disappeared in less than five minutes. They paid the tab, visited the toilets, and reconnected at the van in the parking lot without completing any checkout procedures, which would have drawn more attention than they wanted. Should anyone ask, they'd promised to return later.

Kim glanced at her Seiko, which was barely visible under the parking lot's sparse lighting. Daylight savings time had ended two weeks ago and Matamoros was in the Central time zone. Maybe civil twilight here should be a bit brighter at 5:45 p.m., but cloud cover deepened the darkness to what the weather people called astronomical twilight levels. A mixed blessing. Bright flashlights were out of the question for tonight's activities, but they certainly would be helpful.

Gaspar said, "I'll drive."

Morrie opened the doors with the remote and said, "Let's get down the road first."

Gaspar settled himself in the navigator's seat. Neagley and Kim took the two captain's chairs in the back. Morrie retraced the route they'd traveled twice already. The dashboard lights illuminated the van's interior well enough.

When they were a few miles south of Matamoros and still northeast of Valle Hermoso, Morrie pulled the van off the road and parked behind a stand of trees. No one traveling the road could see them if they left the lights off, but they were visible to satellites and drones. Couldn't be helped.

Neagley set up her high-tech radio interference. It wasn't good enough to block the Boss's ears, but maybe it would work against casual eavesdroppers who weren't specifically focused on them.

"Let's see that bunkhouse," Gaspar said. Kim opened the laptop. The screen glowed eerily blue in the blackness. She passed it to Neagley, who did what Kim had already done. Committed the building's layout and surrounding terrain to memory.

Neagley handed the laptop to Gaspar.

While he studied, Neagley asked, "Where's the equipment?"

"Behind Otto's seat," Morrie said. "Move the carpet and

pull up the false floor."

Gaspar opened the side door, which turned on the overhead dome light. He slipped out onto the shoulder, facing away from the van while Morrie emerged from the driver's side and walked around the front. The two men stood shoulder to shoulder a few seconds longer than necessary. Anyone watching would conclude they'd stopped to urinate and change drivers.

While the men established their diversion, Neagley stood, bent slightly at the waist, and slid between the captain's chairs. She rolled back the carpet, found the pull ring on the false floor, and gave it a solid yank. It came up easily, but it wasn't hinged and she was now at an awkward angle. She couldn't move the heavy metal false floor panel away from the storage compartment.

Kim unbuckled her seatbelt, raised the right armrest on her seat, crouched, and slid through to the cargo area. She took the false floor panel and moved it aside while Neagley unpacked guns, ammunition, night vision headsets, four untraceable cell phones with earpieces, coveralls, boots, gloves, watch caps, and Kevlar. Kim passed gear up to Gaspar and Morrie in the front seats and placed hers and Neagley's in the rear captain's chairs.

Kim rooted around in the storage space until her hand rested on a familiar smooth leather sap. The weapon was the perfect size for her small hands. Durable, heavy gauge leather casing filled with molded metal weight. A two-ply leather hand strap looped at one end for a secure grip. She'd used this model before. Small enough to be concealed, it would allow a strike with the flat part ranging from a stun to an instant knockout. The side edge could target large muscle groups and even break bones when applied with high force to a small area. Ideal for an up close and personal defense, she knew from experience. Tried and true.

She slipped the sap into her trouser pocket and left the storage space open so they could re-stash the weapons and equipment quickly. Just in case.

Then Morrie entered the navigator's seat and Gaspar settled himself behind the wheel. Both doors closed, extinguishing the dome light.

Neagley and Kim returned to their seats.

Morrie memorized the bunkhouse layout and all four quickly donned coveralls and boots and Kevlar and loaded and checked their weapons and night vision and tested the burner phones and earpieces.

Elapsed time was less than ten minutes. Too long, if the wrong people were watching. Gaspar restarted the van, moved the transmission into drive, and eased forward around and away from the stand of trees.

They didn't move far. An unusual spate of traffic clogged the highway headed south from Matamoros. "Where did all these vehicles come from all of a sudden?" Morrie asked, as if one of the four would know. No one did.

Gaspar merged into an open spot in the traffic line and turned on the headlights.

Drove the speed limit.

Observed all traffic signs.

No one talked.

At TAM 12, they turned west for the third time today. Narrow feeder roads Kim hadn't noticed before added vehicles at each isolated rural intersection. The line of traffic became increasingly heavier, seeming to converge from far away in all directions because the entire local population couldn't possibly have owned so many vehicles.

Three miles from Valle Hermoso, they were boxed in by trucks and a few cars and SUVs. Gaspar was forced to slow his speed. No more than fifteen miles an hour.

Travel time to this point from Matamoros on their recon trip had been twenty minutes. Tonight, they'd already been on the road for an hour. They had plenty of time, but the unexpected delay made Kim nervous anyway.

Neagley appeared as unconcerned as ever.

Traffic crawled through Valle Hermoso, which was alive with activities tonight. Was it a local holiday? Did that explain the heavy traffic, the crowds? Kim didn't know.

On the other side of Valle Hermoso, travel speeds began to increase and the bottleneck, whatever it was, slowly opened up.

At El Riolito, at least half the 3,208 people who lived there were moving around the town. Parents with children, elderly couples, a few young women.

Curiously absent in both towns were teenage boys and single young men.

Gaspar traveled safely through the crowds and reached Las Olas Boulevard eighty minutes after leaving the hotel. Full nautical twilight now made it too dark to read the pretentious overhead sign. In fact, it was too dark to see the sign at all.

For almost a mile as the van approached the intersection, Kim had been watching the compound's approach. It was blindingly lit by banks of stadium lights, as though they were on their way to a professional sporting event and not the stealthier game ahead of them.

CHAPTER 35

Monday, November 15
7:08 p.m.
Villa Alto, Mexico

Las Olas Boulevard was deserted, but even from a quarter mile away at the foot of the Boulevard on TAM 12, they could see vehicles parked on the sides of the road, on the weedy aprons, in every available space around the front of the compound. Kim had downloaded the latest satellite photos before dusk when the compound was practically deserted. Whatever drew these people here had happened during the past two hours.

The compound itself was lit by massive stadium lights that spread ambient light well outside the parking areas. Darkness surrounded everything beyond. Very few people could be seen wandering on foot. Activities were focused in the center open space and shielded from view by the perimeter of buildings and vehicles.

Gaspar turned the armored van onto Las Olas Boulevard and traveled ten miles an hour toward the main building.

When he reached the campus, he drove slowly past. Kim and the others peered through the van's dark tinted windows in an effort to solve the puzzle. When they reached the wide driveway, they managed an obstructed view of the open space under the lights because the driveway was jammed with cars, trucks, SUVs, and buses. Kim ticked off 124 vehicles before she stopped counting.

Gaspar drove past the last building and when he reached the corner, he executed a three-point turn and lowered all four windows. The moment the sound seal released, they heard the cheering and booing crowd. Gaspar drove slowly toward the open space; noise volume increased with every inch of covered ground.

Morrie said, "The good news is that no one will notice us with all these other people here."

Gaspar replied, "The bad news is there's no way to sneak in and out under cover of darkness like we planned."

Neagley contributed her usual plain sense. "We only have one option. We're out of time. We go in, find the hostages, bring them out."

Gaspar snorted. "Or die trying."

Kim shrugged in the darkness. "More likely they'd beat you to a pulp." She gestured to two of the buses. Both sported reflective bumper stickers depicting boxing gloves.

Gaspar said, "It's brighter than daylight out there."

She had already moved to the back of the van again and pulled out her laptop and connected once more to the satellite. The connection might be discovered later, but at the moment, she figured everyone was involved with the big show in the compound's center.

Neagley asked, "Can we use the path to the bunkhouse like we planned?"

"I think so," Kim replied when she found what she was looking for. "Each of you should take a look." She downloaded the images and saved them and disconnected the feed. Then she passed around the laptop as she'd done earlier.

The compound's center was now a boxing ring, complete with bleacher seats on all four sides. Which meant the spectators were facing each other and the contestants, not watching the bunkhouse building they'd decided was most likely to hold the hostages. The feed showed four armed guards walking the perimeter of the crowd, but when she snapped the image, two were standing at a break in the sight line to watch the match. She figured the other two were doing the same. Everyone was preoccupied with the big match.

Their first bit of good luck, maybe.

The bleachers were full, which explained the bottlenecked inbound traffic that had lightened up and disappeared the closer they came to Las Olas Boulevard. She noted a few female spectators, but mostly males, which explained the absence of males walking the streets of the towns on the way.

The fight might have been in its first round; the boxers were unbloodied so far. Whatever the match was, hundreds of spectators and participants had gathered to participate. If they were in the opening rounds, the matches could go on for at least a couple of hours before the crowd broke up and dispersed.

Kim didn't figure on being here that long, but they now operated in a fluid situation, which was not ideal and not what they'd planned.

Two heat sensitive images of the main house and the outbuildings were almost identical to the earlier versions. No human forms inside most of the buildings. Only two inside the house; several more inside the target bunkhouse.

After Neagley, Gaspar, and Morrie memorized the new images, Kim relocked the laptop and returned it to the hidden compartment in the floor. Gaspar parked the van in the shadow of one of the buses, raised the windows, and cut the ignition. They collected their equipment and exited the vehicle.

Neagley led, crouched and hanging to the shadows as well as possible. Followed closely by Gaspar, Kim and Morrie at the rear doing the same.

They traveled along the east side of the road until they reached the first building on the northeast corner of the compound. All hugged close to its eastern edge, reached the corner and turned behind the building out of the glare of overhead lights. Still, enough ambient light flooded the weeds in the back that Kim had no need to don her night vision. Nor did the others.

Kim had snugged the earpiece firmly into her right ear and made sure it worked, but she hadn't once used it after they spent ten minutes back at the stand of trees storing one another's numbers in their burner phones and learning how to connect by conference call. Nor did the others.

Neagley made her way quickly along the darkened north side until she reached the northwest corner, where a gap of fifteen feet between buildings presented an opportunity for discovery. One at a time, they dashed across the gap and then continued along the north side of the second building. At the second building's northwest corner, the second fifteen-foot opening gaped. Neagley stopped and waited until Gaspar, Kim, and Morrie reached her.

Across the gap was their target.

The bunkhouse was concrete block construction, one-story, long, and windowless. Its main entrance was on the open compound south side, ten feet from the dead center of the bleachers holding the crowd of raucous spectators.

Using the main entrance was not an option.

The bunkhouse back was the north side of the building. Only one exit door, resting square in the center. Whether the door was locked or armed with an alarm system or guarded by other means was unknown.

Without speaking, Neagley lifted her weapon of choice, a Glock 17 she'd snagged from the hidden compartment in the van. Kim had chosen a Glock 19. Morrie and Gaspar selected Berettas. All four were using the same ammunition, 9mm Parabellums. More efficient. More anonymous when they disposed of all the equipment, too.

Kim refused to think about the consequences should

they be caught with any of these items before they returned to Brownsville, Texas. They'd be lucky if they only ended up in a Mexican prison.

Morrie passed Neagley and approached the bunkhouse's back exit. From Kim's vantage point, the door looked like heavy grey steel and seemed to have been snugged securely shut. No light leaked from cracks around the edges. When Morrie tried to turn the knob, nothing happened. He'd equipped his Beretta with its sound suppressor back in the van. Now, he slipped on his night vision and lifted the gun. The next time the crowd roared he shot three precise, quick, quiet, shattering rounds into the wooden jamb around knob's locking mechanism. When he grabbed the knob again, the door slid easily away from the busted wood.

Still wearing his night vision, he pulled the door open, counting on the darkness behind the bunkhouse as camouflage, which was okay. Morrie entered the bunkhouse, followed by Gaspar, Kim and finally Neagley. The room felt cavernous. Damp. Hot. And empty of all life forms, human or otherwise, which wasn't okay. Not okay at all.

CHAPTER 36

Monday, November 15
7:38 p.m.
Villa Alto, Mexico

Pervasive darkness inside the bunkhouse required night vision, and Kim slipped hers on. She saw an open cement block building lined with cots on either side of the rear exit door. But the cots were nothing more than mattresses on frames. Each cot had a storage locker on the floor at the foot of the bed. The bunkhouse had no windows and only one additional door, this one identical to the first, but on the front compound side of the building.

The short ends of the room were divided by small rooms large enough to house toilets and showers, but not big enough to hold more cots. Along the front wall on the east side of the door were two picnic tables with benches to sit on. On the opposite side of the door was an open kitchen, of sorts. A white porcelain sink, low, round, white refrigerator, and a two-burner propane stove with a child-sized oven. Nothing more.

The entire room was almost soundproof, but when the boxing crowd vocalized pleasure or its opposite, high-decibel wildness penetrated like it was muffled in gallons of viscous syrup.

Kim had studied the proof-of-life videos. From memory, she confirmed the surroundings inside the bunkhouse were similar to what she'd seen. She simply wasn't certain whether the videos were recorded here. Perhaps the hostages had been held here, and perhaps not.

She waved the others outside. They'd made their own assessment of the building's contents. They followed without protest.

When they reconnected behind the bunkhouse, Gaspar said, "Try the main house next?"

Morrie said, "Too risky. The main house is guarded like Fort Knox. Those heat signatures we saw less than an hour ago were probably involved with what's going on in the boxing ring. Las Olas wouldn't risk holding hostages this close to all those spectators."

Neagley replied, "It's possible the hostages were moved to the main house since we checked the satellite. More than possible—it's the only place that makes sense. We've come this far. One way or the other, we need to know if they're here. Let's be quick about it. I'm not a big boxing fan, but these matches can't go on indefinitely."

Every alarm in Kim's stomach was doing backflips. "We need to be on the road before this group breaks up." She checked her Seiko. "Twenty minutes more. Then we've got to go, whether we've found them or not."

Neagley said nothing. Kim figured she didn't agree, but Kim would leave Neagley and Morrie behind if she had to. The woman was maddening. And fully capable of taking care of herself.

They retraced their route until they reached the first building's northeast corner again and then carefully hugged the east wall and moved inside the building's shadow. At the driveway, they split up and crouched low behind and beside the vehicles, zig-zagging toward the main house.

The cheering, booing crowd seemed to be constantly in a state of agitation now. Perhaps the fight was nearing the last round. Would there be more than one bout? Was this the last of the night? Impossible to know. But Kim's gut said time was running out. She felt it the way she felt danger at 30,000 feet. Palpably.

Kim figured the house had been a fortress for at least a decade. Armed guards patrolled as if guerilla warriors were likely to attack and be swiftly repelled. With no crowd or battering contestants to distract them, these sentries were more dedicated to the task at hand. Kim saw four in front, two pairs walking toward each other, passing in the middle, turning at the edge of the yard, walking toward and apart again. Repeat.

She saw four more guards on the north side of the building performing the same routine. She guessed there were four on the west side and four on the south side, too. Meaning two pairs of eyes watched in every direction at all times. It would be impossible to pass unnoticed.

Sixteen sentries with assault rifles and probably side arms as well. It would be equally impossible to take out fewer than the entire gang of sixteen without raising an alert of some sort.

How many more were inside protecting whatever needed protecting? Quite a bit of firepower to guard an empty house, Kim thought. A lot of firepower for seven comatose hostages, for that matter.

Gaspar said, "I'll go ask one of them what's going on."

"Why you?" Neagley asked.

"I look more like them than the rest of you. I speak fluent Spanish with the right accent." He shrugged. "And I know something about boxing. It's a popular sport in Miami, too."

Before anyone could argue, he pulled off his watch cap and gloves and stuffed them in the pockets of his coveralls. Handed his night vision to Morrie. And settled the Beretta comfortably in his right hand, held it casually behind his thigh.

Kim touched his arm briefly. "Let's connect the phones. Leave your connection open. Say 'knockout' and we'll be there."

Gaspar grinned. "But what if I don't see any good-looking women?"

Kim let his levity slide. "You need motivation," she said, and punched him on the bicep. "Think about what I'll do to you if you screw this up, Chico."

"I love you, too." He nodded, stuffed his left hand in his pocket and sauntered jerkily forth as if he'd maybe had a bit too many shots of tequila. He'd traveled about twenty yards toward the front of the house before the first sentry noticed him and headed directly for a confrontation.

Gaspar continued straight ahead, seemingly unconcerned about the man with the AK-47 approaching.

When Gaspar was within hailing distance, the guard said in commanding Spanish, "No one is allowed here, *Senor*. Return to the event, please."

Gaspar acted as if he didn't hear or, perhaps, didn't comprehend. He staggered and stumbled a bit. Righted himself. The guard's steady forward pace brought them closer.

"*Senor*. Return to the event. You are not allowed here," he said, as if rearranging the words and speaking slower would increase the chances of compliance. He didn't raise the gun but didn't back down, either. Of the east side four, Kim figured he was probably the commanding officer. If cartels had any formal structure at all, which they probably didn't.

By now, the guard's partner had reached the northeast corner and acknowledged the two north side sentries at the usual spot, after which all three turned and paced in opposite directions. Meaning the second east side pair were now pacing toward Gaspar, unhurried, unconcerned, thereby confirming that the first guard was the quartet's leader. Maybe the protocol was that he could handle one drunk spectator and he'd let them know if he needed assistance.

None of the others made any attempt to investigate Gaspar or support their colleague. In an unbalanced fight, the thing to do was to take out the leader. After that, maybe one more will try as a show of support. But the last ones left standing will turn and run. Usually.

When the leader's partner and the north side team had traveled back about twenty feet, the remaining east-side team was still fifty feet away from Gaspar and the leader. Gaspar saw his chance. Clearly enough to be heard over the open cell connection, he said, "Knockout."

The leader looked briefly confused by Gaspar's reply. In that instant, Gaspar slid his Beretta from behind his thigh and slammed its butt across the sentry's temple. He crumpled to the ground. Gaspar pulled him into the shadows, bound wrists to ankles with heavy cable ties, and collected the AK-47.

Kim had pulled her Glock and now, crouched low, was hurrying toward Gaspar. On her right, she felt rather than saw Neagley and Morrie approaching from behind a parked van and a parked Toyota. She kept her field of vision trained on Gaspar, prepared to shoot the fallen guard if he stirred.

The second team of east-side guards continued marching toward Gaspar as if they hadn't seen anything. Maybe they hadn't. They had a clear sight line to the open space where their leader had been, but didn't seem the least bit concerned. Nor did they slow their rate of advance.

When Kim reached Gaspar, he said, "One down, seven to go. No pun intended."

She grinned, but said nothing.

He bobbed up again, resumed his drunken saunter and headed closer to the east-side pair of sentries. This time, the two stayed together, suggesting neither was the second in command.

Kim advanced by tucking between parked cars until the pair was ten feet from Gaspar, who was five feet ahead of her.

The first north-side pair had to be close to the turning point now, too, Kim thought, and glanced over in time to see Neagley and Morrie subdue the pair and lie in wait for the second pair.

Kim heard Gaspar say, "Knockout," again. As before, she dashed toward him. Gaspar took down number three and Kim subdued the startled number four with a sold whack of the sap.

The second east-sider continued marching away. He'd be at the southeast turning point in three seconds. The pair coming toward him would learn he was alone. What would they do next?

Kim left Gaspar to pull guards three and four into the shadows and hobble them while she loped up silently behind number two. She flattened her back against the east side of the main house and waited until he turned at the pivot point. He marched ten steps north, came even with her and she thumped his temple with the heavy sap she'd found in the van's cache of weapons. She pulled him into the bushes and cabled him. While she worked, she heard the crowd cheering in the center compound.

Half the project was finished. Eight more sentries to handle and they could enter the building. Which took another four minutes. Fifty-three seconds after that, they'd entered the house through the front door with the booing crowd a Greek chorus behind them.

CHAPTER 37

Monday, November 15
8:22 p.m.
Villa Alto, Mexico

Once inside the main house, they split up, each following a direction of the compass. Kim hurried counter-clockwise from the entry door. She found the house alight but empty as she scanned each room. She met up with Gaspar at the back. He lifted his shoulders as if to say, "Who knows?"

Thirty seconds later, Neagley and Morrie had searched the second floor with the same result. Kim had located a locked door that might have led to a basement. She gestured for Gaspar to handle the entrance. She pulled back the deadbolt, pushed the door inward, and slipped her night vision down over her eyes before she crept slowly down into what could have been a dungeon. It smelled close, damp, musty. Cold. No windows. No light.

Neagley and Morrie followed.

At the bottom of the stairs, they found a single cavernous room. The eerie green glow provided by her night vision revealed the scenes Kim remembered vividly from the flash drives. Everything was there—except the hostages. No mistake about it. Cots, IV poles, cinderblock walls. Newspapers. The same total silence. Not even the noisy boxing spectators could be heard down here.

Sensory deprivation was a form of torture and this was purposely constructed as a perfect spot to apply those methods. Something like a vortex sucked Kim into the maw. She stood at each footlocker and cast her gaze on each cot.

The first thing she noticed was five beds, not eight. Meaning the Sanchezes had been here but not Dixon or the Franzes. Briefly, she wondered where Dixon, Angela and little Charlie had been held and where the seven remaining were being held now.

The second thing she noticed drew her to cot number five. Dark splotches amid the green glow drying on the walls, the floor, and the bed, but still shiny-wet on her pillow could only be the grisly remains of the grandmother's murder.

Kim grabbed the burner cell phone from her pocket and closed her eyes and snapped several quick flash photos. She stashed the phone and pulled an evidence bag out of her pocket, turned it inside out, used it like a glove to scoop up as much of the blood and brain and bone tissue as possible. She carefully pulled the evidence bag over her hand and zipped it closed before sliding it into her pocket. When they returned to the FBI, she'd have evidence that the woman died here, at least, whether it mattered to governments or not. She'd have something to provide closure to her daughter and grandchildren.

If Kim got caught with any of this—she wouldn't think about that right now.

She felt a slight whiff of air behind her. She felt it very firmly. It was exactly the kind of whiff she'd trained herself never to miss. To her antennae it was a complex but complete assault moments before the large paw engulfed her shoulder. The kind of adverse possession she'd trained for, practiced responses to, developed a sixth sense about. The kind that could end her life unless she reacted before it happened.

Without thinking, she raised her gun in front of her to shoot precisely where she knew his center mass would be. One shot was all she'd need. She rested her weight on her right foot and quickly pushed with her left into the pivot, aiming true. She was in the zone where her mind was fast but the physical world was slow. Which was what saved his life.

At the last possible fraction of a second, she recognized Morrie's giant-sized frame and forced her finger from the trigger. She felt her muscles tense with the effort of not shooting. She couldn't muster the extra control she'd need to speak aloud.

Morrie pulled his hand back without touching her, tilted his head toward the stairs. Kim looked in that direction. Saw Neagley's retreating calves almost at the first floor again. Kim controlled her pulse, slowed her breathing, lowered her weapon and headed toward the stairs and the exit. Morrie followed. If he had any suspicion that she'd almost killed him, he didn't show it.

At the top of the basement stairs, Gaspar remained alone in the kitchen. "The last match is ending. A few early birds have already been walking past on the way out. Someone will be looking for those sentries. We've got to go. Now."

"Where's Neagley?" Kim asked. Neagley should have been able to hear the question through her earpiece. No response.

"There was an office of some sort on the second floor she wanted to take another look at," Gaspar said.

No response from Neagley again. Damn the woman. Couldn't she just be a member of the team for once?

Stealthy was a word that didn't do justice to Neagley's particular skills, but the team was functioning on borrowed time. From Neagley, non-response to the open communication channel wasn't mere thoughtlessness. Kim figured she was likely unconscious or coerced to silence. Or worse. "Neagley?" She called directly. Nothing. "I'll get her." Kim headed toward the staircase as she said, "Morrie, get the van and pull it up to the front door. Gaspar, you see anybody coming, shoot first and talk later."

Morrie didn't move. He took orders from Neagley, not from Kim. He'd made that plain more than once.

"Which side of the house is the office, Morrie?" Kim asked. "Right or left of the stairs?"

"Left," he said.

Still nothing from Neagley.

"Make it snappy," Gaspar said, looking out the back windows, weapon ready.

"Morrie. Go. Now." Kim ordered again, putting the commanding officer's tone to the words. She looked at her watch. "We'll be with you in twenty seconds."

She gave him a little push. It was like trying to push a brick wall. Kim thought he might refuse. But then he turned, took long strides to reach the front door in a split second and continued outside.

Right behind him, Kim reached the foot of the stairs and bounded up two at a time.

At the top of the staircase, she turned left, crouched low and followed along the corridor guided by nothing but survival instinct and the green glow of her night vision. Scanning, Kim led with her Glock.

Twelve steps into the hallway, she tripped over a splayed corpse and fell across. She looked down, under her stomach. A man. Wearing fatigues and a broken neck. She checked his pulse. Nothing. Cooling fast.

Kim pushed herself onto her knees and then stood upright. This time as she advanced, she looked ahead but checked along the floor. A few feet further, she saw a second corpse in the same condition. She bent to feel his carotid. No pulse. Stepped around.

Kim quickly opened and closed doors along the left-side corridor. She found nothing but empty bedrooms.

Several doors led off to the right, south side of the corridor.

Except for the two bodies, the entire floor seemed deserted. Kim heard nothing.

Light seeped below one doorway at the very end of the hallway.

Neagley had to be in that room. And she was probably not alone.

Kim crouched and rode the wall with her back as she eased toward the end.

In her ear, Kim heard Gaspar say, "Company headed this way. Fifteen to twenty seconds out."

Morrie replied, "Be there in twelve."

No response from Neagley.

Kim kept moving forward. She said nothing.

Neagley was in trouble. The woman was lethal, but she wouldn't put her team in harm's way. Something had gone horribly wrong.

At the end of the corridor, Kim removed one hand from the Glock and slid the night vision down on its strap to hang around her neck. If she burst into the lighted room wearing the goggles, she'd be blinded.

She took a breath. Grabbed the doorknob. Turned and stepped into the room. Stood crouched, ready to fire. Registered a spacious room, Spanish colonial furniture, desk, chair, loveseats facing each other, a heavy coffee table between, lamps, heavy chairs opposite the desk, large draperied windows along the wall opposite the door.

Nothing unusual or out of place.

Except for Edward Dean standing in her sights, behind the sofa with a Glock 19, Gen 4, pointed directly at the back of Neagley's head.

"Good evening, Agent Otto," Dean said, as if he'd expected her, which he probably had. He held Neagley's earpiece up and wiggled it around. "Loyalty's a bitch, ain't it?"

Kim first had to warn Gaspar and Morrie and tell them to stop using the cell phone channel. She said, "Let her go,

Dean."

"Or what? You'll shoot me? I don't think that's likely. At least, not until I tell you where to find the hostages." His tone was smug.

He thought holding a gun to Neagley's head gave him an advantage.

Kim almost laughed.

"Where are the hostages?" Kim asked because she knew he expected her to.

"Not here, as you've already discovered. We moved them a few hours ago," he said.

"Where?" she asked again, still holding her gun steady on him.

"You brought my money?" Dean replied, as if she was both expected and prepared for a peaceful exchange instead of invasion and rescue.

"Sixty-five million dollars," Kim said.

"Where is it?" Dean asked.

"Where are the hostages?" Kim repeated.

"You disabled my guards, yes?" Dean said. It wasn't a question. "But I called backups when Neagley showed up here without my cash. You've got maybe three more minutes before they arrive to persuade you. Remember Sanchez?"

Mentioning Sanchez was the wrong thing to do.

In a flash of movement Kim barely saw, Neagley turned, grabbed Dean's gun, tossed it aside, and held him by the neck in a bare-handed choke hold that threatened to crush his larynx. His eyes bulged. His mouth opened and closed like a fish.

But she didn't kill him.

Instead, after a moment or two of intense discomfort, she released her grip. Slightly.

Kim said, "Tell me where the hostages are or I'll shoot you in the head."

Dean's voice croaked a whisper. "You will anyway."

"Oh I'd love to," Kim replied. "But I'm an FBI Special Agent. My boss would never get over it."

Dean nodded as best he could with Neagley's grip still firm around his neck. "Are we making a deal here?" he croaked.

"Where are the hostages?"

He waited another moment and Neagley pressed a bit harder to help him decide. His eyes bulged again and his mouth opened and closed without sound.

She relaxed her grip slightly so he could answer.

"Black Star," he wheezed out with the slight bit of air that escaped around Neagley's thumbs. "Texas."

Dean's claim startled Kim.

She knew about Black Star. It was a horse farm in South Texas. Fine quarter horses were bred and sold there. It was also a money laundering operation for the Las Olas drug cartel and two other cartels the ATF and Homeland Security had identified so far.

Black Star had been the subject of intense multi-agency undercover work for months. Work that had stretched as far as the Detroit FBI field office. Kim had seen some of the paperwork. She'd examined the forensic accounting.

"Texas? Try again."

Unlikely that Dean and Berenson would have risked smuggling people across the border to Black Star when there must have been easier, more secluded places closer to Valle Alto. Places where hostages were common. The cartel's daily business involved kidnapping for ransom as well as selling drugs and guns and other contraband. Anywhere inside Mexico, hostages would receive less scrutiny and less interference from US authorities.

"Black Star," he rasped again. "I swear."

"I don't believe you. And we're out of time," Kim said. "Bring him, Neagley. Let's go."

Briefly, Kim thought Neagley would ignore the order.

Neagley squeezed Dean's throat a bit harder. His eyes bulged and his mouth did the trout impression again. For a brief moment, it could have gone either way. Leave another corpse or take another hostage.

"We need him alive to get out of here," Kim said. "And he can help us with Berenson when the time comes."

Another moment elapsed before Neagley let him go. She reached into her pocket and pulled out one of the cable ties she hadn't used on the guards outside. She yanked it hard around his wrists and shoved him between the shoulder blades.

Kim turned and headed back the way she'd come, not sure whether Dean would be alive when they reached the front door or not. And she wasn't sure she cared, one way or the other. Either option had its problems.

"On our way. Meet you at the front door," she said into the headset.

"Ten-four," Gaspar replied.

"Ready," Morrie said.

Kim smiled and kept moving. She heard Dean stumbling along behind her. Neagley was as quiet as a ghost wearing socks.

Gaspar waited at the ready. When they reached him, he waved all three out ahead.

They hustled out the front door, crouched low to hide themselves as well as possible, Gaspar behind, turning to be sure no one ran out after them.

Kim heard more cheering and booing as they raced quietly toward the armored van Morrie had parked directly at the front entrance.

Morrie clicked the automatic unlock, they jerked open the doors and piled in. Neagley shoved Dean onto the floor between the seats. "Raise your head half an inch and I'll break your neck," she said.

Neagley hopped inside and Kim jumped in after them. Gaspar slid the van's door snugly into place, yanked open the front passenger door and struggled inside.

Before Gaspar had dragged his right leg inside and slammed his door, Morrie pulled out onto Las Olas Boulevard behind a late model sedan departing at a measured pace.

When they reached the intersection of Las Olas Boulevard and TAM 12, Morrie followed in line behind the vehicles leaving the compound and turned east. Empty tarmac stretched as far ahead of the short line of vehicles as she could see in the darkness. With this brief head start, they might have an easy trip back.

Unless Dean's guards figured out where he was and came after them.

Kim said, "Let's get this gear stowed. The last thing we need right now is to be stopped while we're armed like an FBI extraction team."

Morrie unfastened his Kevlar. "Spending time in a Mexican prison doesn't appeal to me much, either."

"You might want to leave that on," Gaspar said. "We'd be lucky to make it into a Mexican prison if we get caught before Brownsville."

Neagley said nothing, but she put her booted foot briefly on Dean's neck and pressed before she pulled off her Kevlar, night vision, watch cap, gloves, and coveralls and dropped them into the secret compartment.

Kim's gear went in next, followed by Gaspar's. Morrie removed his gear, too, although it took a bit longer because he was driving. Kim noticed all three kept their guns within reach like she did.

They settled into their seats as if they'd been mere spectators at tonight's boxing matches while Neagley returned the false floor into place.

Kim felt the evidence bag, soft and pliable, inside her blazer pocket and adjusted the sap low into her trouser pocket against the side of her thigh where she could easily retrieve it. Maybe she'd have a chance to use it. Maybe not. But just in case.

When they reached Villa Hermosa, she'd upload the photos from the burner cell phone to the secure satellite and delete them. Manual deletion wouldn't be enough and sending anything to the satellite was risky, but she had to do it. Only one choice.

Neagley settled herself in her seat and returned a booted foot to Dean's neck where he lay in the wheel well. Maybe he was still breathing. She crouched near him and patted him down. Expertly. Thoroughly.

"What are you looking for?" Gaspar asked.

"Dunno," Neagley said.

She pulled his wallet and a cell phone and flipped both onto her seat. She found a switchblade tucked into his boot, which seemed to piss her off. She unbuckled his belt and pulled it out of his pants. She used it to tie his feet together. She pulled off his shirt and boots and tossed them into the back of the van. Then she returned to her seat, put her foot back on his neck, and stared at the cell phone for a while.

"You know you're broadcasting a signal to his crew, right?" Kim asked. "They'll find it and they'll come to get him with heavy firepower."

Neagley looked her straight in the eye as she turned the phone on and scrolled through the call log. "Nothing would make me happier, Otto."

Before Neagley guessed what she'd planned, Kim reached over and grabbed the phone from Neagley's grasp. Reaction was swift. Neagley raised her hand to strike but Kim had leveled the Glock and aimed it center mass.

"I don't plan to die tonight in Mexico," Kim said.

Neagley's nostrils widened and her brow creased and her breathing quickened with the effort of restraining her impulses. Maybe she wanted to smite Kim. Maybe she wanted Kim to think so. Hard to tell. Kim held the gun steady until Neagley worked it out.

Neagley replied, "Everybody dies, Otto."

"I'm aware," Kim answered. She glanced up to catch a road sign. Matamoros 78 kilometers. Which meant forty-nine miles until they reached the Veteran's Memorial Bridge and crossed safely into Texas again. God willing.

She opened the cell phone and disabled the battery, knowing that would only buy them an extra few minutes at best.

CHAPTER 38

Monday, November 15
9:54 p.m.
Matamoros, Mexico

Morrie drove the van across the bridge and into Texas without mishap. He chose a particular booth and had a quiet conversation with the agent, but no one asked to look inside the van. Nor did the agent take notice of a man in the back wheel well.

First time for everything, Kim thought. She'd never smuggled a human being across the Mexican border. It was frighteningly simple. Maybe moving hostages across the border was easier than she expected. Maybe Dean and Berenson had moved the hostages to Black Star after all.

Which wasn't necessarily good news.

Ten miles past the border crossing, Kim said, "Pull over at the next gas station. We need a break."

Morrie did as she ordered without seeking Neagley's permission. When he stopped the van, Kim nudged Dean with the toe of her boot. He groaned. He was alive, which was all she cared about right now. He was shirtless, shoeless, shackled, and seriously dehydrated. She rolled him onto his side with her foot. His throat was bruised and swollen where Neagley had choked him. His temple lay against the floor. His eyes were open.

"Where are the hostages?" Kim asked him again.

He cleared his throat. Again.

Kim waited. She pulled the Glock and held it pointed loosely in his direction. "Shall we let Neagley ask?"

His eyes grew wide, wild. Barely audible, he whispered, "Black Star."

"I don't believe you," she said.

He nodded, scraping his face against the floor of the van. "Black Star. Black Star," he said, as if repeating the words would make them more believable.

Kim stuffed the Glock in her jacket and opened the passenger door. Night breeze rushed into the cabin, bathing her face in welcome coolness. Exhausted by tension and exertion and lack of sleep, she almost fell onto the pavement. Gaspar reached her side in time to steady her.

She felt wobbly. "Let's walk a bit."

"What about them?" he asked, meaning the rest of the van's occupants.

She shrugged. "With any luck, maybe they'll leave us here."

Gaspar's fatigue-lined face lifted into a relieved grin. "You're in a mood, aren't you Susie Wong?"

She walked away from the van to the sidewalk and kept going. Gaspar limped by her side at first. As always, his leg seemed to stretch out and strengthen with exercise. He would be okay. He could take care of himself.

Which was a good thing because it meant she didn't need to worry about him. She was tired. Tired of the Reacher file. Tired of being watched. Tired of Neagley's psychopathic behavior. Tired of being tired. She wanted to sleep, eat a decent meal, call the Boss, and figure out what the hell to do next. In that precise order.

They walked a couple of blocks, then turned to head back. From this distance, Kim saw Morrie buying gas and Neagley stretching her legs around the van. Dean had to be feeling the cramp, but Kim didn't have the energy to care. She hadn't wanted a hostage and now they'd transported one across the border. They hadn't gotten caught, but that didn't make the action any less criminal.

When the Boss had recruited her because her ex-husband had been arrested for stealing and selling military secrets, she'd vowed then and there never, ever to unwittingly be on the wrong side of the law again. Before The Reacher File assignment, she'd never violated a rule in her life. It seemed every moment of this job took her farther away from the solid, secure world she preferred to navigate. She was tired of that, too.

What happened to the real Kim Otto?

She died. Reacher killed her.

"What's going on with your family, Chico?" Kim asked, seeking a respite from the craziness she found herself in now. "Maria okay? The kids?"

Gaspar tensed. "It's complicated."

"I'm good with complicated."

"Not a distraction we need at the moment."

"Seems like you're too distracted already."

When he didn't explain further, Kim shrugged. "What happened to your leg, anyway?"

"You're a bundle of questions tonight, aren't you? What happened to your husband?"

She sighed. "Okay. Let's talk about Reacher. Crazy as it seems, that's a safer topic."

"What about him?"

"Dean thinks Reacher has $65 million that in some twisted way belongs to Dean and Berenson. You think he does?"

"Probably not."

"Where did the money go?"

"Was the money ever there?"

"What do you mean?"

"Dean seems to think someone was going to pay him $65 million for missiles. He never delivered the missiles. He never collected the money. Maybe there never was any money. How many arms dealers have you met that are all that trustworthy?"

"But Neagley said the missiles were ready for delivery."

"Doesn't mean the money was there, does it?" Gaspar asked. "You wrestle with pigs, you both get dirty, as my grandpa used to say."

"Meaning?"

"Meaning this cash-for-weapons deal was made between killers and thieves. Maybe they both got screwed."

"Neagley knows. I think it's time she told us, don't you?"

"Long past time," he said, then chuckled. "Who's gonna make her do it?"

"The problem is that Black Star isn't ready to be raided. There's a solid year's worth of work to be done there. If the government goes in too early, a lot of work will be lost. Dozens of scumbags will get away scot free because we can't prove anything against them." She smoothed her palm over her head. Weary. "Dean holding hostages at Black Star is brilliant, even if he doesn't know why. Almost as good as putting them on Mars."

"It's the same as Mars to them. Dean is a rocket scientist," Gaspar replied. "Berenson's no dummy, either. They chose the one spot they knew Uncle Sam couldn't touch them."

She thought about that for a minute. Shook her head. "I don't think so."

"What?"

"*We* know Black Star is under investigation. But *they* don't know that. They think Black Star's real business activities are still a secret."

Gaspar shrugged. "Either way, whether they're aware of the investigation or not, the result is the same. Our hands are tied. What can we do?"

"I say we leave that up to the Boss." She pulled out her cell phone and made the call.

He picked up on the first ring, as he usually did.

She said, "We need an extraction."

"Who? From where?"

"Seven hostages. Black Star."

Silence.

"Can you do it? Or should Neagley call the Pentagon?"

Silence.

"Tomorrow morning at 5:00 a.m. Central. On the dot."

She could hear him breathing a second longer before he finally said, "It's tricky. Might take some time. Requires inter-agency cooperation. Not a good idea for *your* assignment."

Kim noticed he wouldn't say Reacher's name aloud, even on the untraceable, encrypted cell.

She wasn't in the mood for fencing. "I've got a high degree of confidence in your ability to make it so," she said. "Call me to confirm."

She disconnected and slipped the phone into her pocket.

Kim glanced at her Seiko. 10:55 p.m. They had less than seven hours left to get into Black Star and get the hostages out alive.

Which would be a lot harder than it sounded. Too bad they couldn't send in a couple dozen anti-terror teams.

"Come on," she said. "We've got a lot to do."

When they reached the van again, Morrie drove to the closest roadside hotel. They registered under false names and paid cash and chose rooms on the backside, away from the road.

Morrie drove around back, pulled up close to the stairway, and let the engine idle while the three of them got out. He would clean the van of all trace evidence of their actions in Mexico and get rid of it. Once he accomplished the job, he'd return to the hotel.

Kim hauled Dean out of the van and pushed him ahead of her up the stairs and into his room. She let him drink water. She asked again. "Where are they?"

"Black Star," he said, glaring into her eyes.

"Dixon, the Sanchez family, Angela Franz and Charlie? All seven are being held there?"

"Yes." His voice was raspy, but firm. Defiant.

Kim believed him because she had no evidence to the contrary. And because it made a crazy kind of sense.

The challenge now was to keep all seven alive until the Boss's extraction team arrived, all while keeping the Black Star investigation undercover. And to do it before Berenson killed another hostage.

Okay, so that was more than one challenge.

"Morrie should be back in an hour," she said.

"Everybody gets a shower and clean clothes and coffee," Gaspar replied. "We'll be ready when you are."

Neagley and Kim left to shower and change and gulp coffee and make phone calls.

When everyone reconnected in Dean's room, they were ready.

CHAPTER 39

Tuesday, November 16
12:07 a.m.
Chacho, TX

Edward Dean was strapped to a straight desk chair placed in the center of the room. Gaspar lounged on the bed as if he'd never been more relaxed. Neagley stood in the corner, back to the wall, watching Dean. Morrie leaned against the door as if he were body-blocking it to prevent entry.

Kim paced as she talked, like a caged tiger. She felt like one, too. She'd opened up the laptop and displayed the satellite images of Black Star Ranch. The Boss had sent two encrypted videos showing workers and residents going about their business. Kim didn't share those. She wasn't sure how much cooperation they could expect from Dean.

Everything about Black Star was under intense scrutiny. As soon as the ATF and FBI and Homeland Security had collected enough evidence to nail them, the Las Olas Black Star farm would be shut down. The plan was to close the arrests in six months.

Until then, the operation was as undercover as it was possible to be when several hundred people already knew about it and some of those people were politicians.

She looked straight at Dean and pulled out a syringe filled with yellowish liquid. She held it up to the light, pulled off the protective plastic cap, pushed the plunger to prime the needle and release any potential bubbles.

"This is our most sophisticated truth serum. Way better than anything we've ever used before," she said. "Three minutes after this hits the bloodstream, people feel euphoric and extremely talkative. They know what they're saying. They feel like we're their best friends in the world. They tell us everything we want to know. Not that they want to reveal all secrets. But they simply aren't able to lie."

She recapped the needle and laid the syringe on the desk.

Dean's face had reflected snarling contempt and now showed something like alarm. He was prepared to resist questioning. He was defiant. But chemical interrogation was another matter entirely. Resistance was futile and he knew it. He also knew he was a dead man the second Las Olas learned he'd been compromised. He sneered, but he was appropriately sweaty.

Kim continued, "Agent Gaspar and I are going to get coffee for everyone. You like yours black, right? We'll leave our colleagues here with you."

He glanced at Neagley and his smirk lost a bit of its edge.

Kim said, "When we come back, we're going to ask you about the hostages. And you'll tell us where they are and how to collect them. After we're done here, a half-dozen FBI agents will arrive to question you and record your answers. You'll confess to everything you've done. You'll identify all of your Las Olas pals. You'll help us bring them down. If you're lucky, you'll be tried and convicted and since this is Texas, you'll be put to death pretty quickly. If you're not lucky, your Las Olas friends will reach you before trial."

She stopped pacing and stood directly in front of him, eyes steady on his face until he blinked and looked down.

She put her index finger under his chin and lifted his gaze back to hers. "Be back in a few. Looking forward to it."

Gaspar got up off the bed and followed her out into the hallway. When the door snugged closed behind them, he said, "Where are we going to get good coffee at this hour?"

"You know what La Quinta means?" she asked.

"The Fifth," Gaspar replied, puzzled. "You think he's going to refuse to answer? Try to stonewall until it's too late?"

She smiled and said, "It's a joke. LaQuinta. The hotel chain. I saw one two doors down. La Quinta means next to Denny's."

"Denny's. Right."

They walked toward the lighted sign three blocks away. The sidewalk was in good shape. No cracks or lifted sections. No grass or landscaping on the dry shoulder, but that was okay. Kim felt good to be outside in the breeze. She'd been cooped up too long. Too much tension. Too many antacids.

Gaspar asked, "So you asked the Boss for a raid on Black Star and he sent you the syringe?"

She stuffed her hands in her pockets and slowed the pace a bit. Neagley needed time to give Dean the injection and let it get to work.

"The Boss said they aren't ready for the raid yet. There are too many lives at stake if they don't get enough evidence to shut down Black Star and make a serious dent in Las Olas when they go in for the raid."

"You knew that was the situation before you asked for help."

"True. But negotiations have to start somewhere," she said.

"He made the right decision," Gaspar said. "Simple math. Seven lives are at stake here, but thousands more are impacted by Las Olas' money laundering and drug and kidnapping-for-ransom businesses."

"Agreed. But we can't go in there alone, either. That place is fortified like a bunker."

Gaspar shrugged. "We can't expose the undercover work, but local law enforcement is available. We are back in Texas, after all." He stopped walking at the second intersection to wait for a green light.

"True."

"We escaped Valle Alto, and we were outgunned there, too," Gaspar pointed out.

"We had limited options in Valle Alto and we got lucky," Kim said, tersely. "It was dark. Las Olas was distracted. We were all conscious and able to run."

The light changed. Kim stepped off the curb and over a dead raccoon in the middle of the street and continued to the other side. Denny's was next to LaQuinta half a block ahead.

She said, "Berenson is focused like a laser. She hasn't heard from Dean. That'll make her more cautious. The hostages are deeply anesthetized. It's too risky to wake them up without medical supervision and we can't possibly carry them all."

At Denny's they took a seat and waited for the waitress. Gaspar gazed longingly at food on the plates of four nearby patrons, but there wasn't time to eat right now. They'd come back after they learned whatever Dean could tell them.

Kim checked the time. Even though they had Dean in custody, she fostered no illusions that Berenson or another Las Olas member wouldn't shoot a second hostage if they missed their deadline by half a second.

"What's your plan?" Gaspar asked.

"Black Star pretends to be a legitimate business. So I figure we should treat them as if they are what they claim to be."

"Meaning what?"

"We get Dean to tell us exactly where the hostages are located on the ranch. We call four civilian ambulances to go in there and pull them out," she explained.

He thought it through, nodding. "Are there four ambulances in this town?"

"No. There's two here and two in a town about ten miles away. We'll have to stagger the calls so they arrive at the same time."

The waitress came and took Gaspar's order for nine coffees to go and left.

"Nine?" Kim asked.

"Two each, and one for the throw-away," he said. "Where will the ambulances take the hostages?"

"There's a military hospital thirty minutes away. They'll be guarded there. When they wake up and we're sure they're okay, the Boss will get them home again."

"What about Berenson?"

"We'll have to find her, take her out at the same time."

He raised his eyebrow. "Without a SWAT team?"

Kim wagged her head back and forth. "Dean will help us isolate her. After that, I'm guessing Neagley will take care of Berenson. No way to stop her, even if anyone wanted to try."

The waitress returned with the to-go cups stacked inside two large takeaway bags. Kim paid cash for the order and took one bag. Gaspar took the other. She glanced at her Seiko. They'd been gone fifteen minutes. Plenty of time.

On the walk back, Kim stepped over the dead raccoon again.

"Nocturnal animals end up as road kill because they think they're safe when they're not," Gaspar said. "What if your plan doesn't work? What's plan B?"

"It has to work. It's the only option we have," she replied. "One choice, right choice, Chico."

CHAPTER 40

Tuesday, November 16
12:49 a.m.
Chacho, TX

Gaspar knocked on the motel room door.

From inside, Morrie called, "Yes?"

"Room service," Gaspar said.

Morrie opened the door, stood aside until they entered and then closed, locked, and stood in front of it again. His posture looked much the same as the day Kim first met the man standing guard outside Neagley's office.

Seemed like a lifetime ago.

Which it was.

Neagley was stretched out on the bed in the position Gaspar had formerly occupied. She'd propped two pillows behind her and rested her back against the headboard. Her eyes were closed.

As if she felt Kim watching, without opening her eyes Neagley said, "It's the Army way, Otto. Sleep when you can. You never know when you'll get another chance."

Dean was still strapped to the chair. Neagley had tightened the cables around his wrists and ankles and his flesh had started to swell. He had to be uncomfortable anchored there. But the expression on his face was pleasant, almost happy. The drug had entered his bloodstream and coursed around. He was ready.

Kim set the bag of coffee on the desk. She noticed the empty syringe. She handed it to Gaspar, who took it into the bathroom for secure disposal. He'd disassemble, wash with soap to remove as much trace evidence as possible, and flush each component down the toilet. Not perfect, but good enough.

Kim stood in front of Dean with a cup of black coffee. "I brought your coffee. Would you like a sip?"

He smiled like the offer was one of gracious hospitality. "Please," he said.

She held the cup to his mouth as he drank.

"Thank you," he said. His demeanor proved he was ready enough.

Neagley smirked. Morrie looked amazed. Gaspar watched.

Kim was satisfied. "Where is Margaret Berenson?"

"She's with our folks at Black Star," Dean said.

"Are Angela and Charlie Franz there?"

"Yes, they are."

"Is Karla Dixon there?"

"She is."

"How about Tammy Sanchez and her children?"

"Yes. All with our folks at Black Star. With Margaret."

Good to know. Next, she asked a question to test whether he was being truthful, although the drug never failed. "What about Tammy's mother?"

He frowned and seemed bewildered for a moment. Then, like a cloud passing, his frown disappeared as his memory cleared. "I'm sorry. She died."

"How did she die?"

"Margaret shot her in the head. She had to kill one of

them and the old lady was the best one to get rid of." His tone was conversational. He might have been discussing a football team trading players. He made no effort to conceal or offer any excuse. Again, an objective indication that the drug was doing its job.

Another test question. "Were they at Black Star when Margaret shot Tammy's mother?"

He wagged his head back and forth. "No. That was a couple of days ago. At Valle Alto."

"Where is her body?"

"We had a cookout going already, so we included her."

"A what?"

"You're FBI. You know," he said.

Her stomach cramped and flipped and twisted. She did know. She'd been focused on the job at hand, but she knew the way the most brutal of the Mexican cartels worked. They ruled by extreme violence. A cookout was their euphemism for burning people alive. It was one of many brutal execution techniques she'd seen.

Dean shrugged. "We cremated her at the compound," he said. "We didn't want people to find her. We don't like to shoot hostages. We usually just maim them a bit so we can give them back when the ransom is paid, you know."

So there would never be any proof they'd killed Mrs. Orozco, except the proof-of-life video, which might never be tied back to Dean or Berenson and could have been faked, anyway. But the bag of evidence Kim collected that still rested in her pocket could change all of that, maybe.

"I've been to Black Star," Kim said.

He seemed surprised. "You have? Nice place. Lovely this time of year. The horses are spectacular."

"There are quite a few places out there to hold hostages."

He nodded. "That's right."

"Where, exactly, is Margaret staying?"

"She's in the same building as the hostages. We can't trust anyone else with them. This group is special."

"Why are they special?"

"Because Margaret and I get all the ransom this time. This was a deal we did before we joined Las Olas. So we're handling it on the side. If Las Olas helps us, we have to share. See?"

"I understand," Kim said. "Where is Margaret staying with the hostages, exactly?"

"She's in the extra bunkhouse. It had enough beds already and Las Olas wasn't using it right now."

Kim opened the laptop and showed him the satellite photos of Black Star ranch. "Which building is the extra bunkhouse?" She pointed to each of the small buildings one at a time, methodically, starting near the ranch house. "Is it this one?"

"No. It's farther back."

She pointed to the building close to one of the barns. "This one?"

"Yes. That's it."

"Does this building have a name?"

He shrugged. "We call it the extra bunkhouse. As far as I know, that's the only name it has."

Kim handed the laptop to Gaspar. He looked at the extra bunkhouse and passed it to Morrie, who did the same before passing it to Neagley.

"You know that extra bunkhouse and the whole ranch pretty well, don't you?" Morrie asked.

"I guess."

"Tell us about it," Gaspar said.

Dean went over it, describing the layout. Gaspar made notes. He asked about the doors, the distances, the details. He made the sort of drawing an architect would have been embarrassed about, but it filled in the blanks the satellite photos were missing.

Kim pulled Dean's phone out of her pocket. She'd taken the risk of bringing it from Valle Alto and she'd checked it earlier. She found a number that had been dialed several times. "Is this Margaret's phone number?"

Dean nodded. "Yes. Sometimes it takes her a while to answer and there's no voice mail, so you have to call back."

"Good to know," Kim said. She offered him another drink of coffee because it seemed humane and useful to keep him hydrated. "Anything else we should know about Black Star and Margaret and the hostages?"

Dean seemed to think about the question. Maybe trying to decide what sort of things Kim would want to know. Like he was being helpful giving directions to the local gas station.

"There's a lot of guns out there. And people who know how to use them. It's protected better than the compound at Valle Alto, really. If you try to break into Black Star, you probably won't get very far. You certainly won't get out alive."

Kim asked, "Which building houses the fuel for the farm's equipment? They've got trucks and tractors, and they need to be gassed up. And there's probably propane, too."

Dean considered the question. Maybe the drug was wearing off and he was able to self-censor again. Maybe he didn't know. Maybe he was finally figuring out what they planned to do and didn't want to help.

"Where's the fuel storage, Dean?" Morrie said, a little rougher. "Do I need to give you another injection?"

He shrugged, said, "I was thinking. It's behind the third barn. The one at the end of the row. There's an underground tank. And there's a propane tank there, too. They need to keep it away from the horses. It's toxic you know."

"You said Margaret and the hostages were with your 'folks.' What do you mean? Your family?"

He chuckled. "I guess. Las Olas is our family now, I suppose. Las Olas and our kids. But the kids are almost grown. Daughter in college. Son at boarding school. Margaret and I are just an old married couple now. Empty nesters, you know?"

Kim felt bewildered, like she'd been hit on the head without warning. She wasn't sure she'd heard correctly. Gaspar's eyes widened. Morrie cocked his head as if he'd misheard. Even Neagley opened her eyes and sat up straight on the bed.

Neagley said, "You and Berenson are *married*? Berenson's son and your daughter? The *two* of you are their *parents*?" She made it sound like the idea was more preposterous than intelligent lizards living among us disguised as humans.

Her reaction startled Kim more than the intel. If Berenson and Dean were married, why would Neagley be surprised they had kids?

Before Kim could ask Dean chuckled again. Nodded. "Twenty-two years now. Hard to believe, I know. But she was a looker once." A small cloud crossed his face. He shook his head slightly, as if he felt regrets. "I didn't mean to cut her face like that. She started it. And she's not the only one with scars."

Involuntary shudders ran through Kim's body. Sure, she was exhausted and hungry and barely keeping it together, but the feeling was caused by none of that. No. It was pure revulsion. What kind of man slices his wife's face with a knife like that? No woman who looked like that could ever live a normal life. Maybe Berenson was one of Dean's victims, too. Maybe she wasn't a willing partner. Which meant she might be persuaded to release the hostages.

Neagley's tone was as cold as Chicago winter. "What do you mean she's not the only one with scars?"

Dean said, "We were fighting a lot back then. Things got a little out of hand."

"Out of hand, how?" Neagley asked.

"She cut me, too. Worse. Blood was everywhere. It looked like a butcher shop in there before we were done."

Margaret Berenson's facial scars were hideous. Picturing them freshly inflicted in her mind set Kim's stomach roiling again, worse than the first time she'd seen Berenson's face.

Kim steadied her voice and asked, "How could she have cut you worse?"

He replied, "I'd show you, but you wouldn't want to see. Good thing we already had the kids by then."

Kim had been in the presence of evil many times. She

had no doubt she was looking evil in the eye again now. Edward Dean had taken hostages for ransom, including four children and three women. He'd ordered a grandmother executed when the ransom wasn't paid. He'd made a deal to trade missiles to terrorists, missiles that were to be used against U.S. targets. He was heavily involved in drug trade, which ruined more lives every day than all terrorist activities added together.

A moment ago she thought Edward Dean might be the worst evil she'd ever encountered.

If what he said about Berenson was true, they shared the title equally.

She felt she was drowning in evil now.

Kim turned away from the sick bastard. She picked up her equipment.

"Gaspar, let's go," she said. "I can't breathe in here."

Morrie opened the door, Kim walked through it with Gaspar following right behind her.

Somewhat surprisingly, Morrie followed after Gaspar and closed the door behind him, leaving Neagley alone with Dean.

She joined them in the parking lot less than a minute later.

Kim stood taking deep breaths to steady her stomach, trying not to think about Neagley alone in the room with Dean. Thinking through what she'd just learned from Dean and how to integrate his intel with what she'd already planned. A random thought flashed into her mind.

What would Reacher do?

She grinned to herself in the darkness.

She didn't realize she'd spoken the thought aloud until Neagley replied, "First thing Reacher would do is eat breakfast at that Denny's over there. Another Army rule. Eat when you can."

Kim and Neagley set out, shoulder-to-shoulder, in that direction. Gaspar and Morrie followed.

CHAPTER 41

Tuesday, November 16
1:26 a.m.
Chacho, TX

Denny's, a chain diner, was predictable. Open 24 hours and almost deserted at this hour before breakfast. The only people inside were the waitress who'd sold them coffee earlier and the cook.

They walked across the parking lots, weaving between parked pickup trucks, and jaywalked across the side streets and reached the empty diner lot. Inside, they walked right past the *Please Wait to Be Seated* sign and slid into a booth by the window with a view of the motel. Gaspar and Neagley on one side, Morrie and Kim on the other. Just worked out that way.

The waitress delivered coffee and menus. Neagley ordered a cheeseburger and fries without looking. The guys said her order sounded good. Kim's stomach was twisted by revulsion since Dean's confession and couldn't handle the grease. She ordered toast. The waitress said it would be ten minutes to fry the patties. She left the coffee pot and moved back to her newspaper at the counter.

Neagley said, "Cooper going to be of any help in this or is he as political as ever?"

Kim replied, "He'll oil the wheels, but we're on our own. We've got backup and some local support. But they aren't going to send in the Marines, if that's what you're asking."

Neagley snorted. "Of course they're not. Can't be bothered, I suppose. It's only four kids and three women and none of the women are sleeping with Cooper."

Gaspar glanced at Kim. Understanding passed between them. The joint task force had been working to bring down the Black Star operation for three years. They were so close to wrapping up. Careers would be made or ruined on the success or failure of those involved. There were bigger stakes. Simple as that.

Not that they could tell Neagley the Boss's reasons; not that she'd care if they told her.

When neither Gaspar nor Kim offered a rebuttal, Neagley said, "We can't drive a bus in there and snatch them back. For one thing, there's the medical issues. For another, we'd be dead before we reached the bunkhouse."

"Agreed," Morrie and Gaspar said simultaneously.

"We'll go over all the details. But the basic plan is simple, solid," Kim said. "Neagley and Gaspar can handle the diversion. Morrie and I will confirm the hostages are in the bunkhouse, then call in the ambulances." She told Neagley about the need to stagger the calls to the two communities to ensure they'd arrive together. "Once we have them loaded, Cooper will make sure they are evacuated to safety."

Morrie asked, "How will we get in and get out?"

"Our vehicle should be in the motel lot, fully loaded, when we're done here."

"*Should* be?" Neagley asked.

Kim ignored her. "When Berenson's arrested, she'll be highly motivated to save her hide. That'll be problematic for all of us and an even bigger problem for Neagley, Dixon, and Reacher. She'll start talking about why she and Dean were so interested in Reacher's crew in the first place. She'll use the missing money as a bargaining chip. Might even manage immunity in exchange for testimony, assuming we get all the hostages out alive."

Morrie looked at her as if she'd grown a third head.

As Kim had expected, Neagley said, "Berenson won't be a problem."

The waitress returned with the food and they stopped talking while they consumed it like a Shop-Vac sucks up dust.

"What about the timing?" Neagley asked.

"We've got some set up first," Kim replied. "But we go in at your lucky time of the day. Four o'clock in the morning. What did you call it? KGB time? Are you feeling lucky?"

CHAPTER 42

Tuesday, November 16
3:56 a.m.
Chacho, TX

The Boss had delivered on the first of his promises. A state-of-the-art armored SUV was parked at the motel, equipped with everything they'd need and a few extras Kim hoped wouldn't be necessary. Gaspar behind the wheel driving with his usual lead foot, they arrived slightly before dawn's weak light first bathed the countryside in soft haze.

Black Star Ranch nestled in a Texas Valley near the Rio Grande a few miles north of Mexico. Close enough for frequent visits and exchanges. Far enough outside Mexico's jurisdiction to be both a blessing and a curse, depending on the crime. According to her intel, Las Olas laundered money by the truckload through this operation. Money laundering had to be done stateside. Murder and kidnapping and assorted mayhem was better handled in Mexico where corrupt authorities were more easily persuaded by extreme violence or bribery to look the other way.

In photographs, the scene was benign, enticing. No outward evidence of the evil within existed. Less like South Texas ranches, more reminiscent of Louisville, Kentucky horse farms.

Unlike its dusty neighbors', Black Star's lawns and pastures were well watered. Quarter horses grazed peacefully on lush grass divided by a bright white running board fence. Maybe 200 horses were visible from the last satellite photos she'd downloaded, but there were probably more. Horses were trained, bred, and raced here.

Black Star's layout was similar to the compound in Valle Alto. Maybe Las Olas liked familiarity, which was fine with Kim. She liked familiarity, too. More predictable.

While not as bright as the stadium lighting in Valle Alto, the ranch was well lit from without and within. Each of the buildings was bathed in floodlights similar to those lighting buildings in Washington D.C. or Paris. Runway lights lined the drives and entrances.

Through the binoculars, Kim saw a spacious, ranch-style home sprawled at the end of the private drive maybe a hundred yards from the road where Kim sat inside the SUV with the blackened window lowered. The driveway widened to provide parking spaces large enough for horse trailers. But no vehicles rested there now. Barns and other outbuildings were scattered behind the house. Kim counted eight buildings in all, but her view was partially obscured.

She found the building Dean had identified as the extra bunkhouse where the hostages were being held. It looked similar in size and construction to the bunkhouse they'd found on the Ville Alto compound, but it was obviously newer. The FBI reports she'd read said Las Olas used it for human trafficking and as a holding cell for kidnapping victims for whom they expected to collect ransom.

The interior photos the Boss sent were a couple of months old, and consistent in every respect with Dean's descriptions. The interior of the bunkhouse was equipped with the usual conveniences. A small kitchen and eating area on the front, two bathrooms with toilets and showers and sinks across the north side. The remainder of the interior space was divided into two large dormitory rooms and one smaller private sleeping quarters with its own toilet and sink and shower.

Kim could see four small, high windows on the front of the bunkhouse reflecting the yellow glow of incandescent bulbs. Someone inside was already awake. A sedan and a black pickup truck were parked perpendicular to the building, blocking the doorway from her line of sight. Nor could she see the back of the building from this vantage point, but the photographs had shown the same window layout on the back. Windows too high and too small to enter or escape through. Unless you were a tiny Asian woman with a tall dude to boost you up.

She found the third barn. It wasn't far from the extra bunkhouse. Through the binocs, she saw two trucks and a tractor with a trailer parked at the side.

She counted seven ranch hands moving around outside, even at this early hour. There were lights on in the main house, too. This was a working ranch and there were horses to feed, chores to do. Maybe horses and other things were being shipped and received, too. People were on the job.

"Are we clear on what we're doing here?" Kim asked. "Morrie and I will take the bunkhouse. Gaspar and Neagley, you get the barn. Open communication between us."

Morrie said, "We're going into the bunkhouse to confirm the hostages are still here. Assuming they are, I call and bring in the ambulances to take them to the hospital."

"Exactly," Kim said. "Neagley?"

"We'll get the diversions going. Worry about your end, Otto."

Why did she have to be such a constant prickly female?

"Don't ignite the explosions until we confirm the hostages are actually still in there," Kim pressed. "If they've been moved again, we'll need to find them before we launch the plan. And we can't get too far ahead of our timeline."

"As I said," Neagley said, "you worry about your end."

Gaspar said, "You left out the part where Black Star is guarded around the clock by Las Olas, inside and out. Those guys would love to have a nice big guy like you for a cookout, Morrie."

Morrie frowned. "They do that in Mexico. Not here."

"Don't count on it," Neagley warned. "There's almost nothing they can't do here, Morrie."

Kim said, "We've also got Berenson to deal with."

"I'll be back to take care of her," Neagley said.

"No." Kim was a Federal agent. She wouldn't authorize Neagley's brand of justice. "She's in our wheelhouse. Morrie and I will deal with her."

Neagley said, "Suit yourself. I'll be there anyway. Let me know if you change your mind."

They tested their earpieces and opened the conference channel on their burner phones. The entire operation had the feel of *déjà vu*. They'd tried this same operation without the diversion or the ambulances last night at Valle Alto and failed to get the hostages out. They had to finish before Berenson killed another hostage, if she hadn't already.

The one thing Dean couldn't confirm was whether Berenson had followed their plan to keep all of the hostages alive until 6:00 a.m. Kim and the others had no choice but to assume Berenson was on plan.

"You think this is going to work?" Morrie asked.

"Only one choice, Morrie. It's got to work," Kim replied, with more conviction than the situation warranted. But there was nothing else she could do.

They waited until a truckload of workers pulled into the long driveway and Gaspar pulled the SUV in behind them, following them past the house and toward the barns.

"You really think it's going to be this easy?" Morrie asked. "Driving right in?"

Gaspar shrugged. "We can hope. It's awful early."

"That's our plan?" Morrie said. "Hope?"

"And a prayer," Kim added. "If you're so inclined."

"Can we cut the chatter?" Neagley said.

As they drove past the third barn, Gaspar turned off at the bunkhouse, pulled the SUV around back and cut the engine. They all sat still, listening to the ticking of the engine and watching out the windows for Las Olas security forces to sweep down on them.

Morrie said, "This prayer thing's pretty impressive."

Gaspar pulled the keys from the ignition and tossed them on the floor by the brake pedal. "Anybody needs to drive besides me," he said, leaving the sentence unfinished.

All four left the SUV and gathered behind it for last minute equipment checks. When they were done, Neagley held her fist out, shoulder height. "Fist bump. It's what the special investigators always did before and after a mission."

"Who knew you were so superstitious," Kim said. But they all bumped fists, just in case.

Neagley and Gaspar crouched low behind the building and moved ahead in the shadows while Morrie and Kim waited below the high windows of the extra bunkhouse.

Across the back of the bunkhouse were four windows. They were sixty-five inches off the ground. Kim guessed each one measured twenty-four by thirty inches. She'd studied their wood frame construction and metal lever operations on the manufacturer's website earlier tonight.

Each window was hinged on the top and opened at the bottom. An interior handle swung from right to left, pushing two metal arms on a track that opened the base of the windows outward about ten inches. The handle and arm mechanisms operated in reverse to close. Pop a metal pin from the arms and open the window wider for cleaning or to replace them, the online directions said.

No light emanated now from the four back windows, which might be okay. The hostages were sleeping and if there were no lights in the wards, then maybe that meant no one was guarding them. Or, if someone was watching, the guard could be asleep. Either way, Kim took it as a good sign that the wardrooms were dark.

She'd need to create muffled noise to pry the bottom of

the window open slightly, pop two pins, remove the metal arms, and lift the window wide enough to slip inside.

The old interior photos and Dean's recent drawing showed an interior door between the two wardrooms and the front living spaces. At least one person, and maybe more, was awake and moving around in the front of the building. She'd need to be armed and ready, should someone hear her drop to the floor inside.

Kim checked her watch. Neagley and Gaspar should have reached the third barn by now. They should be setting up the propane triggers at the gas pumps and the 500-gallon propane tank. They'd be ready in three minutes.

Kim figured she'd need two for herself and one for Morrie.

"Going in," she whispered.

"Okay," Gaspar whispered back in her earpiece.

Kim slipped on her night vision. Morrie made a bridge with his paws and Kim put her petite foot in it. He lifted her as if she were lighter than a teddy bear.

She looked inside the window first. Even with the night vision, she couldn't see much. A thin line of light showed under the interior door coming from the kitchen, but it provided little illumination. She pushed her night vision down to hang around her neck and grabbed the micro flashlight out of her pocket and shined it into the dark cavern.

She lifted one foot out of the palm of Morrie's hand in the brief signal they'd agreed to in advance. He lowered her until she could jump onto the soft earth, landing quietly. She whispered loud enough to be picked up by her headset.

"Looks like there's no wall between the two wards now. There are ten beds. Hard to tell how many are occupied, but a few are. I saw the IV poles and probably people lying under light blankets. I'm going to go in there. Hang on."

"Ten-four," Gaspar said.

"Smartass," she replied.

She pulled out the screwdriver she'd brought along for this purpose.

Morrie made his palm-bridge again. She stepped into the

lift.

At the top of the lift, she used the screwdriver to pry the bottom of the window open wider. Reached into the opening with her tiny hand. Forced the opening wider until she could reach her arm inside, grab the lever, and throw the window open wide enough to pop out the pins that held the metal arms in place.

Morrie shifted her weight to his right hand and reached up with his left to hold the window open with his palm while Kim wiggled inside. Briefly, she bent double over the window casing at her waist. She put her toes against the outside cement block wall and slithered the rest of the way into the room and dropped quietly to the floor.

"I'm in," she whispered into her earpiece.

"Ten-four," Gaspar replied.

Okay. Now that was just annoying.

Inside, the room was darker than she'd expected, even with the thin light ribbon under the door. She slipped her night vision up from her neck and over her eyes and looked around.

The room was the one from the videos. Dark, rectangular, barren. Cots rested perpendicular to each wall, lengthwise along both sides, like an old Army barracks. A narrow walkway lay open between the ends the beds. She counted twenty-four beds, twelve on each side.

Seven were occupied.

"Seven present," she whispered.

"Ten-four," Gaspar said.

She approached the first bed and looked down at its occupant. She saw a woman she barely recognized as Karla Dixon. Quickly, she made a positive ID on the other six.

Then she whispered into her headset, "Visual ID. Seven accounted for."

She looked at the time on her Seiko. She'd shaved her time estimate by thirty seconds. "Good to go when you are."

She had ninety seconds to wait.

CHAPTER 43

Tuesday, November 16
4:43 a.m.
Black Star Ranch, TX

Kim approached each bed and placed two fingers on the carotid arteries of each hostage. Although Charlie Franz's pulse was faint and thready, she felt it. Maybe. The Sanchez children had been anesthetized much longer. So had their mother. But they were all alive.

Angela was so fragile. She looked like an angel, for sure. Kim tried several times to feel her carotid pulse, but couldn't. Long-term anesthesia was tricky to manage, even in a hospital setting. Which this definitely was not. Was Angela breathing? It was hard to be sure. All Kim could do at this point was to get help as soon as possible.

Finally, she returned to Dixon. Not as petite as Kim, but smaller than Neagley. Sturdy looking. She was breathing. That was the best Kim could confirm for now, but she'd probably make it.

"Seven. Alive but weak," she whispered into her headset.

She checked her watch. Another minute more.

She pulled her night vision off and let it hang around her neck, allowing her eyes to adjust to the darkness. The light sliver guided her to the door. She remembered the layout from the videos. On the other side should be the common room where ranch hands could read or watch TV and take meals.

Kim reached for the doorknob and found it missing. Instead, she felt a lever resting in a hook on the jamb. The lever could be lifted easily from the other side with a case knife or a credit card. Probably a practical solution for a bunkhouse. Privacy wasn't required here.

She lifted the lever slowly to avoid a noise that might alert the occupants on the other side.

When she cracked open the door slightly, a long, vertical slice of light entered the ward, almost blinding her. She felt her wide-open pupils contract to pinpoints. She blinked several times and her pupils began to resize.

Line of vision from this vantage point included the kitchen area. Berenson and a man were seated at the table, eating, speaking in low tones. Maybe they worried that the comatose hostages could hear them. Maybe it was just the early hour. Either way, Kim strained her ears to hear.

"The girls are weaker than the boys," Berenson said, speaking Spanish.

"All four of the children are weak," he replied in the same language. "We have to wake them up for a few days."

"We can't do that."

"They need solid food."

"Don't worry about it."

"Their lungs are filling with fluid."

"I don't care," Berenson said, showing a mouth full of eggs and sausage and white gravy over biscuits.

"You brought me here because I'm a doctor. Listen to me." His tone was stern.

"We don't have the resources to manage them if we wake them up. You know that."

"You're wasting my time. If you want hostages instead of corpses, wake them up," he demanded.

Berenson glared at him. "Corpses work just as well for my purposes."

Kim glanced at her Seiko. Twenty-five seconds.

The man pushed back his chair, stood, and threw his napkin into his plate of congealing gravy. He walked toward Kim.

"Where are you going?" Berenson demanded.

"I'm a doctor. Not a mortician."

Kim closed the door and flattened her back against the wall and squeezed her eyes shut to avoid light-blindness again.

When he pushed the door open, light flooded the room like a movie premier Klieg.

Berenson's footsteps clomped along closely behind him. "Pablo! Pablo! Stop right there."

Kim opened and closed her eyes slowly.

Pablo kept coming, intently focused. If he happened to glance back, he'd see her. But it couldn't be helped. There was nothing to hide behind.

He approached the first cot where one of the Sanchez boys lay.

Berenson stopped at the threshold, barely inside the room, focused on Pablo. Kim opened her eyes just in time to see Berenson's gun arm extended in the same way and holding the same weapon she'd used to kill the child's grandmother.

Before Kim could stop her, Berenson fired twice and shot the doctor in the back.

Morrie's voice, hard, loud enough in Kim's ear even after the deafening gunshot, "Otto? Otto? Are you there?"

The doctor fell forward. Kim dropped silently to the floor and rolled behind one of the footlockers, peeking over the top.

Berenson walked up to the doctor's side, nudged his head with her booted foot. His head turned. His gaze looked toward Kim, but if he saw her, he indicated nothing. He wasn't dead, but he was close.

Gaspar's voice, urgent, "What happened? Morrie?"

"Two gunshots inside," Morrie said.

"Come on, Sunshine. Let us know you're still breathing," Gaspar coaxed. She could barely hear his voice, which seemed muffled by a loud, ringing bell.

Kim readied for incoming. Surely, ranch hands would investigate.

Holding the weapon at her side, as if she might have to shoot him again, Berenson watched the doctor until the life left his eyes.

Kim rolled under the nearby cot. Now, she could see only along the floor. Berenson's boots and the doctor's lifeless body.

Berenson left him lying on the floor inside the arc of the door's closing path, and returned to her breakfast. Kim scooted from under the cot, watching Berenson's every move as she laid the gun on the table within easy reach near her plate. Berenson seemed unconcerned. She didn't glance toward the open doorway again.

No one else rushed in. Dean said this hostage project was a separate deal for them. Maybe use of the extra bunkhouse came with a privacy clause or something. She'd planned to kill another hostage in less than an hour. Maybe Berenson had ordered them to stay away if they heard gunshots. Whatever kept reinforcements outside for now, Kim needed that system to continue for another sixteen seconds.

"Ten-four," she whispered, hoping she'd spoken loud enough for the team to hear over the rudimentary communicators they'd devised. She returned to stand at the wall by the doorway where she could watch activities in the larger room.

Berenson stretched, and seemed to consider what to do next. She picked up her dishes and walked them over to the sink. She pulled the plug on the old-fashioned percolator and refilled her coffee cup. Then she turned, leaned against the sink drinking the coffee and looking toward the open doorway where the doctor's boots were soles up.

Kim heard a toilet flush, followed by footsteps advancing from the bathroom near the kitchen.

Morrie said, "Ten seconds."

"Good to go," Gaspar replied.

A young man approached Berenson. Maybe seventeen years old. Attractive in the way young men are when they've yet to reach their potential but the fullness of their maturity beckons from the horizon. Sandy hair similar to hers, maybe a little darker. Her build, her eyes. Dean said they had kids. Could this be their son?

"Where's the doc?" the boy said, in Dean's voice.

"In the ward," Berenson replied.

He walked toward the room where Kim was hiding. She tensed, ducked back, flattened herself against the wall.

"Did I hear gunshots?" he asked, as if gunshots were commonplace in his world, which they probably were.

The boy reached the threshold and stepped around Pablo's legs and extended his hand and brushed against Kim's bicep twice as he groped around the wall.

He turned his body toward the switch plate when he couldn't find it by tactile exploration.

Simultaneously saw Kim and flipped the light switch, flooding the room with blinding fluorescent light brighter than an operating theater.

"Seven seconds," advised Morrie's voice in her ear, as Kim brought the sap out of her pocket and smoothly applied it to the boy's temple. He crumpled to the floor, unconscious but not dead.

After he fell, Kim heard Berenson's boots slam two long strides to the kitchen table where she'd left the Glock, and rush across the room.

Kim moved away from the line of fire.

"Who's there?" Berenson said, coming ever closer. "Edward?" she called to the boy.

Kim said nothing. She'd exchanged wild gunfire with

Berenson before. This time, Kim would place precise shots.

Berenson moved into the open doorway, her gun held firmly in her right hand, outstretched in front of her body.

Kim applied the sap to Berenson's extended forearm. Hard.

Berenson's arm made a sickening sound as it bent oddly and jagged bones poked through her skin. Blood spurted and spread, dripping to the floor.

But something inside her skin, muscles or tendons or both, must have remained intact because Berenson's right hand did not drop the gun.

Only now did Kim see the military grade bayonet switchblade in Berenson's left hand.

Tinnitus battled Morrie's relentless voiced countdown in her ear. Berenson's blood slicked the floor.

But Kim's total concentration focused on the arcing knife in Berenson's left hand.

What had Dean said? *She's not the only one with scars.*

In one slow, graceful movement, Berenson lowered her bloody right arm. She dropped the gun into the blood-pool underneath. She crouched like a wrestler and lunged as she sliced upward toward Kim's face.

Kim jumped aside, barely avoiding the vicious blade.

Kim scrambled back, unable to fire.

She didn't want to screw up their plan.

The compound was lousy with Las Olas members who might still invade the bunkhouse. And the undercover investigation would be ruined. Years and thousands of hours of hard work. She couldn't screw that up.

Berenson advanced, knife extended, slicing fast.

Kim's intense focus anticipated each thrust, but barely.

If she could avoid the blade until the right moment—

Morrie said, "Now."

The first explosion came immediately after Morrie's last word. The blast felt like a sonic boom in the room next door.

It came just as Kim leapt away from another lunge, but Berenson managed to knock Kim off balance.

She fell to the floor. Landed hard on her back. Slammed her head against the concrete.

Berenson saw her chance and lunged forward.

Kim aimed and pulled the trigger.

Berenson kept coming.

Kim fired again and again and again.

The first explosion was followed by three additional explosions, but Kim barely heard them.

Berenson fell on top of her.

Kim struggled to break free of the woman's heavy body.

Scrambled and crabbed and escaped, finally, from under the dead weight.

The fifth explosion was much smaller.

Kim stood near Berenson, gun pointed, prepared to finish the job. But the move was unnecessary.

Morrie rushed in from the front entrance, weapon drawn. He saw the seven hostages still comatose in their beds. He bent to check the three bodies on the floor, confirmed two dead, one unconscious.

"Otto? You okay?" he looked up from his crouch by the unconscious Edward to ask.

Kim was shaky. Her stomach was about to give up the dry toast she'd eaten hours before. Temporary gunshot tinnitus in her ears made it difficult to hear his question. But she read his lips, said, "Fine. Thanks."

Morrie probably knew otherwise, but he was chivalrous enough not to say so. He did make sure she could see his face when he spoke. "Ambulances on the way. They'll be here in four minutes. Do you want to wait?"

Gaspar burst into the room. "It's chaos out there. We've got to go."

At least, that's what Kim thought he said. She could hear the chaos faintly, like loud white noise beyond her range.

Neagley walked in last. She looked down at Berenson and the doctor. Then she looked at Berenson's unconscious son. She walked over to the beds and looked at each of the hostages. She put her hand on Dixon's neck, feeling for a pulse as Kim had done. Satisfied, she turned and said, "Morrie, pick her up and bring her with us."

"Morrie, don't," Kim countermanded, laying a hand on his monstrous forearm. In response to Neagley, she said, "Dixon could die if we screw up. Cooper's sending medics. They'll take her to Ft. Lincoln."

Neagley said, "Morrie, pick her up. Bring her with us."

Kim urged Neagley to think about the big picture for a change. "They're expecting seven hostages. If we take her, they'll come looking. We don't want that, either. Leave her here with the others."

Morrie looked from Neagley to Kim and back. He didn't argue. There was no time.

Neagley said, "You go ahead. I want to just say something to Dixon and Tammy and Angela."

"They can't hear you," Gaspar said.

"We don't know that for sure," Neagley replied.

Kim thought a signal of some kind passed between Neagley and Morrie, but she couldn't read it.

Morrie said, "Come on. She'll catch up."

"We can't be caught here," Gaspar said to Kim before he followed Morrie outside.

"Neagley," Kim said. "Gaspar and I are not civilians like you. We're putting hundreds of our colleagues in jeopardy by being here at all. Anyone finds out we were here, too many questions will be asked."

"I owe it to my unit," Neagley said, stubborn to the end. "I need to watch out for their families."

"Cooper will take good care of them," Kim said. "You can see them in an hour at Ft. Lincoln."

"I can't leave Dixon behind," Neagley replied. "She's the only member of my unit left alive."

"Don't make us leave you behind, either. Please."

Neagley's lips lifted in a thin smile. "You worry too much, Otto. I can take care of myself."

Kim grimaced, nodded, knowing what Neagley said was true. There was no way to force her. And she'd never leave

Dixon and the others behind. She'd find her own way home, of that Kim was certain.

"We're confirming all seven hostages are loaded into the ambulances," Kim said. "Then we're leaving. We'll wait for you as long as we can."

"Ten-four." Neagley grinned.

Kim smiled back.

Neagley offered a fist bump. Kim wanted to give her a hug, but she accepted the only touch Neagley had ever offered.

"You'll never find Reacher until he wants to be found, you know."

Kim shrugged. "Then we'll just have to make him want to be found, won't we?"

Neagley's grin widened. "Good luck with that."

"Take care, Frances," Kim said. "Until we meet again."

She stepped outside into Armageddon.

The ranch was indeed in chaos.

Frightened horses had galloped away from the explosions. Now they were scattered everywhere like a frustrated child's toy set.

Rescue vehicles of every stripe were on the way or on the premises already.

Consuming fires burned hotter than funeral pyres, igniting smaller explosions each time the heat reached another fuel tank.

The noise of sirens and choppers and screaming horses and screaming people was deafening.

The stench of gasoline fires and billowing black smoke consumed the very oxygen Kim needed to breathe.

Four ambulances had pulled into the long driveway and were headed toward the extra bunkhouse, sirens blaring.

The Boss had kept his word once more.

Kim found herself a bit surprised. Despite the assurances she'd given Neagley, each time the Boss came through seemed like a fluke. But Kim was grateful he'd done it this time.

The first ambulance streaked to a halt in front of the extra bunkhouse. The driver jumped out and called to Kim, "Seven victims?"

Briefly, she considered correcting the count to eight, including Edward. But Neagley had been alone in the ward too long to be sure Edward was still alive.

"Inside," she called back over the thunderous noise. "Hurry."

And then she loped away toward the SUV, looking back, counting the seven gurneys as they loaded the ambulances and headed back the way they'd come, sirens blaring, dodging incoming vehicles along the way.

Despite what she'd said to Neagley, Kim wasn't worried. Just the opposite. Kim felt confidant Neagley was not alone. Reacher was there to help clean up the mess he'd helped create. He was the kind of man who saw things through.

Neagley would finish her business and reach the van within her window of opportunity or she wouldn't.

Either way, Kim would see them both again. Dixon, too.

For now, there was nothing more she could do here.

Unlike Neagley and Reacher, Kim had only one choice.

She had to go.

CHAPTER 44

Tuesday, November 16
2:15 p.m.
Houston, TX

Hours later, they waited for flights at the Houston airport. Gaspar stretched out into his usual waiting position, ankles crossed, hands folded over his flat abdomen, eyes closed. Kim finished her reports and uploaded them to her own secure server, paying her insurance premium once again. Like all insurance premiums, she hoped she'd never need to collect on the policy. But better to be safe than sorry.

"What do you think happened to the rest of that $65 million?" Gaspar asked from behind closed eyelids.

"I'm guessing you were right."

"What? You're giving me credit for something?"

"We don't know whether there ever was $65 million, really. But when Dixon recovers, she's going to have some questions to answer. She's the one who converted the funds and disbursed them, according to O'Donnell."

"The Boss could have it," Gaspar suggested after another couple of silent moments. "We know he's got Swiss bank accounts. O'Donnell said some of the money was in Switzerland."

"We'll probably never know," Kim replied, although she'd considered the possibility thoroughly in her secure reports. "Neagley's convinced the Boss is her enemy."

"Which means he's Reacher's enemy, too."

"Probably."

"That money could be more than sixty-five million good reasons, with the miracle of compound interest and all." He grinned again, but ruefully this time.

"Pure speculation." Kim changed the subject. "We learned a few things we can put into The Reacher File, though."

"Such as?"

She shrugged. "He's a good tactician. He inspires intense loyalty as well as intense hatred. From both sexes."

Gaspar added, "He's broke. Homeless. Uncommunicative."

"He's no Superman," she said.

One of Gaspar's eyebrows jumped up. "Based on what?"

"He didn't bother to help Neagley keep her only brother alive, did he?" Kim knew the judgment was harsh, but for all the loyalty his unit lavished on Reacher, in the end, he'd failed them all.

In Kim's view, Neagley was the superhero. Neagley had more heart and more courage than any of them would have ever needed. Maybe the SPTF should be recruiting her for whatever secret job the Boss had in mind.

Kim wondered whether Reacher's unit had known all that about Neagley all along. Did Reacher know it? Then? Or now?

Gaspar stretched his shoulders by rolling them around a bit, extending his neck, too. "At least it doesn't look like Reacher left Neagley or Dixon with any extra progeny."

When she closed the laptop and slipped it into its case, Gaspar grinned and, mocking her question to him at the end of their first Reacher assignment, said, "Now what?

Back to Detroit, complete your rotation, request a transfer, become Director, finish your thirty and collect your pension?"

She laughed, but repaid him in kind. "What is going on with Maria? Is she okay? Is the baby all right? You're worried, I'm worried, Chico. That's how it works."

Gaspar's grin faded, but only for an instant. "For a while there, I thought you and Neagley might have been separated at birth or something. But she'd never ask me anything the least bit personal." He opened his eyes and raised his eyebrow. "You're not so tough after all, are you Susie Wong?"

Her spine straightened. She felt her face heat up. Her tone was hard. "That's not a theory you want to test, Chico. Trust me."

The announcer called his flight. Gaspar rose, stretched his bad leg, straightened his jacket, pulled up the handle on his rolling suitcase. "Do you think Reacher was there? At Black Star this morning?"

She'd thought about this particular question while she finished her reports. In the moment, she'd been convinced that was why Neagley stayed behind. Maybe Neagley was a little in love with him, like the other women they'd met from Reacher's past. Who knew?

Kim shrugged. "Dunno. I thought I smelled him a couple of times."

"*Smelled him?* Literally?"

"Yes."

"How could you possibly know what he smells like, for God's sake?"

She shrugged again. "It's not so much that I recognized his scent. But I noticed a scent that was different from the others. Several times. In different places. And each time, there was physical evidence that someone had been there, too."

"Now who's acting crazy?"

The announcer called his flight again and simultaneously she felt the Boss's cell phone vibrating in her pocket. By now, she wasn't surprised that his timing was always perfect.

She held up one finger to stop Gaspar's departure, fished the phone out and clicked the connection open. "Yes."

He said, "Just sent you both an encrypted file. You should have it in another few seconds. Download it now on the secure channel while you can."

"My mother expects me home for Thanksgiving," she said, even as she unzipped her case and rebooted her laptop.

"Thanksgiving is nine days away," he replied. "And you've got no vacation time."

"Gaspar's wife is pregnant, you know. Baby due any minute."

The silence lasted barely a nanosecond.

"Your flight leaves in ten minutes. Plane tickets are waiting at the United Counter. Call me when you get there," he said before severing the call.

ABOUT THE AUTHOR

Diane Capri is an award-winning *New York Times, USA Today*, and worldwide bestselling author. She's a recovering lawyer and snowbird who divides her time between Florida and Michigan. An active member of Mystery Writers of America, Author's Guild, International Thriller Writers, Alliance of Independent Authors, and Sisters in Crime, she loves to hear from readers and is hard at work on her next novel.

Please connect with her online:

DianeCapri.com
Twitter.com/DianeCapri
Facebook.com/Diane.Capri1
Facebook.com/DianeCapriBooks